Praise for

DIM SUM OF ALL FEARS

"Provides plenty of twists and turns and a perky, albeit conflicted, sleuth."
—*Kirkus Reviews*

DEATH BY DUMPLING

"Vivien Chien serves up a delicious mystery with a side order of soy sauce and sass. A tasty start to a new mystery series!"
—Kylie Logan, bestselling author of *Gone with the Twins*

"*Death by Dumpling* is a fun and sassy debut with unique flavor, local flair, and heart."
—Amanda Flower, Agatha Award-winning author of *Lethal Licorice*

"A charming debut, with plenty of red herrings. The heroine's future looks bright."
—*Kirkus Reviews*

Also by
Vivien Chien

DEATH BY DUMPLING
DIM SUM OF ALL FEARS

Available from
St. Martin's Paperbacks

MURDER LO MEIN

VIVIEN CHIEN

St. Martin's Paperbacks

MURDER LO MEIN

For information address St. Martin's Press, 175 Fifth Avenue, New York, NY 10010.

ISBN: 978-1-250-12919-2

Our books may be purchased in bulk for promotional, educational, or business use. Please contact your local bookseller or the Macmillan Corporate and Premium Sales Department at 1-800-221-7945, ext. 5442, or by e-mail at MacmillanSpecialMarkets@macmillan.com.

Printed in the United States of America

St. Martin's Paperbacks edition / April 2019

St. Martin's Paperbacks are published by St. Martin's Press, 175 Fifth Avenue, New York, NY 10010.

10 9 8 7 6 5 4 3 2 1

For Effie,
You will live on forever in my heart

ACKNOWLEDGMENTS

Many thanks to the following:

To the fantastic Gail Fortune, for sharing in my excitement and caring about this series just as much as I do. I couldn't have wished for a better agent. To my editor extraordinaires, Hannah Braaten and Nettie Finn, for their expertise and eagle eyes. Both of you have made my writing better AND caught plot holes I was too blind to see. Here's to sharing many more "duh" moments together. To Sarah Schoof, Allison Ziegler, and Mary Ann Lasher for everything they do to help my books shine. All of you are my dream team. And extreme appreciation goes to St. Martin's Press, for allowing this wonderful series to exist. I can't say thank you enough.

As always, I express my sincere gratitude to the Sisters in Crime, both locally and nationally, for their sheer existence. We may not all know each other, but it's nice to know you're out there.

To the best dad in the universe, Paul Corrao, who I am

grateful for every day. There are no words grand enough in any dictionary or thesaurus to thank you for everything you've done for me. To my mother, Chin Mei Chien, and my sister, Shu-Hui Wills for passing along their wisdom and advice. I was listening more than you realized. To my soul sister, Rebecca Zandovskis, whose friendship I would be lost without. One of the best days of my life was March 18, 1996. If those two gals could see us now . . . what a wild ride it's been!

To Lindsey Timms and Mari Crespo, for the good times in Irvine and beyond. We'll always have "Shanghai Donuts" . . . literally . . . I put it in the book! To Mallory Doherty, for the constant cheering and words of encouragement she gives me on a daily basis. Thank you from the bottom of my heart, little buddy. Much love goes to Lea Miller for being one heck of a mama bear AND baker. Your support has meant so much to me. Lots of love to my gal pals, Alyssa, Holly, and Tiffany. I am fortunate to have you in my life.

A giant thank you to the book store employees, librarians, bloggers, and reviewers who have supported this series and helped spread the word. I appreciate everything you've done. Big hugs to my readers for their support, their kindness, and the time they've allowed me to entertain them. You make every minute of this worth it. And thank you to those who have reached out to me . . . keep it coming! I love hearing from you!

To all the unnamed friends and family who have encouraged me along the way, I thank you always.

And last, but never least, it is with great reverence that I wish to thank my grandmother, the late Effie Corrao, for whom I dedicate this book. Her guidance and wisdom taught me much about life and shaped the woman I would eventually become. Not only did she offer life lessons and valuable advice, but she passed on an immense love of reading that would end up taking me on journeys I could never imagine in my wildest dreams. For that I am eternally grateful.

CHAPTER 1

There I was, staring at my doom . . . surely; this was a fate worse than death. "I am in so much trouble. This is a complete and total nightmare!"

Kimmy Tran, childhood friend and fellow Asia Village employee, gawked at me as we stood side by side inside the enclosed plaza, staring at the cause of my nervous breakdown. The sloppy bun on her head wobbled as she lectured me. "Lana Lee, calm down. It's not that serious. You're a grown woman, for Pete's sake."

"There couldn't be a more horrible circumstance. Why is this happening to me?" I tugged on the locks of freshly dyed, black-and-magenta-streaked hair that framed my face. "What did I do to deserve this?"

She puffed out her already chubby cheeks. "This is ridiculous, you need to relax."

Peter Huang, the head chef at my family's restaurant, walked up behind us. "What's up, ladies? What are we lookin' at?"

"This . . . this monstrosity," I said with a shiver. "This horrible, horrible monstrosity."

Peter adjusted his black ball cap, and tilted his head. With a chuckle, he asked, "What? The doughnut shop?"

As he said the word *doughnut,* I heard my stomach rumble. Standing before us was the newest tenant of Asia Village, Shanghai Donuts. They were due to open in the next few days, and sadly I knew that I would be their very first customer.

On top of my addiction to noodles and book buying, I had a weakness for doughnuts. For the most part, I was able to refrain from indulging on the delicious, round pastries of doughy goodness, but with the new shop opening up right next door, I had to wonder about the current status of my willpower.

At the age of twenty-seven—on the brink of twenty-eight—I was warned by many that my metabolism was on its way off the fast track. Those "many" included members of my family who seemed to be tracking my eating habits.

I squeezed the side of my waist and felt the pounds I had put on since I'd started working at the restaurant. My pants were starting to feel tight. With my credit cards dancing on the edge of maxed out, I found my two favorite food groups to be excellent stress relievers.

Peter laughed, giving my shoulder a nudge. "Don't worry, Lana, I'm sure you'll get sick of them after a while. You can't eat doughnuts every day."

"Says you," I grumbled.

He grabbed my arm and pulled me in the direction of my family's noodle house and current place of employment. "Come on, man, let's get to work, we have to prep for the noodle contest."

Kimmy looked between the two of us. "I can't believe it's tomorrow. Are you guys prepared?"

They were referring to the Cleveland's Best Noodles contest, set to be held at Asia Village. Peter had been prepping and perfecting recipes for weeks in anticipation of winning the competition.

"Super stoked," Peter replied. "This year we're taking first place. No more of this third-place stuff. No, it says right there on the sign." He pointed above his head to the restaurant's gold-lettered sign.

It read: HO-LEE NOODLE HOUSE, #1 NOODLE SHOP.

We served all sorts of Taiwanese and Chinese cuisine, but our specialty, of course, was noodles. And Peter's noodles were the best in the whole city. I might be a little biased, but if you've tasted his cooking, I think you'd agree.

Kimmy gave Peter a flirtatious grin. "If there's anybody that can beat out the Shen family, it'll be you."

He blushed. "Um, thanks."

Peter and Kimmy were in the midst of a budding romance. They weren't the likeliest of couples, but so far it seemed to be working out for them.

Kimmy was a touch on the outspoken side and didn't mind being the center of attention—that was putting it lightly. In recent history, to help her parents with some money problems, she had taken a secret job at a strip club as a cocktail waitress. Needless to say, there were plenty of eyes on her there.

Meanwhile, Peter was on the introverted side. He kept to himself and participated in solitary hobbies usually involving video games or something artistic, like painting or drawing.

We said our good-byes to Kimmy, who shuffled over two storefronts to her own place of business, China Cinema and Song, which she helped run for her parents.

I unlocked the door to the restaurant, and we stepped into the darkened dining room, making our way to the back with little effort. When I say that I've lived a lifetime in this restaurant, it is not an overexaggeration. Ho-Lee Noodle House has been around since before my own creation, and there isn't a time I can remember when it wasn't a part of my memories.

A few weeks ago, I had officially become the permanent restaurant manager, now taking care of the main responsibilities while my mother tended to my grandmother. A native of Taiwan, my grandmother was on her first trip to the United States, and her English was less than stellar. And that's being nice about it.

My parents had spent considerable time in Taiwan recently, tending to my grandmother's medical condition. While there, they had decided the best thing to do was to bring her back with them. I still didn't have any idea what was supposed to be wrong with my grandmother, but every time I asked my mother what the deal was, she told me to mind my own business. I had stopped asking.

The restaurant life wasn't what I originally had been searching for, but it was turning out better than I'd thought. My older sister, Anna May, wasn't thrilled with me taking over the family business, but with her well on the path to becoming a high-powered attorney, she didn't have much say in the matter. There might be a small part of me that took pleasure in that fact.

Outside the kitchen, I flipped on the lights, and the

black and red dining area sprang to life. The touches of gold accent sparkled under the soft yellow lighting and bounced off the black-lacquered tabletops.

We passed through the kitchen and made our way to the back room, which had been turned into an employee lounge. A beat-up couch and small TV from my childhood still occupied the room, and I wondered if my parents would ever replace them.

"So," Peter said as he grabbed his apron from the hook. "I'm ready for the contest, but I want to test my recipes one more time before tomorrow. Are you cool with taste-testing them for me?"

"Twist my arm," I joked. "Of course, I'll taste them. We can't let the House of Shen win . . . or Ray for that matter."

Ray Jin, last year's contest winner, beat out both us and our rival, the House of Shen, by winning the coveted award.

The grand prize winner's restaurant would be featured in *Cleveland* magazine with a special profile on the chef and their award-winning recipes. Not only that, but the winning restaurant also won free advertising in the magazine for a year, a cash prize of five thousand dollars, and an engraved plaque to hang in their restaurant.

In the five years that the contest had been in existence, we had always placed in the top five, but never made first. This was going to be our year. I could feel it.

Peter shook his head. "No, didn't you hear? They asked Ray to be one of the judges this year."

"You're kidding!"

"I swear on my own life, dude."

"But what about all the rumors that spread around last year after the contest was over? So many people thought he cheated."

"Yeah, but no one could actually prove it. Especially when the whole scenario came from Joel Liu . . . totally made him look even crazier than he already did. Losing that contest really threw him over the edge."

"True. I just assumed they would want to avoid the controversy."

"They probably did that so he couldn't enter again. If the rumors are true, what would stop him from doing it again this year?"

I contemplated that while we headed back into the kitchen and got into our morning zones. Peter revved up the appliances while I prepped the dining room to perfection before our first customers of the day arrived.

After all the chaos at Asia Village in the past handful of months, we needed something good to happen at the plaza. And winning this contest would definitely be good.

CHAPTER 2

Asia Village, nestled away in the city of Fairview Park, was my home away from home, and not just because the restaurant was conveniently tucked inside. No, these days, I spent a lot of time in the enclosed shopping center taking advantage of everything it had to offer. When I wasn't browsing the shelves of my favorite bookstore, the Modern Scroll, I was getting drinks with my newest friend, Rina Su, at the karaoke bar, the Bamboo Lounge. And you can't forget the salon, Asian Accents, where I always went to get my hair cut and dyed by Jasmine Ming, who I say is the "best in the Midwest." Aside from that, we had an Asian grocery, an herbal shop, a gift shop, and just about anything else you could think of. It was your one-stop Asian shopping experience.

It was lunchtime at the plaza and my mother and grandmother had stopped by for some noodles before heading off to do whatever it was they did during the day. We were huddled in a circle in Esther's store, Chin's Gifts, talking about the upcoming contest. Esther is my mother's best friend and an aunt of sorts. She does things like lecture me on my behavior and comment on my posture.

"If the Shen family wins this year, Ho-Lee Noodle House will lose face again," my mother told the group. "We must beat them."

My mother, Betty Lee, is best described as a spitfire. She's small, sassy, and will tell you how it is whether you want to hear it or not. Her apple cheeks and quiet smile draw you in, but don't underestimate her. Especially if she doesn't like what you're wearing.

"We will, Mom," I replied. "Don't worry about it so much. Peter and I have everything under control."

Esther nodded in agreement. "Yes, this year you will win. I can sense these things." She tapped her temple with her index finger, and her jade bangle bracelets slid up her arm almost to her elbow. She shook them back into place. "This year, you will have good luck."

My grandmother, who was standing next to me, barely came up to my shoulders. And I am not by any means a tall person—I come in at a solid five feet four on a good day. She observed my mother and me, watching our lips move and trying to follow along. She blurted something rapidly in Hokkien—the Taiwanese dialect that my family spoke more often than not—and stared expectantly at my mother.

My mother replied, and they both nodded.

"What did she say?" I asked. My knowledge of the language was slipping and continued to dissipate for lack of use as I got older. I caught the word *eat* and that was it.

"She said that she would like to have lunch now. She is bored because she does not understand us."

I turned to my grandmother who met my glance with a smile. Her two front teeth were silver and they glistened in her mouth. She grabbed my hand. "A-ma . . . hungry."

"Okay, A-ma . . ." I pointed to the door with my free hand. "Let's go."

"Go!" She tugged on my hand to follow her.

We said good-bye to Esther, and headed out into the plaza. Construction for the noodle contest was under way, and a team of workers hustled to construct a temporary stage over the koi pond.

Ian Sung, our property manager, had insisted that the contest be held indoors in case of unexpected weather. A Cleveland spring could be extra rainy and he didn't want to take the chance.

"Hey, guys!" Rina Su waved at us from the threshold of her new cosmetics shop. The Ivory Doll specialized in Asian makeup and skin-care brands like Shiseido, Wei East, and Amorepacific but also carried more familiar brands like L'Oreal and Revlon. The introduction of the Asian cosmetic lines to the area had been a big hit, and she was drawing in new business for the plaza. Since she'd moved in, my cosmetics collection also had . . . gotten healthy.

Rina was the sister of a friend I'd made not long ago who'd been the victim of a senseless murder. Isabelle Yeoh, and her husband, Brandon, had opened a souvenir shop next to Ho-Lee Noodle House and it seemed like just yesterday that they'd opened the doors to their first business.

After Isabelle and Brandon were murdered, I'd met Rina at the memorial services, and we bonded over the loss of her sister. An unexpected turn of events led to Rina taking over the property that her sister and brother-in-law had previously owned.

However, since the murders happened in the store, Rina had convinced Ian to let her move the property over to a different empty space in the plaza. Now she resided in the spot that had formerly been owned by a man named Charles An. In case you were wondering what happened to him, well, he turned out to be a very bad man, and he's now sitting in a state correctional facility for first-degree murder, and attempted murder. The attempted murder was on yours truly. The nightmares from that ordeal were still waking me up from time to time, but I tried my best to brush it under the proverbial rug.

That is also how I got stuck with Shanghai Donuts right next to the noodle shop. My mom and sixty percent of the Village believed that the space was cursed. This percentage included the older-generation employees who are a little more superstitious than us younger folk. But for once in my life, I wished that were true. I couldn't have this doughnut shop be the exception to the rule. How many pants sizes would I gain in the long run?

My mother grabbed my grandmother's arm. "We will meet you at the restaurant. Go talk to your friend."

I separated from my family, and walked over to greet Rina. "Hey, girlfriend, whatcha up to?"

She pushed off the wall she'd been leaning against and gave me a hug. "Watching these handsome guys work their magic."

I laughed and followed her line of sight to the group of men working, completely oblivious to the two of us staring at them. "I see. Anyone in particular that you've got your eye on over there?"

"Not really, they're all pretty cute. That one there is the new community director, Frederick Yuan." She pointed to a slightly muscular Asian man in a white T-shirt and jeans. "He doesn't start until Monday, but he offered to help with the contest. Isn't that so sweet?"

"I didn't know that Ian had picked someone for the job already."

"He made the decision yesterday. I guess him and Frederick go way back or something. I think he said they went to school together."

I watched him as he worked. He talked and laughed with the others as he helped lift one end of the stage. His biceps stretched the material of his shirt, and a sliver of tattoo was exposed.

"How's Adam?" Rina asked, breaking my stare.

"Huh, what?"

She laughed. "I asked, how's Adam?"

"Oh, right. Adam." I straightened and turned my back to the crew. "He's okay, I guess."

"I haven't seen him around lately. Is everything all right with you guys?"

Adam, also known as Detective Trudeau, was my sort-of-maybe boyfriend guy. I say *sort of maybe* because we have yet to seal the deal on the whole relationship bit. At the present moment, we were dating and not seeing other people—at least I wasn't. But lately, we had been seeing less of each other. I kept reminding myself that it was his work that kept him away and not secretly his lack of interest. "He's been busy with a case so he hasn't had much time to stop by and visit."

Rina frowned. "Hopefully things will lighten up for him soon. Starting new relationships can be hard if you don't put in the time."

"Yeah, you're telling me." I turned back around to the workers who were now taking a break. They had covered the koi pond with their makeshift stage and lounged on benches nearby. "Well, I better get to the restaurant, my mom and grandma are waiting for me."

"I'll talk to you at the contest tomorrow! I have my fingers crossed that you guys win!"

As I walked to the restaurant, I kept my eyes on the cobblestone pathway that trails through the plaza. I could feel four sets of eyes fixed on me as I walked by. Just as I was about to reach for the door handle of the noodle shop, someone yelled, "Hey!" and the natural reflex to turn and look kicked in.

Frederick Yuan was jogging up to me, a dimpled smile on his full lips. "Hey, hi, I'm Freddie," he said as he halted inches away from me. He extended a hand. "You're familiar . . . why is that?"

I took his hand and he gave me a firm shake. "I'm Lana . . . Lana Lee. I work here . . ."

"Ah, that explains it. I'm the new community director. I'm starting next week." His chocolate-brown eyes focused intently on mine, and I could feel the heat rising up my neck into my cheeks. "It's nice to meet a friendly face . . . I look forward to seeing you around."

"Yeah . . . me too." I realized he was still holding on to my hand, which was beginning to sweat. I jerked it away and hid it behind my back. "I'm sorry, it's nice to meet you, but I have to go. My family is waiting for me."

"Oh, don't let me hold you up. Just wanted to introduce myself." He jerked a thumb at the stage behind him. "Are you going to be at the contest tomorrow? Your restaurant is in the competition, right?"

I nodded.

"Cool, I'll see you then." He gave me a wink before jogging back to the other guys.

I turned on my heel and pulled on the door handle. Come Monday, Shanghai Donuts wasn't going to be my only problem.

I pulled into the parking lot of my apartment complex a little after six o'clock. Making my way down the sidewalk to the two-bedroom apartment I shared with my best friend, Megan Riley, I spotted her car parked a few spaces away from mine. That was unusual for a Friday night because she worked at a bar.

When I opened the door, my black pug, Kikkoman, who normally greeted me upon arrival, was nowhere to be found. "Hello?" I scanned the room. "Where is everybody?"

"In here!" a muffled voice yelled back.

I locked the front door and headed down the short hallway where I noticed the bathroom door was closed. The water was running and I could hear splashing. "What are you doing in there? Where's Kikko?"

"Open the door. You'll see."

I twisted the door handle and poked my head inside. Immediately I burst into laughter.

Megan twisted around from her kneeling position over the tub. Her long blond hair was pulled into a tight ponytail that whipped around as she shifted to face me. "Today, this little girl decided to roll around in some other dog's poop. So now we're having bathtime."

I continued to laugh. On my dog's head was a mini shower cap stretched over her floppy ears. She looked up at me and her mouth dropped open. "Kikko, is this true?"

Her little pink tongue flopped out and she panted in reply.

Noting my best friend's choice of black leggings and racerback tank top, I said, "I hope you're not missing work because of this."

"Nope, I took off tonight so I could get up and go with you to the noodle contest in the morning."

"Aw, you did? That's so nice!" I leaned against the bathroom wall, watching Kikko squirm in the tub.

"I know how much this means to you. With everything that's been happening, Asia Village needs a win."

"That's exactly what I said earlier today. Business is still doing pretty well despite everything, but having an award-winning restaurant at the plaza would definitely help."

"Is Adam going to be there tomorrow?" she asked, shifting her focus back on the dog. "You haven't mentioned him in a couple of days."

"That's because there's nothing to tell. And no, I don't think he'll be there tomorrow."

Megan pulled Kikko from the tub, carefully covering her in a towel. "He's still busy with that case?"

I nodded. "He sent me a few text messages, but nothing exciting. Just checking in and saying hello."

"I'm sure once things are wrapped up, he'll be around again. It's gotta be tough juggling that type of job and normal life."

"Right now my main concern is this noodle contest. We have got to beat the Shen family no matter what."

She released Kikko from the towel and the little pug shook the remaining water from her body before zipping out of the bathroom. "Peter is the best cook in town, I'm sure there won't be any problems."

"There better not be. Or my mother won't let me hear the end of it."

CHAPTER 3

Saturday morning I trudged out of bed, caffeinated myself heavily, and managed to leave a little earlier than planned with Megan in tow. She handled the early hours better than I did, but neither one of us were what you'd classify as morning people.

The drive was a short one, and fifteen minutes later we were at Asia Village. The contest wasn't scheduled to start until noon, but the restaurant managers, owners, and cooks had to begin preparing their stations two hours beforehand. Parts of the plaza were sectioned off with velvet rope to discourage stragglers from wandering into the contest area ahead of time.

"My mom said to meet everyone at the restaurant," I told Megan as I steered her toward Ho-Lee Noodle House.

"Hope we can grab some food before the contest. I'm starving."

When we entered the restaurant, there was a commotion in the dining area. My mother was off to the side of the room flapping her arms up and down as she yelled at Esther and my grandmother. My sister was at the hostess station with her head in her hands, her jet-black hair covering her face and spilling onto the lectern. The Mahjong Matrons, our resident gossips and early-morning regulars, were half listening to my mother and half whispering among themselves. And Peter, well, my guess was that he was hiding out in the kitchen.

I walked up to Anna May at the hostess booth and patted her arm. "Hey . . ."

Her head shot up and she jumped up from her seat at the hostess station. When she realized it was me, her eyes narrowed to slits. She held a hand to her chest as if to catch her breath. "Lana! You scared me half to death! Don't do that!"

"Didn't you hear the chimes?" I pointed to the bells hanging above the door. "What the heck is going on in here?"

Anna May removed a hairband from around her wrist, and pulled her hair into a ponytail. "Mom is freaking out because Penny Cho entered the contest at the last minute."

"So?" My eyes traveled back to my mother and I watched as Esther tried to calm her down. She had a hand on my mother's wrist and was whispering to her. "She has a right to compete in the contest just as much as we do."

Penny Cho was the owner of the Bamboo Lounge, a karaoke bar that served a light menu to their singing patrons. I was a little surprised she would enter, considering most of her menu consisted of appetizers. But she did offer a few noodle dishes, and as long as noodles were somewhere on your menu, you were welcome to compete.

"Well, Mom is freaking anyway," Anna May said, taking a quick peek over her shoulder. "She doesn't want there to be any competition within the plaza. She said it will pit people against each other."

Megan stepped up from behind me and nodded in agreement. "I can see why your mom is upset. Up until last year, you guys were the only restaurant in the plaza. This has got to be awkward for her. Remember how upset she was when the Bamboo Lounge first opened? I think if Penny had ended up serving more than an appetizer menu, your mother would have had a coronary."

"Yeah, I know. She needs to take it down a notch though. Her spazzing out about this isn't going to help anything."

"Do you want to tell her that?" my sister asked. "Because I certainly don't."

"Where's Dad?" I asked, scanning the room for him. He wasn't hard to miss. He was six feet and two inches of white guy. In our crowd, he kind of stood out.

"He had to show a house this morning, but said he'll be here in time for the actual contest."

"I better go talk to Mom . . ." I turned to Megan. "Want to come with me?"

"Lead the way."

"Good luck to both of you." Anna May plopped back down on the hostess stool and put her head in her hands. "The yelling is giving me a headache."

My grandmother, who appeared uninterested in my mother's ranting, was the first to notice me. She grinned, exposing her shiny silver teeth. "Laaa-na." She greeted me with a hug and held my arms as she inspected my face. Reaching up, she patted my cheek.

She grinned at Megan and gave her a polite nod. *"Ni hao."*

Megan looked at me. "That's like *hello* in Mandarin, right?"

"Yes."

Megan turned back to my grandmother and smiled. *"Ni hao . . . A-ma."*

My grandmother clapped and gave Megan a thumbs-up. "Very good!"

While this exchange was going on, my mother and Esther had stopped their conversation and turned their attention toward us. "Did you hear what happened?" my mother asked. Her hands were on her hips and the scowl on her face confirmed that she wasn't going to drop this any time soon.

"Anna May told me about it . . . it's gonna be okay, Mom. Really."

"You say it will be okay, and Esther says it will be okay." My mother turned to acknowledge her friend. "But it is not okay with me."

"There's no way she can compete with Peter's cooking skills," I assured her. "Her chef has nothing on us. Where is Peter anyway?"

She waved an arm toward the back room. "In the kitchen."

"Okay, I'm going to talk to him." I gave Megan the signal. "In the meantime, try to calm down; you're going to make Peter nervous."

She clucked her tongue at me as we walked away.

In the kitchen, I found Peter busy at the stove. He was dressed in his usual black attire complete with backwards hat. The only thing different were his shoes, which appeared to be a new pair of black Converse instead of the ratty old ones he wore on most days.

"Hey, dudes," he said with a nod. "How's Mama Lee doing out there?"

"Still the same . . . freaking out."

He smirked. "I told her not to sweat it. But you know your mom."

"I do indeed." I glanced around the kitchen at the things Peter had already packed up. "Do you want help taking anything over to the cooking station?"

"Um, sure, can you grab some of this stuff?" He pointed to a stack of boxes on the counter by the sinks.

Megan went for a box of cooking utensils. "Where are we taking this?"

Peter picked up a box of ingredients. "Follow me, ladies."

Like a row of ducks, we marched through the restaurant past my mother and Esther who were still going at it. They observed us as we walked by, but did not offer to help. My grandmother was now up front with my sister.

"We're heading over and getting set up. Are you stuck here during the contest or are you going to come and watch?"

Anna May nodded. "Vanessa is on her way in and she's going to hostess. Esther is covering the tables so Nancy can watch Peter during the contest, and Lou should be here any minute to take over in the kitchen. We're all covered."

"Great." I hoisted up the box I was carrying. "We'll be back."

Peter led us through the maze of velvet ropes and up the steps onto the stage we had watched them build the day before. The area was busy with activity as the other restaurant owners set up their individual workstations.

The chef stations were set up in a square formation with bleacher-style seats surrounding the stage on three sides. The fourth side was equipped with a table for the judges and a red curtain hung behind their stage. Hanging from the top of the curtain was a banner listing the five competitors.

Our booth was directly across from the judges' table which accommodated three chairs. A shiny silver name plaque was placed in front of each chair.

The first one read: NORMAN PAN. It should have read Norman *Pain* because the man was a severe pain in the you-know-what. As a local food critic, he had made a lot of enemies along the way. To put it politely, he was fussy, and his reviews could be scathing. He was not afraid to get down and dirty, completely annihilating a restaurant with a few short paragraphs.

The second nameplate read: STELLA CHUNG. I had heard the name several times as she was a Cleveland success story. After all, who didn't love a good underdog anecdote? Stella had come from a poor family, found a passion for cooking, and struggled to get into culinary school. By the skin of her financial teeth, she'd made it into the Loretta Paganini School of Cooking where she excelled beyond everyone's expectations. Shortly after completing school, she began working as a chef at a world-renowned Asian restaurant in Chicago.

And the final nameplate read RAY JIN, owner and head chef of Taste of the Orient, a restaurant on the east side of Cleveland in an area referred to as Asia Town. Despite Ray's suffering a few bad reviews from Norman Pan, he surprisingly took first prize in last year's contest. A lot of controversy surrounded the news of his win after the results were publicly announced, and many suspected that he'd bribed Norman to take home the trophy. Like Peter had pointed out, it was never proven, and after a while the gossip had died down. I suspected now that he was a judge, it would get brought up again. The Mahjong Matrons would see to it, I was sure.

The three of us began prepping the workstation, Peter mumbling to himself about placement as he went along. After two more trips back to the restaurant, we finally had everything set up and stepped back to admire our handiwork.

"Looks like a mini-kitchen to me," Megan said with satisfaction. "Now can we get something to eat? My stomach is growling and I'm actually enticed by these raw noodles."

"Agreed, let's grab something quick from the restaurant. We still have a half hour before it starts."

We began to walk away, but I stopped when I noticed Peter wasn't following. "Aren't you coming?" I asked him.

He shook his head. "Nah, you guys go on. I'm going to stay here and find my chi or whatever."

"Okay, we'll be back in a little bit. Want us to bring you anything?"

"No, I cook better on an empty stomach."

"What's up with him?" Megan asked as we re-entered the restaurant.

"I'm not sure. But if I didn't know any better, I'd say he's actually nervous about something."

CHAPTER 4

When we returned to the noodle-contest area with our to-go bags of food, a line of onlookers had started to form at the main entrance of the seating area. Freddie Yuan was helping Ian direct people through the maze of ropes to their seats.

"There's the new guy," I whispered to Megan. "Frederick . . . Freddie Yuan . . ."

"That's the community director guy?" Megan asked, following my gaze. "He's pretty cute."

"He's okay," I mumbled.

Megan glanced at me out of the corner of her eye. "Uh-huh."

We took our places in the seats behind Peter's workstation. My family was on their way over from the restaurant, but Kimmy and her parents were already seated in the row behind us.

Kimmy leaned over my shoulder while I chomped on

a spring roll. "Did you see the Shens over there? Looking all arrogant. That daughter of theirs . . . Jackie . . . I'd like five minutes alone with her in an alley."

Nearly choking on my spring roll, I whipped around. "Kimmy!"

"What? She called you a half-breed. I don't like it." Kimmy sneered in the direction of their cooking station.

Megan gasped, craning her neck to see who Kimmy was talking about. "What? Who said that?"

"That girl, right there." Kimmy pointed across the room to my archnemesis, Jackie Shen.

"It's no big deal." I nudged Kimmy's knee with my elbow. "And please, don't bring it up in front of my mother. She hates them enough as it is."

"When did this happen?" Megan asked. "How come I never heard about it?"

"It was at last year's competition. Really, it's no big deal. I forgot it happened actually."

Okay, that was a lie, I hadn't forgotten. Truth was, being mixed has not always been the easiest thing to live with. According to who you were talking to, it could be a great thing or it could be viewed as a negative attribute. In the particular case of Jackie Shen, she looked down on me for it.

I caught sight of my parents, and reminded the girls to keep their mouths shut about it in front of them. My sister and grandmother trailed behind my mom and dad.

"Hey there, Goober!" My dad scooped me into a hug as I stood up to greet them. He was still in his suit from the house showing and I could smell the Aspen aftershave he used on the collar of his dress shirt. "Megan, I didn't know you'd be here today," he said, turning to greet my friend. He gave her arm a gentle squeeze. "Nice to have you here with us."

"Of course. I couldn't miss out on Peter taking home the trophy!" she replied.

Nancy Huang, Peter's mom, showed up next and squeezed in between my mother and grandmother. I noticed how happy she was as she talked with excitement to my mother. Her naturally beautiful, porcelain face had a certain glow of pride to it, and I was relieved to see her looking like herself again. After months of mourning over her secret lover—and Donna Feng's husband—Thomas, she was finally returning to normal.

Out of the corner of my eye, I noticed Ian Sung was walking out onto center stage. The crowd began to quiet as others caught sight of him making his way to the middle. He held a cordless microphone in his hand, and my mind jumped back to the last time he'd had to make a speech in front of several people. To say it didn't go well was an understatement, and I wondered how he would do this time around.

When he was sure that most of the attention was on him, he held the microphone up to his face. The smile on his thin lips was crooked and often reminded me of a villain ready to announce their evil plans. "Patrons of Asia Village, welcome!"

The crowd clapped and a couple whistles were heard around the bleachers.

"Thank you for joining us today as we kick off the fifth annual Cleveland's Best Noodles contest. My partner, Donna Feng—who unfortunately could not be here with us today—and I are thrilled to be hosting this event."

I was shocked to hear that Donna was not attending,

and wondered what could have possibly kept her away. Since the tragic death of her husband, she acted mostly as a silent partner and advisor for her younger counterpart. And even though her involvement was minor since Ian had taken over, she was more often present than not.

". . . and without further ado, I'd like to introduce our amazing panel of judges," Ian continued.

One by one, the judges came out from behind the red curtain and stood in front of their seats while Ian introduced them. Norman Pan—a stout, older man who was beginning to bald—started the lineup and observed the crowd through his bifocal glasses with what seemed like contempt.

Next to step out from behind the curtain was Stella Chung. The Cleveland underdog was a petite girl with a button nose, and big brown eyes. She regarded the crowd with a gentle smile and waved a quick hello as Ian gave a brief background on who she was. The short bio that he presented about her resulted in massive applause from the audience.

Last to join the stage was Ray Jin. He wore a black shirt with an outline of a red dragon across the front and waved like Miss America as he stepped out from behind the curtain. A few people clapped, but he didn't have a lot of friends in this part of town, and if I didn't know any better, I could have sworn I heard someone boo him.

After the crowd became silent once again, Ian spoke into the microphone. "There will be four rounds to the contest. This first round will involve the chefs preparing a simple lo mein dish. They will be graded on preparation, flavor, and presentation.

"But before the chefs start working their magic, let me

introduce you to them." Ian extended an arm, beginning the introductions on his right. "Over here we have the House of Shen with Walter Shen as acting chef."

A mixture of cheers and boos went through the crowd as Walter Shen waved to the audience. Much like Ray, Walter did not have many friends on this side of town. That was partially due to the fact that the Shen family was in constant competition with Asia Village. And they were certainly never quiet about their dislike for our West Side plaza, claiming we took business away from the heart of the original Chinatown.

"Next up is Stanley Gao from Wok and Roll. Stanley is owner and head chef of the up-and-coming Asian fusion bar and grill in the Flats. His specialty lies in his presentation and I'm excited to see what kind of art he cooks up for us today."

Stanley bowed his head graciously and held up a spatula, using it to wave at the crowd.

Ian skipped over our table and went on to introduce Penny, her cook, and the Bamboo Lounge, citing their recent arrival at Asia Village and bragging about the innovative dynamic that they brought to the plaza. I heard my mother swearing in Taiwanese under her breath. If I had glanced over a second later, I would have missed the priceless image of my grandmother pinching my mother's arm and scolding her for her choice of words.

I liked having my grandmother around. It proved extremely entertaining at times.

After that, Ian introduced Joel Liu from Liu's Noodle Emporium. He was a short man with a thick build and a buzz cut. His stance was military and I half expected him to salute the crowd.

Joel was last year's first elimination and sorest loser to date. But with good reason. In true Norman Pan fashion, the harsh food critic had destroyed Joel's contest entry, and even went so far as to submit a review of the contest *and* Joel's restaurant in a scathing article in *Cleveland* magazine. It was so harsh that people had spread the article all over social media, furthering Joel's embarrassment. The *Plain Dealer* and the *Sun Post* in turn picked up the story, not just of the article, but also of the backlash it had created. Liu's Noodle Emporium had earned the reputation as the worst restaurant in Cleveland. And, because of it, Joel had lost a ton of business. It was a miracle that he was even open at this point.

When news that he'd entered this year's contest made its way around the city, the *Plain Dealer* had reached out to him for an exclusive. He'd told the reporter that this was his chance to prove himself worthy, and that by entering the contest again, especially with Norman Pan as judge, he would show that he does not back down easily. The article quoted him as saying that Norman "would not see the defeat of Liu's Noodle Emporium in his lifetime."

Ian walked over to our workstation and caught my eye. "Ladies and gentlemen, I saved this restaurant for last because they hold a special place in my heart." He winked at me as he said it, and I stifled an eye roll. "Allow me to introduce Peter Huang, head chef of Ho-Lee Noodle House, Asia Village's very own prized noodle shop. This restaurant has been around for over thirty years and is the pride and joy of the Lee family."

My mother stood up with a bright smile on her face. "Ho-Lee Noodle House is number one!" she yelled into the crowd.

My face turned bright red and I slouched on the bench wishing that the ability to disappear into thin air I so often daydreamed about would magically kick in.

The crowd laughed and cheered, and I heard a few whistles from across the room. To my surprise, when I looked to see who it was, I saw a handsome man with reddish-brown hair, and a jawline I would recognize anywhere. It was Adam who was doing the whistling. He was sitting by himself near the top of the bleachers adjacent to us. When our eyes met, he acknowledged me with a nod and smile.

Megan nudged me. "Guess your beau showed up after all."

Suddenly, I was paranoid about my appearance and ran a hand through my angled bob, checking for flyaways. I smoothed out the crinkles in my shirt and brushed away a few stray crumbs that had fallen from my spring roll.

"You look fine," Megan whispered.

The audience clapped and I realized that Ian had signaled for the cooking to begin. He moved off the stage and the area was filled with the clattering of cooking utensils and chefs shuffling around at their workstations.

I tried my best to focus on Peter. It was my job to assist him should he need help with anything during the course of his food preparation or cooking.

However, my attention span is similar to that of a squirrel. Before long, my eyes were drifting around the room, occasionally peeking at Adam who was intent on watching the contest. He seemed to be most interested in what Peter was doing and that brought a smile to my face.

I observed the judges and noted their reactions as their focus moved from station to station. They were also instructed to get up and interact with the chefs as they cooked.

I couldn't help but take a glimpse at what the Shen family was up to. Walter Shen, Jackie's father, worked diligently as his family observed him sauté noodles in a wok.

My attention circled back to the judges' table where a crew of servers had snuck in to set up stacks of dishes at each of the chairs. Freddie was seated on the left side of the judges' table, and he watched Stanley from Wok and Roll with mild amusement as the chef dazzled the audience with his preparation show.

"Lana," Peter yelled over his shoulder. "I need you to grab sesame oil from the restaurant. I think I left it on the counter."

Freddie caught my stare and waved.

"Lana!" Peter yelled, turning to face me.

"Uh, yeah . . . I'm on it," I said, springing up from my seat. If I had been paying attention, I would have noticed that my foot was caught on the handle of a plastic bag. It was too late though. I was already on the ground, palms down, my nose a half inch away from the floor. I hurried to right myself, but I should have stayed down longer. By the time I stood up, I realized that Freddie Yuan wasn't the only one staring at me.

CHAPTER 5

After recovering from my fall, I rushed over to the restaurant to grab the things that Peter needed and hurried back. The rest of the first round proceeded without incident, and before long, the chefs were finished with their lo mein dishes.

A server went around to each workstation with a different-colored plate—ours was red—and placed a small portion of noodles on each one to bring back to the judges who were now at their seats.

My eyes followed the red plate back to Norman Pan who was staring down at the table, shaking his head. He looked up at the server and nodded when the plate was placed in front of him.

Peter turned his back to the judges and looked at Kimmy, who gave him a thumbs-up.

Norman took a small bite of noodle and chewed carefully, moving his head from side to side. He nodded in satisfaction and scribbled something down on a pad of paper next to his plate.

"Peter," I hissed. "Look! He likes it." I nudged my head in Norman's direction.

Peter swung around to see what I was referring to. Even though his back was to me, I could tell he was smiling.

After each of the dishes had been sampled by all of the judges, they stepped behind the curtain to deliberate with one another. The rest of us sat waiting in anticipation, to find out who would be eliminated from the first round.

Around twenty minutes later, the judges filed back out and the room grew silent. Ian walked on to the stage area and leaned over the judges' table. Norman handed him a slip of paper, and Ian nodded before turning around to face the audience.

"Ladies and gentlemen . . ." Ian's voice boomed into the microphone mimicking a game-show host. "While the judges had a hard time making their decision, the vote was unanimous! Peter Huang from Ho-Lee Noodle House wins this round! And it looks like the first chef to be eliminated is Joel Liu from Liu's Noodle Emporium."

"What!" Joel screamed from behind his workstation. "This is impossible! This whole thing is rigged." He threw his spatula across the stage toward the judges' table and nearly hit Norman in the face. "Rigged!"

Without hesitation, Ian whistled into the microphone and two uniformed security guards stepped out from behind the curtain and headed toward Joel. When he saw the guards approaching him, he let out an angry groan and stomped off, disappearing behind the set of bleachers closest to his workstation.

Ian laughed nervously into the microphone. "We apologize for that, folks. But as you can see, the restaurants involved all take this contest seriously."

"You're not kidding!" someone yelled.

The audience erupted in laughter.

Ian gestured for the group to quiet down. "Now be sure to join us tomorrow at noon for the next round where we will eliminate another contestant!"

Everyone clapped, and Ian bowed his head before stepping off to the side. He started to make his way around the workstations, exchanging a few words with each of the chefs.

When he made it to our station, he slapped Peter on the back. "Good job, Huang. Norman was impressed with your cooking more than anyone else's. Keep it up and you're going to win this thing."

"Really?" I stepped between the two men. "Over everyone else?"

"Geez, Lana, don't act so surprised," Peter groaned.

"I didn't mean it like that. It's just that he always praises Walter Shen above everyone else. It's different to hear him say otherwise."

"Excuse me!"

We all jumped a little at the booming voice. Oh no! It was Norman. He must have heard us talking about him.

I smiled graciously, pulling out the facial expression I reserved for our customers. "Mr. Pan, it's so great to finally meet you."

He looked down his nose at me. "And you are?"

"Lana Lee." I extended my hand. "I'm the manager at Ho-Lee Noodle House."

Peter turned away from us, focusing his attention back on the workstation as if Norman wasn't even there.

Norman glanced down at my hand, and back up at me. "Isn't that nice?" Turning his attention back to Ian, he thrust a small paper toward him. "Mr. Sung, what is the meaning of this?"

Ian took the little paper and squinted. "I don't understand . . ."

"This was inside the fortune cookie at my place setting. I'd like to know why."

Ian inspected the tiny slip of paper. "I'm not sure . . . we didn't ask for fortune cookies to be placed at the judges' table."

"If this is someone's idea of a joke . . ." Norman's face reddened. "I will not be treated like a fool." He glanced over at the judges' table where Stella and Ray appeared to be having some type of debate.

I inched closer to Ian, trying to read what the fortune said, but I couldn't make out the words from over his shoulder.

While I was trying to get a better look, someone pinched my side, and I jumped, pushing Ian forward. Ian gasped and glared at me over his shoulder. Norman shook his head at both of us.

When I turned to see who had pinched me, I saw Adam standing behind me, his green eyes dancing with amusement from my surprise. He gave a cheesy grin. "Happy to see me?"

"I am," I replied, wrapping my arms around him. "You should have told me you were coming today. You could have sat with us."

"Nah, it's okay. This was your family time. I didn't want to intrude."

I could barely hear what Norman and Ian were talking about and I was dying to turn around and eavesdrop on their conversation. But I didn't want Adam to think I wasn't happy to see him.

"You ready to head over to the Bamboo Lounge? It was nice of Penny to throw a kickoff party."

"Yeah, I'll be right over; I'm going to help Peter take some things back to the restaurant."

"Let me help out," Adam offered. He kissed me on the forehead and turned to Peter, greeting him with congrats and a handshake.

"Yes, absolutely, I'll look into the matter," I heard Ian say from behind me.

"I should hope so." Norman glared at me as I turned around, and then stormed off.

"What the heck was that about?" I asked Ian.

He shook his head. "I'm beginning to think it's impossible for us to have an ordinary day in this place." With exasperation, he handed me the slip of paper.

It read: *If you do not seek out allies and helpers, then you will be isolated and weak.*

I tilted my head as I read it over again. "This sounds vaguely familiar. What is it?"

Ian stared across the stage at the judges' table. Ray and Stella had disappeared and in their place was the cleanup crew clearing away the place settings. He sighed. "Sun Tzu . . . it's from *The Art of War*."

After the contest, the participants, judges, and our special guests migrated into the Bamboo Lounge. Penny had reserved the party room for us and we filed inside finding a long buffet table at the far end. The rest of the floor was cleared and small tables were placed along the edges of the room.

Penny huddled with a group of servers at the door, giving instructions as they nodded and looked over their shoulders at their new customers. There were around twenty of us.

Adam made a beeline for the buffet table. "Watching all that cooking made me hungry."

Megan and I followed behind him. "I still can't believe you didn't tell me that you were coming," I said.

He winked at me over his shoulder. "Thought it might be fun to surprise you."

Megan whispered in my ear. "See? I told you everything was fine."

I had to admit that it made me happy he'd put in the effort. It seemed the longer we knew each other, the more our time together shrank and distance between dates expanded. The struggle not to turn it into a "me" thing was becoming difficult.

The table was filled with spring rolls, lettuce wraps, steamed pork buns, teriyaki skewers, and a number of other Chinese finger foods plus an entire section dedicated to desserts. My stomach rumbled as my eyes skimmed over the table.

"Holy . . . I think I need one of everything," Megan said, peeking over my shoulder. "She really went all out for this, didn't she?"

We piled our plates with food and picked a corner to congregate in. A server ambled over to take our drink orders, and after the excitement of the day, we agreed it would be cocktails all around.

I was chomping on a chicken teriyaki skewer when Jackie Shen sauntered our way. She gave Adam a once-over and a smile spread over her lips. "Lana Lee, who would have thought you'd have such excellent taste in men? Sure beats that last guy I saw you hanging around with."

Adam was mid-bite of his pork bun. He closed his mouth, placing the pork bun back on his plate. "I'm sorry, are you one of Lana's friends? I don't think we've met." He looked at me with a question in his eyes.

Jackie smirked. "Friends? No. But maybe you'd like to be?" She winked.

I almost choked on the piece of chicken I had in my mouth. "What do you want, Jackie?"

"I came over to tell you not to get too excited that your cook impressed Norman today. It's not going to last. My family is going to win. We got cheated last year because of Ray and his connections . . . but with him out of the way, the contest is *ours*."

I felt that Jackie deserved an extra-large eye roll, so I made sure to lay it on thick. "Look, Jackie," I said, pointing my skewer at her, "if you think you're going home with first place, you've really lost your mind. Peter is the best cook in Cleveland, and the judges are going to figure that out real fast."

"Whatever, Lee, you don't stand a chance. Why don't you step aside and let us *real* Asians do our thing?"

I knew that my face was turning different shades of red. I took a step closer to her, my skewer still pointed at her chest. "What did you say to me?"

She matched my step. "You heard me . . ."

Adam put a hand on my shoulder. "Are you really going to start a fight with the police present?" His voice was a mixture of stern and amused.

Jackie snickered. "Gee, I wish I could say I'm sorry about getting you in trouble with your boyfriend, but I'm really not."

"I was talking to *you,*" Adam said to Jackie.

"Whatever. If you ever get some taste, come find me. I'll show you some *true* Asian persuasion." She winked and sashayed off to find her parents.

My mouth dropped. "I can't believe she actually said that out loud."

"Is that girl serious?" Megan asked, her eyes following Jackie across the room.

"Unfortunately, yes." I polished off the remaining chicken on my skewer and set it on my plate. "I'm just glad Kimmy didn't hear it. Jackie would have left here with two black eyes and we'd have to bail Kimmy out of jail."

The three of us laughed, but I wasn't kidding.

The mingling began after everyone had stuffed themselves with as much food as possible. The buffet table was nearly empty, and a few people had dispersed into the main room to sing karaoke.

Megan and I were lounging by the dessert table, finding ourselves overly interested in the tiny cream puff tray that had just been refilled. Adam had disappeared somewhere, probably to talk with Peter about whatever men talk about these days.

"You there, young lady." Norman pointed at me, turning his finger and gesturing for me to come to his table. He sat at a two-seater on the opposite side of the room. On the table in front of him were several plates of food and four empty martini glasses. I couldn't drink four martinis on my best day.

The few people who remained in the room turned to see who Norman was yelling to. My eyes caught Ray watching us from the side of the room. When our glances met, he smirked at me and shrugged his shoulders.

"Uh-oh," Megan whispered. "Mr. Meanie Pants wants to talk with you. Do you want me to come with?"

"Nah, that's okay. You go ahead and find Adam. I'll meet up with you guys in a little bit."

She shrugged, grabbed another cream puff, and scampered off.

I walked over to the food critic's table. "Hello, Mr. Pan."

With a slur, he asked, "What is the purpose of your hair?"

"Excuse me?"

He gawked with disgust at my hair. "What purpose does it serve to dye your hair this odd color?"

I shrugged. "It's something I've always wanted to do."

He scoffed. "You're the manager at Ho-Lee Noodle House, are you not?"

"Yes sir, I am."

"Well, let me give you a piece of advice. Don't dye your hair strange colors. It's not professional and does not suit the appearance of an individual in a management position. I've met your mother on several occasions, and I'm appalled that she would allow such a thing."

I didn't know what to say. If I said anything slightly disrespectful, he could end up taking it out on Peter during the contest. So, I just stood there, grinning and bearing.

He waved his hand dismissively at me. "You can go now."

Without a word, I turned around and scurried away. I could feel my face changing colors again.

In the small amount of time that I'd spent being insulted, more of the room had cleared out to watch the karaoke performances, so I decided to head out to the main room as well.

Stella Chung had been standing in the doorway, observing my interaction with Norman. "He's a piece of work, isn't he?"

"Yeah, that's a word for it."

"Especially when he has a couple drinks. Sober he doesn't have a filter . . . give him a few and multiply his rude behavior by ten."

I looked over my shoulder at Norman as he slurped noodles from his plate. "I've heard stories, but this is the most interaction I've ever experienced with him."

"You're not missing a whole lot." Stella eyed him with an air of superiority. "He'd never last a week in Chicago." She shook her head and turned her attention to me. "I'm Stella, by the way."

"Lana."

"Nice to meet you. Everyone was really impressed with your cook this afternoon. I hope he takes home the win this time."

"I hope he does too."

"I still can't believe that Ray Jin won last year. That guy is a complete disgrace."

"Do you know him?" I asked.

"Nope, just from what I've heard. When they asked me to be on the judging panel this year, I had no idea he'd be on it with me. I might not have accepted if I'd known."

"Well, as a fellow Clevelander, I'm glad that you did."

She smiled. "It's nice to be back. I haven't been home in ages . . . gives me a chance to catch up with people and . . . tie up loose ends."

Clapping erupted from the main room, and my attention was drawn to Rina who was bowing onstage.

Stella looked over her shoulder. "Don't let me keep you. I think I'm going to grab another plate of pastries before heading out. Maybe I'll talk to you later."

I said good-bye and went out into main room to find Megan and Adam.

After scanning the crowded room, I spotted Megan and Adam at a small table off to the side of the stage.

"What the heck did he want?" Megan asked as I slipped into the seat next to hers.

"Oh, he just called me over to criticize my hair."

Megan gasped. "What? Your hair is totally awesome. How could anyone not like it?"

I shrugged. "He's an old-fashioned guy. I shouldn't be too offended. But to call me over just to insult me . . . it was pretty low."

"That guy doesn't have very many friends, does he?"

Adam, who was sitting a little in front of me, leaned back, looking at me over his shoulder. "What are you two gossiping about back there?"

"Just Mr. Pan being a jerk."

Adam shifted in his seat to face me. "He does seem to

have some kind of chip on his shoulder. Is he always like that?"

"Only every day of his life," I told him.

The song ended and everyone clapped. Nancy Huang, who was standing at the side of the stage, walked up to the microphone and spotlight. She had an amazing voice, and I was looking forward to hearing her sing.

She began to introduce herself. Her soft voice was amplified by the microphone. "Hello, everybody, I'm Nancy Huang, and I am going to sing—"

A bloodcurdling scream erupted from the party room. Everyone turned in their chairs.

"Crap!" Adam shouted. "Now what?"

"What the heck was that?" I asked, standing from my seat.

The music from the karaoke machine started to play.

"Turn it off!" Adam yelled. He shot up and headed in the direction of the party room.

I followed behind him.

He spun around and put his hands on my shoulders. "You. Stay."

I pouted but didn't argue.

Megan tugged on my arm. "What the hell is going on?"

"I don't know. It almost sounded like Penny." I searched the room for the Bamboo Lounge owner, but she was nowhere in sight.

My mother came running over with my dad and grandmother following closely behind. "Lana!" my mother yelled. "Lana!"

"I'm right here, Mom."

"Oh good, you're okay. I was worried you were still inside the party room eating."

We all stared at the door in anticipation. The room was filled with whispers and people inched closer to the party room door to get a better view of what was happening. A few minutes later, Penny came out sobbing; Adam followed behind her, a grim look on his face. He shut the party room door behind him and stood guard.

I ran up to him. "What happened in there?"

He took my hands, holding them in his. "I have a team and paramedics on their way."

"Why? What—"

"Lana . . . Norman Pan is dead."

CHAPTER 6

Adam stood up on the karaoke stage. He spoke with authority to the room, scanning the crowd. People huddled around tables anxious to hear what would happen next. "Nobody is leaving until we've gotten a chance to speak with everyone present. Once you've been spoken to by one of my team, you'll be escorted out by your interviewer. We need to keep this area contained, so there are officers posted at the entrance of the restaurant to ensure that everyone stays in or out."

A team of three officers stood at the front of the stage below him, their eyes scanning the crowd as Adam talked.

"I would like to divide the room into two sections. Please stand on the left if you were with the contest party. If you were not with the noodle contest, please stand off to the right. We'll try to make this as efficient as possible so you can get out of here and get home."

After the room was divided the way Adam wanted it,

he stepped off the stage and began instructing the other officers. They nodded diligently as he gave them their orders. One officer followed after Adam while the other two went to the opposite side of the room to question those who were at the lounge for a regular afternoon out.

I huddled together with my parents, my grandma, Anna May, and Megan. Peter, Kimmy, and Rina came over to join us.

"Can you freakin' believe this?" Kimmy said with indignation. "I can't believe it! All I wanted to do was have a couple drinks with my boyfriend before heading home. We had *plans* tonight." She gave me a pointed look.

Peter pretended to be occupied with something happening on the other side of the room.

I didn't want to guess what she meant by "plans" so I decided to pretend she didn't say anything at all.

"Do you think he had a heart attack?" Rina asked.

My dad shook his head. "I don't think Detective Trudeau would ask all of us to hang around if it was something like a heart attack."

"The plaza is cursed!" my mother screamed.

My dad squeezed my mom's shoulders. "It's just a coincidence, Betty. Try not to get worked up."

Penny came over to stand with us. Mascara was smeared on her cheeks, and she wiped at her face with a tissue as she stood next to me. "This can't be happening . . ."

"What exactly went on in there?" I asked.

She sniffled. "I went into the party room to clear away some of the empty plates. The room was empty . . . or so I thought . . . and I wanted to get a head start on the cleanup. When I went in there though, Norman was at his table with his head down. I thought maybe he'd passed out from all the drinks he had, but when I got closer, I realized he was lying with his face in a plate of noodles."

We all gasped in unison.

"I still thought maybe he fell asleep, but when I lifted his head up . . ." She started to sob. "He . . . wasn't breathing! And there were marks around his neck like he'd been strangled—" She erupted into tears, covering her face with her hands. Her shoulders shook as she cried uncontrollably.

I reached out to hug her, giving her a strong squeeze. "It's okay, Penny, the worst part is behind you now."

She lifted her head, pushing me away. "I'm ruined, Lana. No one is going to want to eat *or* sing here after someone died."

"Things will calm down," I reassured her. "Look what happened with Ho-Lee Noodle House. And we're fine again . . ."

"That's different, Lana. Mr. Feng died in his office. Norman died in *my* restaurant . . . in the party room."

I didn't know how to comfort her, and to be honest, I was a little surprised with the direction of her concern.

She sniffled into her tissue. "I'm sorry, I have to clean myself up. I must look a mess." She excused herself from the rest of the group, and I watched her scurry to the ladies' room.

Megan squeezed my arm, and seemed to read my mind. "She's in shock. I'm sure she's just trying to focus on something else."

"I guess."

Our little group decided to sit down at one of the larger tables on our side of the room. A considerable amount of time passed, and despite the fact that I was shaken up by

Norman's unexpected death, I was also kind of restless. I observed Adam as he came out from the back office and moved through the restaurant like he'd done it a million times before. He was constantly assessing everything, and I'd noticed before that he seemed to know where every object was in a room no matter where we went.

I tried to read his face for some type of emotion, but he had his detective hat on and that meant he was damn near emotionless.

He stopped at a table and talked to someone I couldn't see. He turned and headed back toward the office where he was conducting his interviews.

The person that stood up was Joel Liu, and his expression was much easier to read than Adam's: satisfaction.

We didn't make our way home until late evening, so poor Kikko rushed to the door when we finally got back to the apartment. I suspected Adam was worried that if he interviewed me first, it would seem like favoritism to the others. Also, I had been with him when the murder occurred so I probably couldn't offer many clues. But it was protocol to interview everyone, and most importantly, no favoritism was allowed. In the end, he opted out of taking my statement at all. He made one of the other guys do it. Officer Wilkins . . . nice guy.

From the little I learned while there, Norman Pan had apparently been strangled with a thin cord of some type, potentially a metal wire. There were signs of a minor struggle, but I was guessing those drinks I'd seen him with slowed him down a bit. More would be learned on specific details once the coroner could examine him.

I knelt down to pat Kikko's head. "It's definitely tinkle time, my friend."

She wiggled her tail in return.

"So we're gonna get into this, right? I mean, it's what we do now."

I could feel Megan's eyes boring into the back of my head as she said it.

I stood up. "I wasn't planning on it. Adam really wants me to stay out of this one."

After we were dismissed from the lounge, he'd pulled me aside and asked me not to interfere. There was something that bothered him about how bold the murderer had been, strangling Norman in a public area. Someone could have walked in at any time.

"We'll be discreet. We've learned a lot about what to do and not to do. It'll be a lot easier this time around."

I snorted. "Easy? Solving a murder is easy?"

"You know what I mean. We have experience now."

Instead of answering her, I searched the living room for Kikko's leash. Meanwhile, my dog was doing spins by the door.

"Lana."

"Megan."

"I'm being serious." She crossed her arms over her chest to prove it.

"So am I." I found the leash on the far side of the couch and held it up for Kikko to see. Her tongue flopped out of her mouth and she plopped down on her butt. "Maybe we should stay out of it."

"Should, could, would." She followed me out the door of the apartment.

Kikko beelined it for the nearest patch of grass, giving it a good sniff before tending to her business.

"We should at least try, don't you think? Doesn't it bug you that this happened to Penny?"

I couldn't lie to her. It did. It really did.

"Plus, you have an advantage over Trudeau . . . people are willing to gossip with you and give you the inside scoop because you're not a cop."

She did have a point.

"And," she continued. "Clearly it was that Joel guy. I mean, come on . . . totally obvious. Plus, how weird is it of him to have shown up at the afterparty considering the tantrum he threw after he lost today. If it were me, I wouldn't have shown my face out of sheer embarrassment."

Joel *was* the obvious choice. Maybe too obvious. I thought back to my conversation with Stella . . . she had been one of the last ones I'd seen in the room. When I'd left, she said she was heading to the dessert table, but maybe instead she went and strangled Norman Pan.

Now that I thought about it, I wondered how long she'd been in the room with him after I'd left. Were they ever completely alone? Who were the other stragglers? I hadn't been paying attention because it wasn't important at the time.

We finished a lap around the complex with Kikko, mostly walking in silence. Megan knew that once my wheels started turning, it was best to leave me be.

When we were back inside the house and all three of us were situated again, I conceded. "You're right; we can't let this happen to Penny *or* Asia Village. And, like you said, I could probably learn valuable information to pass on to Adam that will make his life easier."

"Exactly."

So, it was settled . . . Detectives Lee and Riley were back on the case.

CHAPTER 7

Sunday afternoon, after my family and I were done with dim sum, I ventured to Asia Village in hopes of chatting with Penny in private. I'd heard from Anna May that Penny was still planning to open the Bamboo Lounge as if nothing out of the ordinary happened the day before. The only room that was off-limits according to the police was the party room. They'd gone through the rest of the restaurant the previous night, but according to Adam, nothing seemed relevant and they released it back to Penny.

Personally, I didn't think it was a wise decision to open the lounge so soon after the tragedy. But I could understand that Penny most likely wanted something to keep her busy.

I found her wiping down the counter, the bar completely empty of customers. She appeared contemplative as she wiped over the same spot repeatedly.

Making some noise as I walked, so as not to startle her, I greeted her with a reserved pleasantry. "Hey, there . . ."

I hoisted myself up onto the bar stool in front of where she was standing.

"Oh, Lana, hi." She lifted her head, barely making eye contact. "Did you want something to drink?"

Glancing around the empty room, I thought it might be best to give her something to do. "Sure, but make it something on the weak side, it's a little early in the day for me."

"How about a mimosa?" she suggested.

"Sure, that'll work."

She pulled a miniature bottle of champagne out of the cooler and poured it into a flute, mixing it with orange juice. Her movements were robotic and I sensed her mind was somewhere else.

"How are you holding up?"

"Hm? Sorry?" She set the glass down in front of me and wiped her hands on the towel she'd been cleaning the counter with earlier.

"I asked how you're holding up."

"Oh, right . . ." She inspected her hands. "I'd like to tell you I've been through worse . . . maybe I have . . . I'm not sure anymore." Her eyes skimmed over the room. "This is the first Sunday since I've opened up that the place has been empty. I'm ruined, I can feel it."

"You're not ruined," I reassured her. "It's just a minor setback. In a few days, everything will be back to normal."

"The party room is my real moneymaker and I don't know when I'll even get that back. There was a pretty big business party planned in there for Monday. I had to call and cancel with them, and it cost me a huge chunk of money."

I took a sip of the mimosa and slid a peek at the party room. The door was shut and crime scene tape was covering it. That right there probably wasn't helping business. "They might be done quicker than you think. After Mr. Feng died, the property office was back open in no time."

"I don't know, Lana. I feel like hard times are ahead."

I know that grief shows differently on everyone, but it was a little concerning to me that she was more worried about her business than finding a dead body in her party room. I remember how Kimmy reacted to finding the Yeohs, and how Cindy from the bookstore had been after she found Mr. Feng. But, in this instance, I thought Penny was completely overlooking the fact that someone had died. It was almost as if it didn't matter to her.

Steering the conversation, I asked, "Do you remember seeing Joel Liu last night? I thought it was odd that he'd show up after his outburst at the contest. I was wondering if he'd been here the entire night?"

Penny scoffed. "Can you blame him? The poor guy has been ripped apart by that . . . jerk. And, I hate to say that about someone who was just killed, but there you have it." She slipped away mentally for a minute, and her gaze traveled out the window into the parking lot. After a long pause, she shook herself back to the present, realizing I was still waiting for her to answer my question. "No, I don't remember seeing Joel until after everything happened. I was pretty busy most of the night. I couldn't exactly keep tabs on certain customers. Maybe he was out here in the main room trying to avoid being in such close quarters with Norman."

I drummed my fingers on the side of the champagne glass. "What do you know about Stella Chung?"

Penny froze. "Why would you ask me about her?"

"I spoke with her a little bit last night. She was pretty nice to me and all, but she didn't seem to be a big fan of Norman Pan."

"Oh . . ." Penny relaxed, resting her elbows on the bar.

"What did you think I meant?"

"Nothing, I don't know. I don't know anything about Stella other than what everyone else knows . . . that she's a witch."

"A witch?"

"Not literally . . ."

"She seemed okay to me. Maybe a shade on the prideful side, but I can't say that I blame her. She's accomplished quite a bit with what little she had."

"Well, she's not that great," Penny spat in return. "She's deceitful and manipulative. Maybe she had something to do with Norman's murder. Either way, I can't say that I saw much of her last night. I tried to avoid her as much as possible."

Another odd reaction. She seemed a little defensive about my mention of someone she didn't know very well. But maybe my brain was being overactive. When I got in this mode, I started to see things that weren't there. Everyone becomes a suspect.

I pointed up at the security cameras above the bar. "Well, maybe those will help things along . . . I noticed you have a few in the restaurant. Have the police taken those yet to investigate? If they could see who came out of the room at the right time that would be a big help." I had to suggest it even though I already knew that Adam would have been on top of any type of surveillance. I needed to get her talking before I lost control of the conversation.

She shook her head. "The cameras are fake . . . I only have them up there to discourage anybody from trying to rob me, but they're not actually recording anything."

How convenient, I thought to myself. A trickle of doubt started to form. Considering the type of business Penny ran and the cash flow that went in and out of the place, you'd think she would have functional cameras at least by the cash register. In recent months, my parents had had four installed in the restaurant: two in the dining area, one in the kitchen, and one in the back room.

My silence must have given me away because she gawked at me, her stance defensive. "Something like this wasn't supposed to happen here. When I moved here, everything was supposed to be right again." Her eyes widened and she grabbed the towel, swiping it carelessly across the bar.

"What do you mean 'right again'?"

"Nothing . . ." She avoided eye contact as she replied. "I mean I love it here because it's supposed to be a safe place . . . nothing ever happens in this town."

"Maybe less than other places, but things can happen anywhere, you know?"

With a sigh, she nodded. "I guess you're right about that."

The restaurant door could be heard by the loud creaking it made as it swung open. Normally the noise inside the lounge drowned it out.

We both turned around to find Adam and two uniformed officers coming our way.

Adam had his game face on, but despite the fact that I remained ever so innocent-looking, he did not appear pleased to see me.

"Lana, what are you doing here?" His voice was gruff and authoritative. "Isn't today your day off?"

I held up my champagne glass. "Stopped in for a mimosa."

His eyes slid to the glass in my hand and then back at me, studying my face. He knew that's where all my emotions liked to come out and play. "I didn't know you liked mimosas . . ."

"Look at you, learning something new every day."

He pursed his lips. "Can I talk to you out in the plaza, please?"

"I'll be right back," I said to Penny as I scooted off the stool.

Adam led me out into the plaza. I watched the tension build in his shoulders as I followed behind him.

"For the record," I said, as the door shut behind me. "I am just enjoying a drink with a friend. I'm not up to anything, I swear."

"You're snooping. I can sense it . . . you had your guilty face on when I walked in."

With feigned surprise, I raised a hand to my chest. "Why, Detective Trudeau, are you implying that I'm not being forthright with you?"

"Knock it off, Lana . . . I don't want you getting involved."

"I was seriously just having a drink. Besides, Penny could use the company. She hasn't had a single customer all day. You saw how empty it was in there."

"We suggested that she remain closed until the investigation was done, but she insisted on opening."

"How long do you think it's going to take before she

gets the party room back? She had to cancel on some potential customers and I think she's hurting for money."

He shook his head. "I'm not sure. I'm waiting to hear back from the lab on a couple different things. I don't want to open up the room if it turns out we need to go over it again. Everything will be compromised."

"Do you have any suspects yet? What about the murder weapon? Do you know what he was strangled with?"

"I thought you weren't snooping?"

"I'm not . . . just morbid curiosity."

"Don't you worry about any of that, Miss Lee."

I huffed. "Fine. I was just making conversation. I don't really want to know those things anyway."

"Uh-huh." He sighed to himself, scrubbing the day-old chin scruff that had begun to form. "Let's get you back in there so you can finish your drink and be on your way. I'm sure you have plenty of other trouble to get into."

As I started to walk in, he grabbed my arm, giving me a little tug. I turned to face him.

"Do me a favor, Lana . . . maybe keep your distance from Penny for a while, okay?"

"Why?"

"Because I do have some suspects, and she's made the list."

When I got home, Megan was in the living room doing yoga. While she was trying to accomplish the downward dog, my own dog was attempting to lick her face.

"Lana, get your dog out of here. I've been trying to

do yoga for the past hour." She turned her face away from Kikko, whose persistence was something to be admired.

I chuckled as I scooped up the little pug and carried her to where Megan had pushed the couch against the wall. "There are some bones in the pantry to keep her busy."

"I tried that. I gave her two . . . they're now buried somewhere in the apartment." Megan looked at me upside down from her position on the floor. "How did it go at the Bamboo Lounge? Find out anything interesting?"

"Penny was sort of skittish, but I can't tell why. She doesn't seem too worried about Norman, so it can't be that."

Megan exhaled. "From what you've told me about his past, I don't see that many people would be."

"Something else did happen while I was there, though."

"Oh?" She flipped over and sat Indian-style on her yoga mat. "Do tell."

"Adam showed up, and he was really concerned about me being there."

"Of course he was . . . he knows how you are."

"It's not just about my snooping around. He said that Penny is one of his suspects."

Megan raised her eyebrows. "Oh, really?"

"Yeah, and on top of that Penny mentioned something about how it wasn't supposed to be like this when she moved here."

"Wasn't supposed to be like this? What do you think she means by that? What the heck was she expecting . . . fairy-tale land?"

"She wouldn't really tell me, and before I could question her more on the subject, Adam and his guys showed up. Not that I think she would have told me much more anyhow. She doesn't usually talk about herself. But the whole thing makes you wonder what she was running from to begin with."

CHAPTER 8

Monday morning came with a mix of emotions. Most of it was centered on frustration. After I prepped the restaurant for opening, I stood outside of Shanghai Donuts, waiting for the new owners to unlock the doors. I really would be their first customer.

A petite, older lady, maybe in her sixties with graying hair, shuffled to the door with a pleasant smile on her face. In some ways she reminded me of my grandmother and I wondered if they would become friends.

The smile extended to her eyes, which I always found to be a form of sincerity. She pushed the door open. "Welcome," she said, stepping aside to let me in.

I smiled in return. "Hi, I'm Lana Lee, I manage the noodle shop next door and thought I should come introduce myself."

With a delicate bow of her head, she shuffled back behind the counter. "It is very nice to meet our neighbors.

Everyone here is so nice. My husband is not here yet. I'm Ruth Wu."

"We're happy to have you at Asia Village." I eyed the case of doughnuts. "Especially me." There were so many kinds. My gaze landed on the glazed doughnuts shaped like eights. "I'll have one of those, please. And some coffee."

She opened the case and pulled out a doughnut. I could feel my mouth watering already.

"I was very sorry to miss the contest this weekend, but after hearing about what happened, I'm very glad we didn't go."

I cringed. The opening of her shop and the noodle-contest tragedy was definitely bad timing. "Normally it isn't like this here. Most days nothing happens at all."

Ruth nodded in understanding, but didn't comment. Instead, she handed me a waxed paper bag.

I peeked inside; the sweet smell of freshly baked dough filled my nostrils.

"I put some extra doughnut holes in there for you." She smiled, sliding a paper cup of coffee across the counter.

"Thanks, that's so nice of you." I reached for my wallet inside my purse, and she held out her hand to stop me.

"Please, this is a gift to my first customer."

"Well, let me be your first tipper at least." I pulled out a five-dollar bill and slipped it in the cookie jar that was marked TIPS.

"What will happen to the contest?" Ruth asked. "Will it be canceled now?"

"I'm not sure," I admitted. I had yet to talk to anyone about what would happen next. Canceling it seemed like the best idea, but I doubted that Ian would even entertain the thought. "I guess we'll find out today."

"Hopefully our business will not get off to a bad start." She glanced around the tiny eatery. A few wooden tables were placed near the front windows and off to the left side against the wall were two blue velvet armchairs with a small end table in between them. It felt cozy and I could hardly believe that the souvenir shop had once occupied this space. "My husband and I are retired now. We moved here from California to be close to our son. We put a lot of money into making this doughnut shop."

"I'm sure you're going to do great. Who doesn't love a good doughnut shop?" I said, holding up my bag. "I better get back to work; our cook is going to wonder what happened to me."

"Thank you for stopping by, Lana. I will be sure to return the favor."

I stepped out into the plaza clutching my doughnut bag and coffee. The abandoned stage still occupied the middle of the plaza and I took a minute to reflect on the current state of Asia Village. Aside from my reservations about gaining another pants size, I hoped Shanghai Donuts would succeed, and that what was happening now wouldn't affect their business or their desire to stay.

The spot had housed a variety of businesses, too many to remember, which is why my mother and her friends insisted the space was cursed and no business would succeed there.

Ian made it a point to remind the Mahjong Matrons, and anyone else who claimed the business lot was doomed, that those types of things didn't exist. I wasn't very superstitious myself—unless of course it was midnight and

I was home alone. But after meeting the nice woman who ran the place, I kept my fingers crossed that things would work out for them after all.

When I returned to Ho-Lee Noodle House, Peter was in the dining room hanging out with the Mahjong Matrons. The four widowed women were our first customers every morning without fail. They sat in the same booth, in the same spots, and ate the same thing every day.

They all turned when I walked in.

"Where have you been, Lana?" Pearl, the eldest of the four women, asked me.

I held up my bag. "I stopped at the new doughnut shop next door."

Peter snickered to himself. "I figured that's where you snuck off to. I was keeping these lovely ladies company until you got back."

Opal, Pearl's younger sister, clasped her hands together. In her soft voice, she said, "I have prayed for the new owners next door. I will bring them a good-luck charm later."

"Well, I better get back in the kitchen and start on your breakfast." He tipped his head and disappeared into the back.

"Lana." Helen, who acted as mother hen, and also happened to be the loudest and most active gossip of the four, glanced around the restaurant before continuing. "Do you know what is happening with the noodle contest?"

"No, I haven't talked to Ian since Saturday. My mother told me he isn't doing so well with what's going on."

Wendy, the most sensible of the women, nodded. "I still think he is too young for this job. We need someone like Mr. Feng to handle these types of problems."

They all bowed their heads in his memory. Mr. Feng, the original owner of Asia Village, had been taken from us not that long ago by his own tragedy. The Village was the first property he ever owned and it was his pride and joy. While Ian came with plenty of fresh ideas to help restore the plaza and its business, no one felt that anyone could give it the same love and attention as its previous owner.

"What does your boyfriend think?" Helen asked, sipping her tea.

I knew they were trying to pump me for information. Anything I told the Matrons would spread around the plaza in a matter of minutes. "He hasn't told me anything," I said plainly.

"He should talk to that Stella Chung girl . . . she was arguing with Mr. Pan the day before the contest. I could not hear what they were discussing though," Helen offered.

Pearl clucked her tongue. "Everybody knows that Joel Liu is the guilty one. He was very disrespectful to Mr. Pan at the contest."

Opal gazed out the window as the others bickered. Barely above a whisper, she said, "I think it is Mr. Shen. He will do anything to make Asia Village look bad."

The other three erupted with disagreements at the Mr. Shen insinuation.

Pearl held up a hand to silence the other two. When they were quiet, Pearl turned to her sister. "This makes no sense, they are very good friends, why would you think this?"

Opal continued to focus on the activity outside the restaurant window. "Ever since Mr. Pan picked Ray last year, their friendship is not the same. Mr. Shen feels jealous, and angry. You can see it in his eyes."

While they discussed who was the most likely suspect, a group of businesswomen walked in and signaled me from the podium. I left the Matrons to their speculations while I took care of our new guests.

One thing was certain. Mr. Pan was not a well-liked man, so the enemy count was going to be high. But if I had to include people who were supposed to be his friends on top of that . . . well, that would make this case even more difficult to solve.

When Nancy showed up for the day, I escaped to my mother's office, which was really becoming mine since she'd promoted me to manager. I had a few reservations about changing anything in the office in case this whole situation turned out to be a fluke. But, aside from random check-ins, my mother was virtually nonexistent in the family business.

And though this wasn't exactly where I saw my life going, I was actually enjoying myself. It felt nice to run something . . . call the shots . . . be the big boss lady instead of constantly taking orders from everyone else.

While I went through the sales slips from the previous evening, I thought about what the Mahjong Matrons had told me. I needed a plan of attack. I didn't even know what I thought yet. My thoughts were still so unorganized. What I did know was that I needed to check out Stella. And, of course, Joel Liu was at the top of my list. But what about one of the other contestants? Did I need to look at them more closely too? If any of them had received poor reviews from Norman, they could also be a potential suspect. How would I ever begin to narrow this down?

Opal mentioned that Mr. Shen could be a possibility. Had their friendship really taken a turn for the worse after last year's contest? I didn't know much about their personal interactions, so it was hard for me to have any solid thoughts on that.

I made some mental notes of potential subjects and wished I had the notebook I kept hidden under my mattress with me now. The notebook first came into existence when I was investigating the particulars of Mr. Feng's death. Writing things down helped keep my thoughts straight and eased the sense of overwhelming anxiety that took control of my brain as I rummaged through the various possibilities and suspects.

As I finished up with the sales slips, there was a knock at the door.

Ian poked his head in. "I'm holding an emergency board meeting at six P.M. We'll meet in the community center."

"Oh, is it finished?"

"Not quite, but we need a private space."

"Okay, I'll be there. It's not like I had anything better to do tonight." The sarcasm in my tone came out a little strong.

"Lana, this is serious business. We have to rescue this noodle contest and we're out a judge. We have to find someone new *and* get the contest back on track before too much time passes."

"Maybe the contest should be canceled for the year." I hated to admit that, but at this point maybe going on with the contest would only bring negative attention to the plaza.

"How can you say that?" He gawked at me. "Lana, this contest is in the hands of Asia Village. And me. It will not fail under my watch."

"I said I'd be there, Ian, don't worry."

He took a deep breath. "Good, I need your support. If the others argue with me, I need you to back me up. We have to stick together in this. People like you; they'll listen to you."

"Okay, okay." I came from around the desk and ushered him out of my office. "I'll see you at six."

"Sharp," he added before walking away.

To kill some time before the meeting, I headed over to Modern Scroll, the plaza's bookstore, and my own personal slice of heaven. As I walked through the door, I took a deep breath, inhaling the intoxicating smell of paper, and a smile spread over my lips. Sometimes I thought maybe I should have opened a bookstore of my own.

I perused the mystery section, sliding out paperbacks to glance at their covers. Out of the corner of my eye, I noticed that Cindy, the bookshop owner, was watching me with amusement.

She adjusted her thick-rimmed glasses and came around the counter. "Do you know, you are the happiest person I've ever seen in a bookstore? It gets me every time."

I laughed as I put a Louise Penny book back in place. "I can't help myself . . . it's the best place on earth."

"You were just in here the other day . . . did you finish those books already?"

"Not even close. But I have some time to kill before a board meeting, so I thought I'd swing by."

"Uh-oh, another board meeting, huh?" She swept a lock of hair behind her ear. "Let me guess, Ian is spazzing out about the noodle contest and needs to meet with everyone pronto."

"Of course he is. He's more concerned about the noodle contest than he is about what happened to Norman Pan."

"I'm not surprised. That man wasn't well liked."

"Everybody keeps saying that, but he's still a human being. And the suspect list is long, for sure. The only saving grace is that it's somewhat limited to whoever was at the Bamboo Lounge that night."

Cindy looked at me sideways. "What are you up to, Lana?"

I blushed. "Just checking into a few things is all. No big deal."

She leaned in closer, lowering her voice. "If you want my opinion, my money's on that Stella woman . . . she's been slinking around this plaza like nobody's business."

That was twice that someone had suggested Stella was up to something. "I'll keep that in mind."

A customer ambled up to the counter, looking around for help. Cindy called out to them she'd be right there.

Before walking away, she turned to me. "Good luck, whatever you find . . . just remember . . . be careful."

As I was leaving the store, Freddie was coming in. His black T-shirt fit him like a glove, and the soft jersey material moved effortlessly with his body instead of restricting his movements.

A smile appeared on his face as he noticed me. "Hey, Lana, how are you?"

We stepped off to the side of the entrance to let a group of women pass by.

"I'm doing okay. Getting ready to head over to the community center for a meeting," I explained. "Will you be there?"

He shook his head. "Not this time. I will be in the future, but Ian asked me to stay back this time."

"Oh?"

"Yeah, he said something about not wanting to expose me to the Yi sisters yet."

I laughed. "He's right. Best to ease you in."

"I've heard stories." He chuckled. "So, I figured I'd kill some time in the bookstore. No better place, right? I love it here."

My heart thudded. He was attractive *and* loved the bookstore? "It's my favorite place to be. I come here at least once a week if not more."

"Same. Michael Connelly has a new book out, so I thought I'd check that out then just browse."

"You like Michael Connelly?" I asked. I couldn't hide my surprise.

"Oh sure, love the guy. I'm more into sci-fi really, but I love a good thriller every now and then."

"I would never have guessed," I admitted.

He winked. "I've got plenty of surprises up my sleeve."

I could feel the heat rising in my cheeks, and I hoped that it wasn't noticeable. "Well, uh, I better get going. I'll never hear the end of it from Ian if I'm late."

"Right," he said with a smirk. "Don't want to hold you up. I'll be seein' ya."

As I walked over to the community center, I told myself it was no big deal that he was into books. We had something in common . . . so what?

CHAPTER 9

This was the first time I'd been in the community center since before they began construction. The whole interior of the space had been gutted so they could start from scratch. The previous interior had been an alarming shade of bright white muddled with scuff marks from chairs rubbing up against the wall or shuffling tables back and forth. Now, the walls were a light almond color and paintings by local Asian artists would be hung up instead of the ratty posters that decorated the walls before. The stained gray carpeting that had covered the floors for over a decade had been removed, and a nice ceramic tile had been laid down in its place.

A large table was set up in the back of the room for the mahjong tournaments that would begin once the renovations were complete. Most of the board members were already there and sitting around the table making idle chitchat. Ian was nowhere to be seen.

Kimmy waved me over and patted the empty chair next to her. "Over here, Lee."

I said hello to the group and took my seat next to Kimmy.

"Why's your face all red?"

"Huh?" My hands flew up to my cheeks. "Oh, I was rushing over here from the bookstore . . . I lost track of time."

A few minutes later, Ian showed up carrying a stack of papers and looking flustered. His forehead glistened with sweat and he was taking deeper breaths than normal. With his free hand, he adjusted his tie and approached the group, clearing his throat to get everybody's attention. "Sorry I'm late. I was talking with Freddie Yuan earlier and going over some details for the next portion of the noodle competition. We got sidetracked and I almost forgot to print out these packets for the meeting." He waved the papers he was still holding on to.

June Yi, co-owner of Yi's Bakery, was the meaner of the two sisters. In all the years that I'd known her, I had yet to hear a nice thing come out of her mouth. "Freddie Yuan? Why are you discussing the noodle contest with *him*?" Her salt-and-pepper hair shook around her face as she rattled her head in disapproval. The bobby pin securing her long bangs started to loosen and she reached for it, putting it back in its place.

This must have been what Freddie was referring to when I talked with him earlier, I thought to myself. Ian probably didn't want him to witness the Yi sisters reacting to the news.

Ian tapped the pile of papers on the table and addressed the group instead of replying directly to June. "I've decided that Freddie will be the perfect stand-in judge for the noodle contest."

The Yi sisters exchanged shocked glances and murmured to each other. June whipped her head back around to face Ian. "Mr. Sung, I think this is most inappropriate."

"What's the big deal?" Kimmy asked before Ian could answer.

June clucked her tongue, giving Kimmy a glare that would rival Medusa. "He has no experience. What will people say?"

"They won't say anything because no one cares," Kimmy spat.

I nudged her under the table. "I'm sure that people will understand." It was the best generic answer I could come up with to back up Ian as he requested. I wasn't entirely sure what he was thinking by asking Freddie Yuan to be a judge, and it did sorta make me feel uncomfortable, but not for the same reasons as the Yi sisters.

Ian settled into the seat he'd been hovering over and folded his hands in front of him on the table. In a calm and matter-of-fact voice, he said, "I tried asking another food critic first, but no one would accept the position because of the circumstances surrounding the event so far. Understandable, I suppose. But Freddie is new to town and doesn't have any reason to play favorites with a particular restaurant, so we know we can count on him to be fair."

June mumbled something under her breath.

Esther raised a hand, her bracelets jingling as she waved her arm to get Ian's attention. "What about the police? Have they found out anything about what happened to Norman?"

"No . . . I'm afraid not," Ian said, looking down at his stack of papers. "Detective Trudeau hasn't been very forthcoming with information."

Everyone turned to me.

I held up my hands in defense. "Don't look at me, I don't know anything."

Shirley Yi scooted to the edge of her seat. Even though she and June were identical, there was something about her that was a little more on the gentle side. Maybe it was the way she carried herself or the fact that she spoke in a more soothing tone. "We all know that it was Joel Liu. He has been after Norman Pan since last year's contest. He's been sending him nasty e-mails for months."

I gaped. "How do you know that?"

June leaned forward, annoyed that I would dare question her sister. "Walter Shen was talking about it at the cocktail party the other day."

Well, now that was interesting. Walter Shen just happened to mention this in front of a group of people? Was he trying to cast off suspicion about himself by throwing Joel into the proverbial fire?

"Let's stop speculating on something we shouldn't be worrying about anyway, and focus on getting this contest up and running again," Ian lectured. "Now, I've created these packets for the revised schedule of the noodle contest." He handed the packets out to each of the board members. "All of you have a job to complete."

When I received my packet, I flipped through the pages, skimming the detailed outline that Ian had organized to a tee. I found my name and learned that my duty was to notify the contestants of the changes. Easy enough.

It would also give me a chance to dig around for information with a solid cover story.

"The contest will resume on Friday and go through the weekend." He turned to me. "Lana, I'll need you to contact the contestants as soon as possible to let them know. I have extra packets for you to drop off with them if you don't mind."

"Sure, I'll see if Anna May or Nancy can cover for me in the morning while I drop these off."

"Is continuing the competition wise?" Mr. Zhang, the proprietor of Wild Sage, asked.

"Of course, why wouldn't it be?"

"A man has died, and to dismiss such things is disrespectful. Bad karma will surely find you, Mr. Sung."

Mr. Zhang, a small man with gray hair and bifocals that covered smiling eyes, was the oldest and most Zen resident of Asia Village. He owned the plaza's herbal shop, practiced what he preached, and was no stranger to philosophical teachings and things like balance, karma, and chi. He was wise in his advanced years, and though the exact number of those years was unknown to us, I suspected the remedies and tonics he carried in his shop helped keep his age a secret.

Ian brushed off the concern. "I don't believe in karma. And I will not let this contest fail. Everyone is watching us right now . . . especially in the Asian community. We need to keep up appearances and show everyone that we can persevere under difficult circumstances. I need everyone to be on board with this."

We all looked at each other and nodded in unison . . . even Mr. Zhang.

"I can't stress the importance of this contest enough. We need to make it work . . . no matter what it takes."

By the time I got home that night, Megan had left for work already. I pulled the tattered notebook out from under my mattress and plopped down on the bed, Kikko joining me with inquisitive sniffs.

I opened the book and memories from the past several months came flooding back. On the very first page I had written the words WHO KILLED THOMAS FENG? Though it had only been a couple of months ago, it felt like a lifetime had passed.

The following pages contained notes from the Yeoh investigation. I hated to recall the memories of digging into my friend's murder. It had not been an easy time for me.

Several times I'd thought about burning the entire notebook for fear of someone finding my notes and jumping to the natural conclusion that I was a crazy person. But for whatever reason, I couldn't bring myself to do it.

With a heavy sigh, I flipped to an empty page and put pen to paper.

The next morning, I woke at my usual time for work, but instead of heading to the restaurant, I planned my route to visit the other contestants. Seeing Penny would be my last stop since she was at the plaza, so I decided to start with Walter Shen and then make my way over to the Flats for a chat with Stanley Gao at Wok and Roll.

The House of Shen was on Rockwell Avenue, which

was the location of the original Chinatown. Their restaurant sat on the corner of the street and was surrounded by a row of Asian businesses that had established their roots long ago.

I parked my car in the lot adjacent to the restaurant, and jogged across the street to the entrance.

When I opened the door, the first person I saw was Jackie Shen at the hostess station. She was dressed in a traditional qipao and her hair wrapped up in an elegant bun. She looked coiffed and perfect.

Self-consciously, I ran a hand through my hair, which had fallen flat since I'd left the house.

"Finally decided to have some real Chinese food, huh?" Jackie asked.

"I'm here to see your father," I told her. "It's about the noodle contest."

"I warned the OCA Cleveland chapter that they shouldn't trust the contest in the hands of Asia Village. Disaster was sure to strike."

The Organization of Chinese Americans was a nonprofit organization that supported advancements and well-being in the Asian community, and the Cleveland chapter was helping fund the noodle contest as a way to promote local Asian businesses.

I stifled a groan. "I'm not interested in having this conversation with you right now, Jackie. I'm here to see your father . . . is he here or not?"

She folded her arms over her chest. "Yeah, he's here."

"Can I talk to him then?" I could hear the exasperation in my voice. It was too early in the day to be this agitated. "I have places to be."

She stared at me, challenging my patience.

I stared back, unwilling to give in. Did she think I was going to leave? I was here on official business and she was trying to play high school games.

With a stomp of her foot, she conceded and headed to the back of the restaurant.

I studied their dining room while I waited. Their setup was decent and resembled a modernized version of 1920s Asian décor. Lattice woodwork bordered the room, and matching partitions separated some of the booths, creating intimate seating arrangements. All of the tables were covered with ivory cloth and came complete with bamboo-shoot centerpieces in ornate oval vases. Calculating the cost of their design setup made my head spin.

Walter Shen came out of the back room, but Jackie didn't follow. I wondered if he'd asked her to stay behind while he talked to me.

"Miss Lee, what a pleasant surprise," he replied in a cordial tone.

"Hello, Mr. Shen," I said, trying to remove some of the tension from my voice that his daughter had caused. "Sorry to interrupt your morning, but Ian wanted me to drop off this packet for the contest."

He took the packet from my hands and reviewed it, nodding with approval. "This is satisfactory."

"I'm glad you think so," I replied. "Frederick Yuan will be taking over Norman Pan's judging duties and there was a little upset over this news. I wasn't sure how the other contestants would feel about this."

He cocked his head at me. "Oh?"

"Yeah, Ian announced the news during our board meeting last night, and some of the members were not very happy with the decision. But I guess Ian couldn't get anyone else to accept the position."

He stared out into the street. "That is very interesting."

"I thought so too. Ian said they were uncomfortable with the circumstances surrounding the contest. I guess I can see their point."

With confidence, he said, "I believe the danger is over now. We have nothing further to worry about, I'm sure."

His answer caught me off guard. "You think so?" I mumbled.

"Norman created a lot of problems for himself. I'm not surprised that this is the way his life ended."

Walter's response caused an involuntary shiver. Not knowing how to reply, I decided to go along with it. "Well . . . he did have a reputation."

"I tried to warn him. But Norman was a stubborn man, and he lived life by his own rules. You couldn't tell that man anything."

"You warned him?"

His eyes slid to meet mine, and there was a coldness in them that was so familiar. After a brief moment, I realized why. I'd seen that same chill in the eyes of Charles An . . . the man who'd murdered Thomas Feng.

"Yes," he replied. "I warned him one day someone was going to pay him back for all his wrongdoing."

Goose bumps traveled up and down my arms. "Oh . . . yeah?"

"He laughed . . . he said karma doesn't exist in this world." His eyes slid away, his focus back on the street. "Guess he was wrong about that."

My breath caught in my throat and the possibility that

I could be standing in front of Norman Pan's killer became very real. "I better get going. I have to make a few stops before heading to the restaurant." I waved the packets for emphasis.

The expression on his face returned to normal. "Yes, of course, sorry to hold you up with my ramblings."

"Not a problem." I backed away slowly toward the door.

"Please tell your parents, I send my best."

"I'll do that," I said, and exited the restaurant in haste. I ran back to my car with the hairs on my neck standing straight up.

CHAPTER 10

In the short time it took to make my way over to the Flats, I managed to compose myself from the uncomfortable encounter with Mr. Shen. Relief set in as I reminded myself that after this stop, I could return to the safety of the plaza.

I'd like to think of myself as an Asian restaurant connoisseur, so I was disappointed to admit that since Stanley Gao opened Wok and Roll two years ago, I had never been in to sample the food.

The outside boasted a neon sign shaped like a wok and a guitar crisscrossed over it with noodles for guitar strings. It was clever and I had to give him points for that.

The hours of operation were posted on the door, and informed me that they wouldn't be open until noon. Thankfully, I could see Stanley roaming around in the back, probably prepping for the day ahead.

I knocked on the glass, startling him. He acknowledged me and came to greet me at the door.

The inside walls were covered with metal sheeting and gave the place a grunge rock ambiance. The dining tables and chairs were also made of metal, and the only thing that appeared not to be was the floor, which resembled the inside of someone's garage.

"Miss Lee." Stanley held the door open for me. He was a tall and skinny man that I hated to refer to as lanky, but no other word came to mind as I walked past him into the restaurant. "You're not someone I expect to see so early in the morning."

I waved the packet in my hand and gave him the lowdown just like I had with Walter. And just like Walter, he flipped through the packet, skimming over the details.

"Cool, cool," he said while nodding and reviewing the last page. "I'll be there, chef hat and all."

"Glad to hear it. Ian seems pretty confident about continuing with the contest, but I wasn't sure how everyone else would feel about it after what happened."

"I wouldn't worry your pretty little head about it." He closed the packet and winked. "As they say, the show must go on. And if anyone knows that better than anyone, it's Ian Sung."

"You're not the least bit concerned even though they haven't caught who's responsible?" I couldn't hide the surprise in my voice. Was nobody worried but me?

He snorted. "I think we know that Norman Pan had it coming. Don't you agree?"

The shrillness in my tone shocked me. "Just because he's a jerk, it doesn't mean someone should have killed him. He's somebody's . . . brother." I said that last bit without confidence as I really had no idea. But it sounded good.

He held up his hands in defense. "Whoa, Lana. All I'm saying is that this happened to him for a reason. It wasn't luck of the draw, you know?"

I took a deep breath. Clearly I was on edge. "So who do you think could have been responsible for doing something like that then?"

Stanley shrugged. "Your guess is as good as mine. But I truly don't believe the contest is the cause of what happened. No . . . it was definitely the man himself."

He did have a point there. Norman's behavior caused him to have a long list of enemies. But an important question remained . . . what was the reason?

As I made my way back to the plaza, I thought about the conversations I'd had with Walter and Stanley, wondering what my encounter with Penny would be like. She'd been acting so strangely since the night of the murder, I didn't know what to expect at this point.

On the drive over, something that I'd said to Stanley kept replaying in my mind. Norman was somebody's brother. Was he? Now that he was gone, who was missing him? From the little that I knew about him besides his being a food critic, nothing led me to believe he was married. But did he have a girlfriend? Brothers or sisters? I made a mental note to find out.

Penny was behind the bar jotting down notes on a pad of paper. The lounge was empty except for a man in a suit sitting by a window with a martini and a laptop. At least someone else was coming to the Bamboo Lounge besides me.

"Hey, Penny." I attempted the most cheerful voice I could conjure.

It was returned with a weak smile. "Hi, Lana." She noticed the packet in my hands and pointed to it with her pen. "What's that?"

I extended the packet to her. "This is from Ian. It's the new conditions and changes regarding the contest."

"He doesn't want to call it quits, does he?" She took the packet from my hand and flipped through the pages.

"No, you know Ian," I replied. I hopped up on the stool and leaned forward. "Do you want to call it quits?"

Penny sighed and closed the packet. "It's not that I want to quit . . . I *can't* quit. How would that look to everyone?"

"I think people would understand . . ." My eyes traveled back to the closed door of the party room.

"Is anybody else quitting?" she asked.

"Well . . . no . . ."

"Then neither will I." She eyed me as if she expected me to challenge her. "I'm not going to be the one that can't take the heat, Lana."

"Of course, I wasn't suggesting—"

She huffed. "It's fine. I should probably go check on my customer . . . seeing as he's the only one I have."

"Yeah, I should get to work myself." I slid off the stool and was about to remind her that she could talk to me any time she needed to, but she'd already walked away.

When I got to Ho-Lee Noodle House, Stella was waiting for me at a booth. There were a few bowls scattered around her table and she was flipping through a magazine while she ate.

"She's been here for over an hour," Nancy whispered to me. "She said it was very important that she talk to you and she did not trust me to leave a message." There was a touch of bitterness in her voice and it made me chuckle. Nancy was so used to being liked and trusted by almost everybody. It was hard for her when someone didn't.

"I'll go talk to her." I stuffed my purse under the hostess station. "Would you mind bringing me a cup of tea?"

I made my way over to the table. Stella was oblivious to my presence as she was immersed in the magazine in front of her. I cleared my throat to get her attention.

Her head popped up and it took her a couple seconds to register who I was. When it dawned on her, she shook her head and laughed. "Ugh, my head is not on straight. Lana, thanks for meeting with me."

"If I'd known you were here I wouldn't have kept you waiting so long."

Nancy came by with my tea, and I thanked her before sitting down.

Stella shoved the plates aside, clearing the space between us. "You have fabulous food, by the way. Peter is a genius in the kitchen. If he wasn't so loyal, I'd try to steal him for Chicago . . . he'd be amazing."

I laughed. "Yes, please don't. We really need him here."

"Don't worry, on second thought, I wouldn't want him to outshine me. With my luck, I'd be out of a job."

"So what brings you by?" I asked. "I'm sure that Ian informed you about the contest changes?"

"Yes . . . I mean no . . ."

I cocked my head at her. "Okay?"

"I know about the contest changes, but that's not why I'm here. I actually came to ask you something on a more personal level."

"Oh?"

"You're dating that detective guy, right? Trudeau or something like that?"

I was hesitant to answer. Why would she want to know about that?

Without me confirming that I was, she continued. "If I were to talk to him about something . . . legal . . . would he tell anybody? I mean, would he tell anybody that it was me who talked with him?"

"No, they keep things confidential all the time."

"Yeah, well, that's what they say, but I don't really trust cops very much. No offense or anything."

"None taken, but can I ask what you want to talk to him about? Maybe if I know more details, I could help you decide if it's something to take to him."

She squirmed a little in her seat and considered what I was asking. If she was anything like me, she was probably also deciding whether or not I could be trusted.

After a few brief moments of mulling it over, she sighed and began digging in her purse. She pulled out a tiny piece of paper and slid it across the table. "After we left the party that night, I found a fortune cookie stuffed in my purse. I don't know where it came from, but when I opened it, this was inside. I almost didn't open it at all. Normally I don't eat fortune cookies, but there was nothing to eat in my hotel room, and I was craving something sweet."

I picked up the paper and read the fortune. It read: *If your enemy is superior, evade him.*

Suddenly, I remembered the fortune that Norman Pan

had shown Ian after the first round of the contest. In all the chaos, I'd completely forgotten about it. I began to wonder if Ian mentioned anything to Adam or if he'd forgotten about it too.

"Do you mind if I look up something really quick?" I asked. I didn't want her to think I was messing around with my cell phone while she was trying to tell me something important.

"Sure . . . why?"

"Norman Pan received an odd fortune similar to this on the day of the first round . . . it totally slipped my mind. I want to see if something checks out with it." I grabbed my phone out of my jacket pocket and typed in the quote written on the fortune paper. I wasn't entirely familiar with Sun Tzu, but if I was right, this was a quote from *The Art of War* too. After skimming over the search that popped up, I saw that my assumption was correct.

Stella took a deep breath. "What did Norman's say?"

I racked my brain trying to remember the verse that had been printed on the tiny slip of paper. "Something along the lines of seeking allies or becoming weak without them as a result . . . it's hard for me to remember the exact wording, but it definitely wasn't your average fortune."

She contemplated this, drumming her fingers rapidly on the table. "It could fit with my theory, but I'm not positive. I guess you can spin things however you want them if you're speculating. Then everything makes sense, right?"

"Yeah, I suppose it does."

"Let's say I overheard something that might be helpful to the investigation. I could tell your boyfriend and he wouldn't rat me out to the person . . . even if they don't end up being guilty of the crime?"

I nodded, handing the slip of paper back to her. "You should absolutely give this to Adam and tell him what you told me. You don't want to end up like Norman."

"But if I show him the fortune, he'll have to bring that up to the person, right? Then they'll know it was me who tattled on them. If Norman and I are the only ones to have received one, who else would it be?"

I hadn't thought about that part. If Stella told Adam about the fortune, then he would have to put those into evidence, and show them to the suspect in question. Then whoever it was would know that Stella had accused them of the crime. "Who are you afraid of and what did you hear exactly?" I asked. "Who is this enemy that you're supposed to evade?"

She sat back in her seat. "I'd rather not say."

We were silent for a few minutes while she considered her situation. I didn't want to press her, but I did want to know what she thought she knew. It might help weed out some of the potential suspects I had in mind.

Her eyes scanned the restaurant, and when she was satisfied that no one was listening, she leaned in and whispered, "But I will tell you that Norman was involved in something illegal . . . I think. At least that's the gist I got from what I overheard."

"Did you hear this conversation at the party?" I asked, trying to remember if I'd seen or heard anything suspicious without realizing it.

"No . . . before that . . . it was before the contest started that day."

"And was that same person at the party? Or do you remember seeing them talking to Norman at all that night?"

"I'm not sure . . ." She bit her lip. "The person was there, but I don't know if they were talking with Norman at the party or not. I don't even know if what I heard was anything . . . it sure seems like something now that Norman's dead."

Her responses sounded wishy-washy to me, and I wasn't sure what to make of it. I thought about bringing up the fact that I remembered *her* talking to him at the party shortly before he ended up dead, but I didn't want her to totally clam up on me. Right now she seemed to believe I was on her side and I needed to keep it that way.

The more I thought about it, I wondered, what if she was playing me? If she was that worried about her safety then why not go straight to Adam with what she knew? She said she didn't trust the police, but did she really want to take her chances with whoever she thought might have slipped her the fortune cookie?

Furthermore, why come to *me* with this information? Unless, of course, she was trying to create a backstory that would take away suspicion that she could be guilty of the murder herself. For all I knew she was here trying to convince me that someone else was involved . . . this supposed unnamed person's identity she wasn't willing to divulge. That could be because there wasn't an unnamed person to identify. Could she have been the one who gave Norman the fortune cookie and then pretended that she'd also received one? It was a possibility I needed to take into account.

She fumbled through her purse and pulled out her cell phone, checking the time. "I better get going; I have an appointment in about a half hour. Would you mind getting my check for me?"

I obliged, and went to get her check from Nancy. We wrapped up her bill and she told me she would be in touch with Adam later that day.

As she was heading out, Penny was coming in. The two women exchanged some heated words that couldn't be heard and Stella stormed off while Penny stood glowering after her. In the brief time that I'd known Penny, I'd never seen her get nasty with anyone. And I hate to use the phrase *if looks could kill,* but there was definitely something murderous in those chocolate-browns.

CHAPTER 11

Penny stood at the front of the restaurant, preoccupied and clearly steaming from her conversation with Stella.

"Everything okay?" I asked, stepping up to the hostess station and nodding my head toward the direction Stella had left in.

"Huh?" Penny gave me a blank stare as if she hadn't realized I was standing there. "Oh, it's nothing . . . she is just a nasty woman. I shouldn't let it get to me."

I shrugged. "I still haven't seen that side of her. She seems all right to me."

"Well, she would. She puts on a good façade, doesn't she? Everyone just *loves* Stella Chung."

Where was all this aggression toward Stella coming from? "I'm sorry . . . I didn't mean to make you upset."

She waved it off. "It's no big deal. I've just read a couple articles about her and she is a total snob. I wish people would see through her act already."

I didn't want to argue with Penny any further on the

subject so I nodded in agreement. "Maybe the success went to her head? You know how that happens to people after they make it big. The media has really fluffed up her story, so I'm sure that doesn't help matters."

"Yeah . . . something like that."

"So, what can I do for you?" It wasn't like Penny to stop by so early in the day.

"I came to ask if Detective Trudeau has mentioned anything to you about giving back my party room. It's been a few days and I really thought I'd have it back by now. I have a booking request from a previous customer and I'd really like to rent the room to them. They're offering me a substantial amount and I'm not in a financial position to turn down the money."

Shaking my head, I told her, "No, he doesn't discuss his work with me. I never have any clue what's going on with a case. I wish I had something better to tell you."

Her shoulders sagged. "I guess I'll try calling the police department again. He's a hard man to get a hold of."

"If I talk to him today, I'll pass along the message for you. It's not much, but it's the least I could do."

"Thanks," she mumbled, and headed out the door.

Nancy came up behind me once Penny left. "She seems to be acting strangely, don't you think?"

"Yeah . . . this whole day is strange," I replied. "I think I need to head next door and grab a doughnut."

I spent some time admiring the doughnut selection and talking to Ruth Wu in between her customers. So far the doughnut shop was doing really well. So well, in fact, she mentioned that the Yi sisters were glaring at her from across the pond. Apparently, their moon cake customers were in the mood for a little something different.

"June Yi is the one to watch out for. She's the meaner one. But you'll get used to them," I assured her. "Before long you'll learn to ignore them like the rest of us do."

Ruth laughed. "I am glad that it's not only me they are mean to. It is hard to be new in a place where everyone is like family."

To make her feel better, I told her about the times that the Yi sisters had been especially rude to me despite the fact that we were all supposed to be "family." Most of that came with the murder of Thomas Feng and how they seemed to think that Peter and I were the guiltiest of all.

I tried not to hold grudges, sometimes they can be a heavy load. But, then again, no one's perfect.

Business at the doughnut shop started to pick up, so I waved good-bye and headed back out into the plaza with my bag of doughnuts. When I peeked inside, I saw that she had added some free doughnut holes just like the other times. I smiled to myself . . . doughnuts made everything better.

Right as I was about to head back into the noodle house, I noticed Joel Liu coming out of the Bamboo Lounge. What the heck was he doing here? I hadn't seen him since the contest. I decided to walk over and find out.

He smiled at me as I came up to him, but clearly had no intention of stopping to chat. Before he could rush by, I stepped in front of him. The expression on his face was borderline surprise mixed with agitation.

"Hi, going so soon?" I asked with a tilt of my head.

"Lana, hey." He glanced toward the main entrance. "Nice to see you."

"Likewise . . . what brings you to our neck of the woods?" He looked like he was ready to run for it, so I figured, why waste time with pleasantries.

"Uh, I stopped by to talk with Penny and see how she was holding up after . . . after what happened."

"That's awfully nice of you . . . I didn't realize that you two knew each other." There seemed to be a lot of that going around lately.

"We . . ." He glanced back at the lounge and then down at his shoes. "We used to know each other, but we drifted out of touch."

"You drifted?" That didn't make any sense; Penny was newer to the area. And I've known Joel Liu to be a Cleveland native, so how would that be possible?

"It's not a crime to stop and visit with someone, is it?" Joel said, his tone sharpening. "Are you the visitation police?"

I held up my free hand, the other clutched my doughnut bag. "Hey, just asking a simple question. No need to get riled up over it."

"Oh, quit the crap, Lana. You are treating me just like everybody else is." He inched closer and I could feel his breath on my face. "And frankly, I'm getting a little sick of it."

"How is everyone treating you?" I asked, trying to appear innocent. For the record, I'm not sure it worked.

"Like I'm the one who killed Norman." His shoulders drooped. "Does everyone really think that poorly of me that they'd believe I'm capable of murder? I may have hated the guy, but I'm no murderer."

"But you did get in a fight with him at the contest . . .

and you *did* threaten him on different occasions. Send any interesting e-mails lately?"

"How do you kno—" He pinched the bridge of his nose and shook his head. "Never mind, I don't have to justify myself to anyone . . . especially you. But if anyone asked me my damn opinion, I'd tell them exactly what I told the police."

"Which is . . . ?"

"Ray Jin. That slimy good-for-nothing wannabe cook. If they're pointing the finger at anybody, it should be him."

"What? Ray? That doesn't even make any sense."

"Sure it does."

"The two of them were friends," I pointed out.

"Ha, okay . . . *friends*. Right. The reviews that Ray got for his crappy restaurant are a little too perfect. Do you honestly think that sort of thing comes free?"

I knew he was referring to the bribery rumor . . . the rumor that he'd started. "To be honest, I've never given it much thought."

"Maybe you should. And maybe your stupid boyfriend should too. That whole police department . . ." He shook his head. "The blind leading the blind."

"Hey! There's no reason to disrespect Adam or the police department like that. They're just doing their jobs and considering every possible lead. Clearly, you have something to be guilty about if they're looking at you," I spat.

He threw his hands up in the air. "You're like a dumb kid, you know that? I insult your boyfriend and you throw a tantrum."

"It's not a—"

"Try focusing on the actual facts, genius. It's like I said to your knucklehead boyfriend . . . if you read all of Norman's reviews, you'll notice they've never gleamed as bright as they have for Ray . . . that's because his payout is probably the biggest. Go ahead, take a look and see for yourself."

"Maybe I will."

"Do whatever you want . . . just stay away from me. I have enough problems as it is." He stormed off, and I watched him stampede through the plaza.

You wanna talk about tantrums? Joel Liu would definitely take first place.

CHAPTER 12

My run-in with Joel bothered me the rest of the day. I went through sales slips and food orders on automatic, the possible suspects rolling through my head over and over. Was Joel telling the truth? Or was he another one trying to move suspicion away from himself with exaggerated accusations? I didn't know.

And, what was he doing at the Bamboo Lounge? Penny had never hinted that she knew Joel besides the fact that he owned a local restaurant. He'd said they knew each other from before . . . before when? I could try and ask Penny, but something told me she wasn't going to be very forthcoming with me either.

At five o'clock, I left for the day, leaving the restaurant in the capable hands of Nancy, and our resident teenager, Vanessa Wen, who was at times more than I could handle.

Megan was at work, and I decided to stop and see her. Maybe an outside perspective could enlighten me.

Happy hour was in full swing at the Zodiac, but thankfully I was able to find an empty stool at the bar. The astrologically themed bar had been our local hangout since college, and they were known just as much for their art murals depicting the twelve signs as they were for their outstanding drink menu.

I caught Megan's attention and she acknowledged me with a wink as she made her way down the bar to where I was sitting. By the time she got to me, she already had a mixed drink in hand. She slid it toward me with a napkin and leaned over. "Your face tells me that you need this."

"It's that bad?"

"Oh, yeah."

Keeping my emotions off my face has always been a difficult task for me. But even when I thought I was successful at hiding them, Megan usually knew the truth. After all, we'd been friends for years—plenty of time for her to observe me.

"What happened?" she asked, her eyes checking the bar for raised hands.

"I ran into Joel Liu today. He was at the Bamboo Lounge visiting with Penny."

"Remind me why that would be weird again?"

Before I could tell her the full story, she was summoned by another patron. I sipped my drink and glanced over the happy hour menu . . . it had been a long time since lunch and the noodles that Peter made for me earlier in the day seemed like a distant memory.

When Megan returned, I placed an order for some boneless teriyaki wings and finished my story.

"Sounds to me like this Joel guy is making things up.

I mean, Ray was supposedly paying Norman for good reviews, but we don't actually know that to be true. That whole thing was a rumor that was started at last year's contest by Joel himself, wasn't it?"

"Yeah, he made sure to pass on his story to the Mahjong Matrons. They basically did the work for him. Aside from that, though, no one thought Ray should have won anyway."

"And why is that? His food is good, no?"

"Well, up until the contest, his reviews weren't that great. And truthfully, his food really isn't either. I've eaten there a couple of times, and it's nothing to write home about. There is nothing on his menu that makes him stand out in any way."

"Yeah, but you're partial to Peter and your family's recipes. Are you sure you can be a good judge of whether or not this guy has a creditable menu?"

"Okay, that's true . . . but . . ."

"But what?"

"I hate to admit this, but if anyone should have won other than us, it should have been Walter Shen. His food is definitely contestworthy. Don't tell my mother I said that though . . . she'll disown me in a heartbeat."

"Then do you think it's possible Norman was worried that if Walter Shen won the contest it would look like favoritism? They're supposed to be good friends, right?"

"Well, yeah . . . but then we should have won."

She smirked. "Take yourself out of the picture and take into consideration that maybe Norman was trying to make the contest look more legit. But instead, it went in the opposite direction."

"But that didn't stop the House of Shen from winning

in previous years. So if he did suddenly care about things appearing to be on the up-and-up, what changed?"

"Maybe someone brought it up and Norman was approached about it. You know as well as I do that some things aren't a problem until someone puts a spotlight on it."

"It is possible, I suppose."

My boneless wings arrived and I realized just how hungry I was. Megan worked the bar while I chomped on my food, contemplating what my next move would be. I knew that I needed to talk to Ray at some point, but I wasn't looking forward to it. In general, I'd never been a fan of his. I found Ray more often than not to be pompous and condescending. He wasn't that much older than me, but he always managed to treat me like I was some kind of child who needed his guidance.

The last time we'd had a run-in prior to the contest, he told me how surprised he was that my parents put such a young girl in charge of the family restaurant. He also made it a point to suggest that if I ever needed tips from an expert, I'd know where to find him.

Besides the obvious need to talk with the people involved, I also needed to take some time and read the reviews that Norman had written for any of the Asian restaurants competing in the contest.

Another thing I wanted to do was check out Norman's family tree. I didn't know if that would lead me anywhere, but it wouldn't hurt to do a little digging into his personal life. Who knows, maybe I'd find something of use.

And at some point down the line, I'd have to talk to Adam about all of this. Since I knew how he would react to me asking questions and bringing up the case, I decided to leave that task for last.

Maybe in the meantime, I'd be able to come up with something more concrete.

When I got home after visiting with Megan, I spent a considerable amount of time walking Kikko around the apartment complex. While she sniffed and marked her territory, I thought about the case and the best way to approach Ray.

The contest was only a couple of days away, and I wanted to talk to him before then if possible.

Back inside, Kikko found her bone under a cushion and I plopped down next to her on the couch with my laptop to do some digging.

My first search consisted of articles written by Norman about Asian restaurants in the area. Most of them were harsh, even when he was giving compliments. Apparently in his opinion there was always something to be improved on.

It seemed the only glowing reviews he gave were to Walter Shen and Ray, but even in those he added touches of criticism. A few times he mentioned that Ray's sauces could be a little overused, making some of his dishes more watery than necessary. The harshest thing he said about Walter was that he needed to spend more time on the presentation of the dishes.

Walter getting excellent reviews, I could understand. As much as I disliked the Shen family, they had a reputable restaurant that had been around for over forty years.

They served traditional Chinese food and they never skimped on ingredients. Their meats, vegetables, and noodles were always of the best quality, and the portions were always big enough that you'd have plenty to take home. Something like picking on his presentation wasn't going to hurt business in the least.

But why Ray?

While I was searching through reviews from customers who claimed to frequent the establishments, Ian called.

"I need you in my office at ten A.M.," he said by way of greeting.

"Oh, is that so?" My patience was thin and easily apparent in my tone.

"Sorry, I'm a little on edge." He paused. "Freddie Yuan is coming tomorrow to talk about the contest, and I'd like you to be there."

My stomach dropped at the mention of Freddie's name. "Why do I need to be there? Don't you want the other judges there instead? That makes more sense, doesn't it?"

"Lana, why must you always argue with me? We act like a married couple and you won't even go on a date with me."

My eyes rolled so far into my head, I thought I might flip over the back of the couch. "Fine . . . I'll be there."

He was silent for a minute, possibly at the shock of my quick agreement. "Do you think the other judges should be there too?"

"Yes . . ." I said with exasperation. "Stella and Ray should definitely be there to meet with Freddie and discuss the particulars and . . . deliberate or whatever it is they do." I realized as I said it that this would be my opportunity to talk with Ray without actually having to go see him at his restaurant. It would be less suspicious *and* save me the trip.

"Okay, I'll give them a call and see if they can make it. I suppose it would be a good idea. See? This is why I bring you along on these things. You always have such good ideas."

"Uh-huh. I'll see you tomorrow, Ian."

"Ten o'clock. Don't be late."

"Okay, okay. I'll be there at ten." My eyes drifted back to my computer screen. "Hey Ian, what do you know about Norman Pan?"

"What do you mean? As in personally?"

"Yeah, you know, like did he have a girlfriend or maybe a cousin . . . nieces, nephews?"

"Not that I'm aware of . . . oh, wait! Yes, of course, I can't believe I completely forgot about his niece, Tammy."

"Tammy? Who's that?" I asked.

"Sweet girl, she owns the Tasty Dumpling over on the east side. From what I understand they weren't really on speaking terms. He gave her a bad review once in *Cleveland* magazine."

"Wow, he actually gave his niece a bad review?" I knew he was a jerk, but doing that to his own niece was a low blow.

"Norman isn't one to pull punches; I guess that applied to family as well."

I thanked Ian for the intel before hanging up and searching for the Tasty Dumpling online. I found an address and jotted it down on a notepad. If I got the chance, I would definitely be paying a visit to Tammy.

CHAPTER 13

"Leave it to that guy to always find a way to involve you in everything. Things that don't even make sense!" Adam tapped his chopsticks on the rim of his plate. "The new judge introduction? How does that even apply to you?"

I'd gotten him addicted to scrambled eggs and scallions for breakfast. When he could, he'd come in for a quick breakfast before heading to the station. It had been a while since he'd been able to come in and it cheered me up to see him.

"It'll be fine, plus I'll be able to see what's going on for the contest. None of the other contestants have that advantage."

"What can you even learn by being there?"

"Maybe the judges will slip and talk about things they're looking for or mention their favorite dishes. You never know what could come up."

Adam refused to ease up. "I don't care. I don't like him."

"I know. Believe me, I'm not his number one fan either."

A couple came in and I got up to tend to them, seating them at a booth on the opposite end. While I got their tea and took their order, Adam finished his breakfast and pushed his plate aside. He sat sipping his tea and checking e-mails on his phone.

"So Ray and Stella will be there too . . ."

"At least that part makes sense." He mumbled this as his attention was split between me and his cell phone.

"What do you think about Ray anyway?"

"Huh?" He looked up in confusion. "What do you mean what do I think of Ray?"

"You know . . . about what happened. Is Ray on your suspect list?"

"I'm not going to discuss that with you, and you know that." His voice transformed into detective mode. "You're not supposed to be snooping around, remember? I specifically remember asking you to stay out of it."

"Well, I am . . . I was just wondering about Ray . . ."

"Why him?"

I fiddled with a loose thread on my shirt. "Because he's someone who doesn't seem to have a motive . . . but maybe he does . . . secretly."

He pointed to a patch of hair on his head. "Do you see this? These gray hairs . . . these are from me worrying about you."

I inched closer and scrutinized his face, crinkling my nose in a dramatic way. "Yeah, there's some in your scruff too."

"Har har."

I stood up, straightening my back, and folded my arms

over my chest. "So you're not going to tell me what you think?"

He shook his head. "Sorry, doll." He gave his hands one last wipe on the cloth napkin and moved to get up from the table. "What do I owe you for breakfast?"

"It's on the house," I said.

Adam kissed me on the forehead and gave my shoulders a squeeze. "I'm only trying to keep you safe. We're still not clear on motive, and for all we know, this could happen again. People in the contest could be a target . . . which is exactly why I want you to keep out of it. I'd ask you to drop out, but I know that Peter would never do that."

"Do you really think it could happen again?" I asked. Almost everyone else seemed to think that we were out of danger. "You don't think this was specific to Norman? I mean, he wasn't the best guy."

"He does have a lot of enemies, I can tell you that. Especially after digging through his history and seeing the number of people he's pissed off along the way. But, in this job, I've learned that everything is a possibility until it's been ruled out."

"Aha!" I yelled. "So that means that Ray *is* a suspect!"

He returned my question with a flat stare. "I'm going to work . . ."

The time flew after Adam left and I thought a lot about what he said. Anything was a possibility. No clear motive had been established, the killer was out there, and we couldn't be sure that he—or she—wouldn't strike again.

Anna May walked in at 9:55 A.M.

"Cuttin' it kind of close, aren't you?" I said to her. "I have to meet with Ian and the judges at ten."

She waved a hand at me. "Oh, Ian will survive if you're a few minutes late."

"Of course he'll survive, but will I?" I asked. "I really don't want to get an earful from him later on."

"I'm here now . . . so go. Quit standing around giving me a hard time." She gave the dining area a quick glance and then hopped up on the hostess stool. "Make sure you're back in an hour, I have a class at noon and I can't be late."

"Uh-huh." I grabbed my purse from under the counter. "Let me ask you something . . ."

"Go for it."

"This thing that happened with Norman Pan . . . do you think that he was the main target?"

She shrugged. "I haven't given it much thought. Why do you ask?"

"A couple of people think that it's possible the killer could strike again. That maybe it has something to do with the contest and not Norman himself."

"Maybe, maybe not. It's hard to say without any other evidence."

"That's what Adam said."

"Well, listen to your boyfriend. He's the cop and all."

"I suppose." I headed for the door.

"Lana!" Anna May yelled as I was heading out into the plaza.

I turned around. "Yeah?"

"He probably also told you to stay out of it. And frankly, if I were you, I'd take his advice."

* * *

I was the last to arrive at Ian's office. He had rearranged the area where Mr. Feng's desk used to be, and now in its place was a small love seat, two chairs, and a coffee table. It was a nice little sitting area and it gave the office a more personal and inviting atmosphere.

He'd also chosen to brighten up the room with better lighting. Mr. Feng never turned on the overhead lights, and only used a small desk lamp that left the office dank and foreboding. It hadn't offered a lot of encouragement for people to swing by.

Everyone turned when I opened the door.

"Oh, Lana, good," Ian said, getting up and greeting me at the door. "Glad you're here . . . now we can get started."

Stella and Ray were seated in the two chairs and Freddie Yuan sat on the love seat. He smiled at me as our eyes met and I immediately felt myself get flustered. There was something about the way he looked at me that made me blush. My only hope was that no one else would notice.

Ian gestured to the open spot next to Freddie. "Why don't you take that seat and I'll grab my desk chair."

Freddie patted the cushion next to him and then rested his arm on the back of the love seat, which now seemed too small. "Nice to see you again, Lana."

"You too, Freddie," I whispered as I sat down next to him. "Thank you for agreeing to help judge the contest."

"Not a problem. It's my pleasure," he replied with a wink.

Stella shifted uncomfortably in her chair. She crossed her legs and then recrossed them. Our eyes met briefly and I saw a tinge of fear in her expression.

Ray appeared unamused. He glanced at his watch, and then twisted in the chair to look out into the plaza.

Ian returned with his chair. "Okay, let's begin . . ."

"Yeah, let's get this show on the road, I need to get back," Ray spat. "I don't have all morning to deal with this."

Ian cleared his throat. "Okay then . . . well, Freddie, let's get you properly introduced. I don't believe you've had the chance to officially meet Ray and Stella."

Ray seemed to size up Freddie. "Wait a minute, isn't he one of the construction workers?"

Freddie leaned forward; the crook of his arm grazed my shoulder. "Yeah, I helped out with that, but I'm the community center director. Always lookin' to help out wherever I can."

Ray scoffed and slouched back in his seat. "Whatever, let's just keep this moving, okay?"

Freddie went into a brief introduction of himself. Apparently, Freddie and Ian knew each other from Chicago and a fast friendship was built while the two men were attempting to establish a foothold in a city they were both unfamiliar with. Turned out that Freddie was originally from South Carolina and moved to the Windy City for school.

He didn't have much to offer in the way of credentials, but assured everyone that he would be more than fair in judging the contestants on their culinary skills. I have to admit that I missed portions of what he said because I was too preoccupied with watching the movements of his lips. Once I caught myself, a silent and thorough scolding began.

Ian looked among the three judges. "Stella . . . Ray . . .

what do you guys think? Are we on board with Freddie being the replacement judge?"

"I'm okay with whatever you decide, Ian," Stella said quietly.

She was a lot different from the boisterous woman I had met during round one. Even when I'd seen her the other day, she wasn't as confident as she'd first appeared. I wondered if she'd talked with Adam yet. I'd have to ask her since I knew that he wouldn't tell me.

Ian nodded. "Great . . . that's the spirit." Turning to Ray, he said, "And how about you, Ray?"

Ray turned his attention back to the group. "Is this really the only guy we could find?"

Freddie's jaw clenched as he leaned forward again. "If you've got a problem with me, man, don't be shy about it."

Ray snickered, seemingly satisfied that he'd gotten under the new judge's skin. "No . . . no problem here. Like I said . . . keep it moving. I really don't care."

"Okay then, it's settled." Ian clapped his hands together, ignoring the tension building in the room. "Now, let's get you brought up to speed on what's happened so far, and what's going to happen next. Everything needs to go as smoothly as possible on Friday."

"Do I need to be here for this?" Ray asked. "I already know the drill."

Ian slumped in his chair. "No . . . I suppose if you need to go, we can take it from here. Mainly I wanted you to be included in the final vote."

"We're running out of time, so there's not a lot of room for argument. This whole meeting was unnecessary." He stood up and headed out of the office without saying a formal good-bye.

While the other three got heavily into conversation about contest details, I slipped out to catch up with Ray.

"Hey!" I yelled after him. He was already halfway through the plaza and past Ho-Lee Noodle House

He turned his head but kept walking.

I broke into a jog to catch up. When I finally caught up to him, I said, "Hey, what's your hurry?"

"I have to get back to my restaurant," he blurted. "Did you need something?"

"You didn't seem too happy about Freddie replacing Norman. Do you not approve of him?"

"It's not really my call, is it? The whole meeting was all for show. Even if we disagreed with Ian, he'd still pick Freddie Yuan anyway. Besides, as long as we can get through this contest, that's all that matters. Hurry up and get it over with."

"Would you rather the contest be canceled?" I asked.

"What does it matter to me? I'm not in it. I already won last year." When we reached the main doors, he finally stopped moving and turned to face me. "What is all this about? Why do you care about this so much?"

"I don't know, I guess I wanted to make sure you were doing okay. I know that you and Norman were good friends. This must be hard for you."

His eyes shifted to the door. "Well, what can you do, right? People go . . . they go."

My mouth dropped. "He didn't just go . . . he was murdered. That's totally different."

"That's a way to go too, isn't it?"

I didn't know what to say to that, and he took my pause of silence as an opportunity to escape. He left the plaza before I could ask him any questions. I stood at the main entrance and watched him disappear into the sea of cars. If that wasn't suspicious, I didn't know what was.

CHAPTER 14

The afternoon was slow at the restaurant once lunch ended, and while we were putting the dining area back in order, my mother and grandmother showed up for a visit.

My mother seemed a little preoccupied and mumbled a hello to me as she and my grandmother went to sit at a booth. Without them asking, I went in the back and warned Peter that they had arrived, got them some tea, and headed back out to their table.

They thanked me for the tea and my mother stared at me and blinked her eyes rapidly.

"Mom, are you okay?" I asked.

"How is everything?" She winked at me this time and glanced at my grandmother.

"Fine . . . how are you? Are you feeling all right?"

"Yes, I am okay. Do you need me to help you with something?"

My grandmother looked up at me and smiled.

"No . . ." I scrunched my brows at her.

My mother winked again.

"I mean, yes . . ." I said, unsure of what was happening. "Yes, can you help me in the office?"

"Oh, yes! I am happy to help you!" My mother exaggerated a smile and hurried up from the booth. She muttered something to my grandmother before grabbing my arm and leading me into the back room.

As we passed through the kitchen, Peter waved a spatula at my mom. "Hey, Mama Lee."

She gave him a dismissive wave and continued to pull me to the back room until we made it to the office. When the door was shut, she finally let go of my wrist.

"Mom . . . what the heck is going on?"

My mother let out a frustrated sigh. "Your A-ma is driving me crazy."

A laugh escaped, and I covered my mouth.

"This is not funny," my mother said with a scowl. "I need you to take A-ma somewhere. I will work for you."

"Take her where?" I asked. "And why is she driving you crazy?"

With a groan, she replied, "She is always telling me what to do, and that I am not doing things right. Even when I am cleaning the house, I am doing things wrong."

We stood staring at each other for a few seconds before I burst into laughter.

My mother folded her arms across her chest. "Aiya, Lana! Do not laugh at Mommy."

"Oh, come on, Mom . . . it's funny. Now you know how it feels." I took a deep breath to calm my laughing fit. "This doesn't sound at all familiar to you?"

"No," my mother replied in a serious tone. "Mommy is very nice to you."

I blurted out a laugh and shook my head. "Okay, I'll take A-ma off your hands for a while. I was planning on going out for a late lunch anyway. But I just want you to remember this moment . . ."

My mother gave me one final glare before I left the office with a giant smile on my face.

With my grandmother in tow, I ventured over to Liu's Noodle Emporium. She was none the wiser that I was giving my mother a break from being around her own mother twenty-four/seven. As far as she knew, this was just a granddaughter taking her grandmother out for lunch.

The parking lot was filled with a decent amount of cars, but a little more business probably wouldn't have hurt.

We ambled inside and I scoped the place out. It was much like any Chinese restaurant you've seen—dark wood trim, a few pieces of Asian art on the walls, and plastic tablecloths.

The hostess greeted us with a cheery smile, pulling two menus from the slot on the side of her lectern. "Just the two of you today, miss?"

"Yes. And I'd like to see the owner if he's available."

"Oh," she said, hugging the menus to her chest. "He's with someone in a meeting right now. Did you have a complaint?"

"No, nothing like that. Do you know if he'll be long?" It's not like I was in a hurry to get my grandmother back, so I didn't mind waiting.

She shook her head. "I can't say for sure. Could be ten minutes . . . could be a half hour . . . or more."

"Okay, well, we'll sit and have lunch while we wait."

She gestured for us to follow her. "Right this way."

We walked past a couple of patrons on our way to a booth toward the back of the room. She placed the menus on the table. "Would you both like some tea?"

"Sure." I slid into one side of the booth while my grandmother slid into the other. Our table came with a nice view of the parking lot. Thankfully the menu was written in both Chinese and English, so we flipped through the pages while we waited for her to return.

The menu was standard stuff, and I decided to go with my usual fallback. It had been a while since I'd eaten at Joel's restaurant, and I couldn't even remember what I thought of the food. I imagined it must not have impressed me much since I never made it a point to come back until now.

When she returned with our tea and glasses of water, we gave her our order. I went with hot and sour soup—mild, a vegetable spring roll, and Mongolian beef with white rice.

My grandmother ordered a shrimp mei fun dish, egg drop soup, and an egg roll.

While we waited for our food, the fact that I couldn't speak Taiwanese or Mandarin in full sentences reared its annoying head. Most days it wasn't that big of a deal, but now that my grandmother was here and her English was practically nonexistent, I was bothered more so than usual at our inability to communicate properly with each other. A lot of our conversations involved hand gestures or pointing at random objects as reference.

I pulled out my phone and selected the translation app that I recently installed. Maybe my grandmother and I could translate this way. Sometimes the translation wasn't exact, but it was worth a shot.

The app didn't have the Taiwanese dialect that my family preferred, but there was an option for Mandarin that I could use. I entered the translation criteria and spoke into my phone explaining what I was doing for my grandmother. When I played it back for her in Mandarin, she smiled and nodded, giving me a thumbs-up. "Okay!" she said.

I asked her if she was enjoying her time in America. And when she seemed to understand the translation, I held the phone up to her mouth and pressed the record option.

She spoke carefully into the phone and the translation came back as, "I like it here very much. I would like to live here."

"You don't want to go back to Taiwan?" I asked.

She shook her head. "A-ma is lonely in Taiwan. Everyone is too busy."

I nodded in understanding. When my parents announced to Anna May and me that they were going to Taiwan because something was wrong with my grandmother, they never specified what the problem actually was. And when I'd questioned my mother about it, she'd told me to mind my own business.

Was my grandmother suffering from loneliness and was that the cause of the trip? The behavior my mother had reported back to me at the time they were away seemed to make sense now. My grandmother's mood improved extensively once my parents showed up, and she'd begun to act like her old self again. Maybe her staying in the States was the best option for her.

I glanced toward the back room door to see if Joel

would magically appear. I couldn't help but wonder who he was meeting with and what was taking so long.

My grandmother gestured that she was going to the restroom so I decided to entertain myself by checking Facebook while she was gone. As I scrolled past photos of cake doughnuts and bears swimming in pools, an idle thought occurred to me. I could be eating lunch at the restaurant of a killer. And on top of that, I'd brought my grandmother along for the ride.

Had I really made the best decision by coming here and bringing my grandmother with me?

Was I making any sound decisions as of late? It was kind of after the fact to take it back now, but I wondered what an alternate time line of my life would have been like. I imagined that maybe I could have been a receptionist or office manager for a nice company where bad things didn't happen to decent people. That had been my original plan. While I waited for my grandmother to return, I pondered at what point I went off my scheduled path of life.

The hostess, who was also our waitress, brought our soup and appetizers right as my grandmother was returning from the restroom.

The steaming bowls splattered onto the vinyl tablecloth as she set each one out in front of us. "Oops, sorry about that," she apologized. "Be careful, it's extremely hot." Between our bowls of soup, she set down a wooden bowl of shrimp chips for us to share and two small plates with appetizer rolls on them. "The rest of your food should be out shortly. Just holler if you need anything in the meantime."

My grandmother bowed her head in thanks, and then smiled down at her food.

I thanked the waitress as well and inspected my soup. If there's one thing I am when I go to another Chinese restaurant, it's picky. When your mother cooks the best food possible, it sets the standard for everyone else at an extremely high level. There were few restaurants in the city that I truly loved outside of Ho-Lee Noodle House.

I wondered what my grandmother, as a newcomer, would think of the different Chinese restaurants we had in Cleveland. I watched her as she sampled her soup. When she noticed me observing her, she pointed to the bowl with her spoon and shrugged.

Focusing back on my soup, I noted that it was a lot thinner than I was used to, and the top was covered with reddish slicks of oil. I put a small amount of broth on my spoon for a taste test.

Awful! And spicy! Too spicy. I quickly took a sip of water. So much for mild soup.

My grandmother laughed at my reaction. She dipped her own spoon into my soup, took a taste and puckered her lips.

Next, I tested the spring roll. Spring rolls are basically foolproof, which is part of the reason why I order them as one of my fallbacks. I took a bite and deliberated. Not bad, but slightly cold in the middle. I focused on my spring roll and slid the soup to the side.

My grandmother poked at her egg roll, took a bite, and gave me another shrug. "So-so," she said.

While we ate in slight dissatisfaction, I gazed out into the parking lot, watching traffic move along Superior

Avenue. It was a nice day with lots of sun, and people were taking advantage of a spring day without the threat of rain.

Our food finally came after what felt like an eternity. The waitress set the steaming plate of Mongolian beef in front of me, along with a nice-sized bowl of white rice. In front of my grandmother, she placed the platter of rice noodles topped with shrimp.

I broke the wooden chopsticks apart and went straight for a piece of beef. This was the deal breaker right here. The quality of meat is important to me and I believe it tells a lot about the restaurant and how well the food is cooked. The care they put into their ingredients speaks volumes.

Taking a bite of the beef, I immediately felt the gristly texture between my teeth. The flavor wasn't bad, but it felt like I was chewing on a piece of fat. The gag reflex in the back of my mouth started to argue with me, and as discreetly as possible, I spat the piece of meat into my napkin and folded it, stuffing it under my dish.

My grandmother caught me and laughed. She poked at her shrimp and frowned. I nabbed a piece from her plate and immediately knew the cause of her unhappiness. The shrimp was overcooked and extremely dry.

She pushed all of her shrimp to one side of the plate and focused on the rice noodles. At least her meal wasn't completely awful.

I decided to stick to the vegetables on my plate, which were overcooked and kind of mushy. And as long as I'm complaining, the rice was kind of dry.

I could see why someone in Norman Pan's position would give Joel a bad review. What was worse was that after all of the reviews Norman had given him, he hadn't changed the quality of his food. Assessing the items I'd ordered, I couldn't believe that Joel had remained in business all this time.

After we had picked through everything we intended to eat from our plates, Joel still wasn't done with his meeting. The unsatisfying food had left me grumpy and I didn't feel like waiting anymore, so I asked the waitress for our check.

"Did you want to-go boxes?" she asked, pointing at our nearly full plates.

"That's okay," I told her, trying not to sound nasty while I said it. "We'll just take the check."

She returned shortly with the check on a black tray along with two fortune cookies.

The fortune cookies reminded me of Stella and I wondered how she was doing.

And then the weirdest thing happened.

Stella stormed out of the back kitchen, her face flushed with anger. Joel followed closely behind trying to catch up with her.

The absurdity of her showing up right as I was thinking about her made me gasp and the sound caused Stella to turn in my direction. When recognition hit, she also gasped, and guilt washed over her face.

"Lana . . ." Stella steered herself in the direction of our table. "What are you doing here?" She smiled politely at my grandmother before turning her attention back to me.

Joel stood a booth away, silent and observing our exchange.

"I should ask you the same thing," I said, trying to regain my composure. "I'm actually here to see Joel."

She looked back at him, and then at me. "Well, he's all

yours." And she stomped out, leaving both Joel and me in an awkward silence.

After Stella left and I paid for our horrible lunch, I explained to my grandmother via the translation app that I was going to talk with Joel and I would be back in a few minutes. I opened up a gaming app and left her with my cell phone.

Joel brought me back to his office. It was similar to my mother's in that it was cramped and definitely not fit for more than one person. The difference between hers and his was that his was actually tidy. He even had room for a plant on his desk.

"You wanted to see me about something?" he asked, keeping his eyes on the desk in front of him.

"I didn't realize that you knew Stella," I replied. "Seems like you know everyone around here."

His eyes flitted up for a minute. "Is that why you came here, to interrogate me again? I'm kind of busy."

"No, I came to ask you some questions about Ray."

"Oh, him." The relief that washed over him was not lost on me.

"So, what gave you the idea that things with Ray and Norman were not going that well toward the end? Did you see anything that might give you that impression?"

He shrugged. "I didn't see anything so much as I've heard things."

"Heard what kind of things . . . where? And from who?"

"You ask a lot of questions."

"I'm not getting back any answers." The sarcasm in my tone was thick, and that was just fine by me.

"What's it to you anyway? Shouldn't you let that cop boyfriend of yours figure it out? He's supposed to be some miracle detective, isn't he?"

"Because a bad thing has happened at Asia Village—"

"Yeah, and I would think that'd be more Ian Sung's problem than yours."

I scowled at him. "It concerns *all* of us at the plaza. And besides, Norman deserves some justice, don't you agree?"

"No . . . I don't think he does." His tone was flat and his stare icy.

A chill ran down my spine. "No?"

"Oh, come on, Lana, look who we're talking about. That man deserves exactly what he got. If he wanted sympathy in death, then he should have treated people with a little more humanity."

"That's a pretty bold statement for someone who is on the suspect list."

He snorted. "On whose suspect list? Yours? I have nothing to fear . . . I didn't kill anybody . . . I didn't do anything . . . and I don't really care what you think." He stood up from his desk. "Now, if you'll excuse me, I have things I should be doing."

"Just tell me where you heard about Ray and I'll be on my way."

Joel took a deep breath. "I said around, okay? Don't you have a restaurant to run? Maybe you should try worrying about your own matters rather than pestering other people during their workday."

I hated to admit defeat, but I didn't feel like Joel was going to give in to me any time soon and I didn't want to leave my grandmother alone for too long. "Fine." I clutched my purse and stood up from the rickety chair. "I suppose I should be going."

"Worry less about where I've heard things from and convince your boyfriend to look deeper into Ray Jin. You'll get your answers . . . one way or another."

I left confused and frustrated. I was confused about what connections Joel had with Penny and Stella, and frustrated with him and his unwillingness to tell me where he'd heard about Ray and Norman. What was the big deal?

His caginess on the matter led me to believe that he was either making it all up or he'd heard something he wasn't supposed to and didn't want to give himself up. At this point, both scenarios could be a possibility.

Debating between the two, I headed back to the restaurant with my grandmother for some real food.

CHAPTER 15

"Something is weird here," I said to Megan when I got home that night.

She was at the kitchen table with her laptop. Her eyes didn't even move from the screen when I walked into the dining area. "About Joel and his associations with Penny?"

Kikko ambled over to greet me, no doubt waking up from a nap. How I envied the leisurely life of a dog.

"Well, add Stella to his list of odd associations. I was just at Joel's restaurant, and Stella was there meeting with him in private. I don't understand how they would know each other . . . any of them. Stella doesn't even live in this city."

"Stella Chung, where did you say she lives now . . . Chicago? It's possible she knew Joel before she made it as a big-time chef."

"Yeah, I guess it could be possible. But that doesn't

explain the connection with Penny. What are you looking at?" I couldn't stand it when I was talking to someone and they weren't looking at me.

Her eyes finally left the screen. "How to ombre-dye my hair."

"You're planning on doing this yourself?" I asked, moving behind her to watch the video.

She shrugged. "Yeah, why not, you know? If it doesn't work out, I'll just dye over it."

"Have Jasmine do it, it'll be safer that way."

Megan clucked her tongue. "Anyway, you were saying . . . Chicago. So, okay . . . pretend they knew each other from way back when. It doesn't really make it a big deal now."

"Then how does that explain Penny? She's still the odd man out."

"Where is Penny from?"

"Miami," I told her. "She only moved here about a year and a half ago."

Megan was focused back on her laptop. "Huh . . . weird."

"Will you pay attention to me?" I asked. "You know, you're the one who was so gung-ho about diving into this whole mess. And now I'm just going in circles all by myself."

"Geez, sorry. What's got you so crabby today?"

I shook my head, attempting to shake away the agitation that I felt. I knew I was on edge, but I hadn't realized how much. "Joel and his attitude really set me off."

With an understanding nod she closed the lid of her laptop and folded her hands over the top. "Okay, you have my full attention."

"This is what I'm thinking . . . tell me if it sounds crazy."

"You know I will."

"What if Joel is who Stella is scared of? Maybe she saw him at the party and knows that it was him. So she goes to confront him at his restaurant and tries to make him turn himself in. Then I caught her in the act and she's embarrassed because she knows that I know something strange is going on with her."

"Okay, but what does any of that have to do with Penny?"

"Maybe Joel went to threaten Penny or . . . *or* . . . he went to see if she knows anything just like I did. She's supposed to have those security cameras running and it's not like he would know that they're fakes. He could think she has evidence on tape or something."

"Possible. It might be a stretch, but it's not crazy."

"What do you think happened?" I asked, plopping in the chair adjacent to her.

"Love triangle."

I rolled my eyes. "Been there, done that."

She laughed. "Just because it's happened before, doesn't mean it couldn't happen again. The love triangle is a very popular circumstance in the murdering world."

"Would you be serious?"

"You ask me that at least once a day, Lana Lee," Megan chided. "And when has that ever worked out for you?"

"Point made."

"I think you should talk to Penny again, see if she'll tell you why Joel stopped by."

"She hasn't been very socialable with me lately. I don't know if I'll get much out of her."

"Doesn't hurt to try. You're at the plaza anyway . . . hey, wait a minute, what about that Walter guy? Did you scratch him off your list?"

"No, I've just been avoiding anything to do with him for the time being."

"Why, because of his daughter?"

"No, because he gives me the heebies." I shivered thinking about our last encounter.

Before bed, I pulled the notebook out from under my mattress, and wrote down everything new that occurred since I'd woken up that morning. I put a giant star next to Joel's name.

While I tried to fall asleep to the sound of Kikko's snoring, I thought about what Megan had said regarding the love triangle. I found it highly unlikely that this was the case for the three of them. There had to be another connection. There just had to be.

All of Thursday was a complete bust. The restaurant was overwhelmed with business, and Nancy was running late because of a doctor's appointment. It was almost time to wrap up for the day and go home when I'd finally finished prepping the bank deposit. I swung by the Bamboo Lounge but found the doors were locked. I had no idea whether or not Penny was inside, so I decided to head to the bank instead.

After I finished up at the bank, I thought it wouldn't hurt to give Tammy at the Tasty Dumpling a quick visit before heading home. The address was in my purse, and I dug it out, typing the location into my GPS.

Twenty minutes later, I arrived at the Tasty Dumpling.

It was a cute stand-alone building with a bright yellow sign that sported a cartoon dumpling with a smiley face. The lot was empty except for one car that I guessed to be Tammy's. When I approached the door, I noticed on the sign that the restaurant was closed for two hours in the middle of the day. The restaurant was open from eleven A.M. until four P.M. and opened again at six P.M. for dinner. That explained the lack of cars in the parking lot.

The doors were unlocked and I entered the empty restaurant, a set of chimes going off as I walked in.

A petite woman in her mid-thirties with light brown hair and a button nose appeared from the back. "Oh, hello there." She was holding a dishtowel and wiped her hands as she came over to greet me. "I'm not open quite yet, would you mind coming back in about a half hour?"

I extended my hand. "I'm Lana Lee, I was wondering if I could talk to Tammy?"

Stuffing the dishtowel under her arm, she smiled and took my hand, giving me a delicate handshake. "I'm Tammy, how can I help you?"

"This may seem kind of strange, but could I ask you some questions about your uncle, Norman Pan."

The smile evaporated from her face, and she released my hand, folding her arms over her chest. "If you're a reporter or something, I have nothing to say about his death."

I let out a nervous laugh. "Oh no, you misunderstand, I manage Ho-Lee Noodle House, my restaurant is one of the contestants in the noodle contest."

"Oh!" She chuckled to herself and seemed to relax. Unfolding her arms, she removed the dish towel and threw it over her shoulder. "I've had a few reporters come through here wanting to do an article about the man behind the reviews, but I told them I wasn't interested. The less association I have with him, the better."

"I can understand that completely."

"Come, have a seat with me." She gestured to the first booth near the entrance. "Would you like some tea?"

"No, I'm okay, thanks. I won't take up much of your time, I just wanted to ask a few things about him and then I'll be out of your hair."

"Can I ask why?" She slid into one side of the booth and motioned for me to have a seat.

I sat across from her, propping up my purse next to me. "I suppose I have some concerns about the safety of the contest. At this point, it's not entirely clear whether or not your uncle was a target or if it's the contest itself."

"Uncle Norman was a man with many enemies. I think it's entirely possible that he was killed for his decision making in the contest. Can I say for sure that he was the intended target and that everyone else is safe now?" She shook her head. "I can't be sure. But I will say that I wouldn't want any part of it if I were you."

"Let's say that your uncle was the target, does anyone come to mind that he might have had problems with?"

"Is there someone *you* have in mind?" Tammy asked.

I sighed. "I'm not sure. I know there were a lot of issues between him and Joel Liu from Liu's Noodle Emporium. But I wasn't sure if you knew of anyone who hated your uncle more."

"I really tried to keep away from my uncle so if there was someone threatening him, I wouldn't have known about it. He isn't close with my parents, so if there was anyone after him, he wouldn't have told them either."

"Was there anybody he was close with at all?"

She teetered her head back and forth. "Not that I know of. The few times we ran into each other he was always alone."

I sat back in my seat. This was a bust.

She seemed to notice my disappointment. Leaning forward, she said with a gentle smile, "I'm sorry I couldn't be of more help. I wish I could tell you more."

"Oh, please don't apologize, it was a long shot to begin with." I started to slide out of the booth. "I should let you get back to work. Thank you for entertaining my questions."

She scooted out of the booth and stood with me, giving my hand another delicate shake. "If it were me in your shoes, Lana, I would have to ask myself if winning this contest was worth the risk of something else happening during the next couple of rounds. Suppose that my uncle wasn't the target and it's the contest this person is looking to ruin; would you really want to put yourself in that position?"

"There's a good team of detectives working on the case, and I have faith they wouldn't let anything like that happen again," I said. I didn't know if I was trying to convince her or myself. Dismissing the thought, I pulled a business card out of my purse and handed it over. "If anything comes to mind that you might believe to be helpful, would you mind giving me a call?"

She looked the card over and gave me a weak smile. "I don't think that's very likely, but yes, I'll call you if anything comes to mind."

I said my good-byes and headed back to the car. As I left the parking lot, I wondered if winning the contest was worth it myself.

* * *

At home, I played with the dog for a little while to take my mind off the conversation I'd had with Tammy, ate cold pizza out of the box, and passed out on the couch while it was still light outside. The day had wiped me out. I didn't wake up again until one in the morning, when I dragged myself to bed with Kikko hot on my heels.

The sleep must have done me some good because Friday morning, I woke up feeling energized and ready to formulate a plan. It was the day the contest was going to resume, and there was a lot to prep at the restaurant. And I still needed to find time and have my talk with Penny about how she knew Joel . . . preferably before the contest began.

My parents and grandmother were coming in, and Anna May was coming to help. I was hoping to slip out once they all got there.

There was a lot of commotion at the plaza when I arrived. The stage workers, including Freddie Yuan, were back setting up curtains and putting together the cooking stations. The noise echoed through the plaza and I repressed the urge to cover my ears.

Zipping through, I made my way to the restaurant, shutting the doors quickly behind me. Way too much commotion so early in the morning.

The muted sounds managed to make their way into the restaurant, and I hid in the back office, organizing paperwork for as long as I could procrastinate.

While I was prepping the dining room for the day, Peter showed up, his eyes shifting back and forth between the restaurant and the stage. "Whoa man . . . I just got freaked out again. I thought I'd be cool today. Round one went pretty good."

"You'll be better once you start cooking." I ushered him into the restaurant and shut the door again. "Plus my mom will be here soon, and I'm sure she'll keep you distracted with all her nervous chatter."

He disappeared into the kitchen and I went about my morning routine. The menu covers were all wiped down, the place settings at the tables were perfect, and the carpet had been vacuumed.

To my surprise, my family showed up before the Mahjong Matrons.

My mother surveyed the restaurant and nodded with approval. "You have done a very good job. Now today, Peter will win again, and we will get even more business."

"I agree, she's doing a great job, Betty," my dad said, giving my shoulder a squeeze. "She's a natural leader, this one."

"Thanks, Dad." I peeked behind him. "Where is A-ma?"

"Oh, she's next door at the doughnut shop talking with Ruth."

She said it with a hint of relief, but I could have been imagining it after our little chat from the previous day.

After my mother went in the back to visit with Peter and give him a breakfast order, my parents settled at the booth closest to the kitchen, and surprisingly kept to themselves. It was out of character for my mother to not be flying around the restaurant giving me last-minute orders or rummaging around in her office.

I was about to ask her what the occasion was when the Mahjong Matrons came filing into the restaurant. "Good mornings" were exchanged and the Matrons took their usual booth near the window. Instead of getting up and going to one another's table, my mother and the Matrons yelled to each other across the restaurant.

My dad winked at me, and I slipped into the kitchen to grab their morning tea. "The Matrons have arrived," I told Peter as I reached for a teakettle.

"What's up with your mom, man?" Peter stepped away from the stove where he was preparing some eggs and scallions. "She's like supercalm today. Do you think your dad spiked her tea or something?"

"I don't know, I'm wondering that too." I finished loading the tray with teacups and the kettle. "Something is definitely up with her."

When I came back out with their tea, I found my grandmother standing at the table talking to them. This was the first time they were officially meeting, and I was anxious to see how it went.

The Matrons, though very sociable, were also very selective. Since I could remember, it was always just the four of them. I thought it might be nice for my grandmother—and my mother—if she made some friends and I knew that she liked mahjong. Maybe they would pick her to be a fill-in if one of them ever got sick. Not that it had ever happened before.

My grandmother smiled when she saw me, her silver teeth sparkling. "This . . ." She handed me a paper bag. "This for you."

I peeked inside and found four doughnut holes and a glazed doughnut shaped like an eight. "Oh, boy . . ." I said, shaking my head.

My grandmother frowned. "No understand."

"You young girls need to learn the language." Helen looked at me. "I will translate?"

"Tell her that it's not good that the doughnut shop owner knows me so well." I pointed to my waistline.

Helen smirked and gave my grandmother a speedy reply.

My grandmother looked at me, held her stomach, and started laughing hysterically.

An hour before the contest was set to begin, I noticed Penny rushing past the restaurant. I'd been waiting for her to show up all morning and was surprised that she hadn't arrived earlier. Peter was already busy prepping his station along with most of the other contestants.

Anna May was wiping down one of the tables, and I sidled up next to her to try and tell her discreetly that I was stepping out for a minute, but she yelped when I said, "Hey."

"Oh my God, Lana Lee!" Anna May gasped, clutching her chest. "Do not sneak up on people like that. You're going to give me a heart attack one of these days with all this slinking around you do."

A few of the patrons turned around.

I smiled awkwardly. "Sorry."

"What do you want?"

"I'm going to step out for a minute; can you keep an eye on things until Vanessa gets here?"

"Where are you going now? Can you never stand still?"

"I wanted to talk with Penny before the contest."

"Are you sure that's a good idea? Talking to the competition right before the contest starts?"

"It's not about the contest."

"What are you up to?" Anna May said, eyeballing me. She put her hand on her hip, imitating our mother. "Are you snooping around in things you shouldn't be?"

I avoided her stare. "No . . ."

"Then what do you need to talk to her about that can't wait until later?"

"Nothing, mind your business."

She pursed her lips at me. "Whatever, Lana, I don't even have the energy to fight with you today."

"Yeah, what's that about?" I asked her. "Mom is not acting like herself either."

"Didn't you hear?"

"Hear what?"

"Auntie Grace is planning on making a trip here. She wants to spend some time with A-ma."

My eyes widened. "When is this supposed to happen?"

Anna May shrugged. "Not sure, but it's definitely got Mom distracted."

Auntie Grace is my mother's older sister. It's an understatement to say that they don't get along. Their feuds may be worse than anything Anna May and I have ever been through.

I stood there scrutinizing my sister and wondering what type of battles our future would hold. Would we end up like our mom and aunt? Or would there actually be a day when we got along?

My sister gawked at me. "Hey! Space cadet, what are you doing? Snap out of it."

"Okay, I'm going . . . geez." Guess us getting along would have to wait for another day.

When I entered the Bamboo Lounge, I heard a bunch

of clanking around coming from the kitchen. "Penny?" I asked the empty room.

No response.

I headed back toward the kitchen and poked my head inside the swinging door. Penny was crouched down grabbing pots and pans from below a steel counter unit.

"Penny?"

She jumped up, dropping the pans on the floor.

"Sorry, I've been having that effect on people today."

"Lana . . . you startled me." She picked up the pans and threw them in the sink. "My cook is running late and didn't even bother to tell me until about a half hour ago. He was supposed to set up for me."

"Is there anything I can do to help?" I asked, looking around the kitchen at the scattered supplies.

"It's probably best if you don't. It might seem odd to the judges if we're working together."

"I was hoping I could talk to you for a minute. It's kind of important. But maybe we should talk after the contest instead?"

"Yeah, if it's not too urgent, would that be okay with you? I'd like to get this stuff out there and set up as soon as possible. I don't even know when my cook is going to show."

"Sure, good luck."

"Thanks, Lana, you too."

CHAPTER 16

If there was any worry that the murder of one of the contest judges would keep people away from the next round, it was soon alleviated by the large crowds of people that showed up to watch today's cooking session.

Though Donna Feng was mostly the silent partner in running the plaza, she did handle a lot of the publicity affairs. For the sake of the contest, she allowed camera crews from the local news stations to attend. Normally she banned media outlets from filming inside the property, but she was hopeful that this would bring more business to the plaza and perhaps shed some positivity on a rather gloomy situation.

Donna now stood at the front of the stage in what I recognized to be a two-piece, pencil-skirt Dolce & Gabbana suit. I remembered fawning over the black-and-white basket-weave suit in a recent issue of *InStyle*. While she waited to give a speech about the recently deceased food critic, she smoothed the sides of her French twist, exposing a delicate diamond bracelet on her wrist.

Approximately five minutes before the contest was set to begin, Ian let out an earsplitting whistle and the crowd hushed. Donna smiled, her teeth immaculately white against her fire-engine-red lipstick.

"Greetings to all, and thank you for joining us for the second round of Cleveland's Best Noodle contest."

The crowd cheered.

"But first, let us take a moment to pay our respects to the ill-fated Norman Pan who was senselessly murdered during the first round of this contest. Norman was a staple in the community and he has reviewed almost every fine Asian establishment in the city. Along with that, he was a friend to many." Her eyes slid toward Walter.

A couple people bowed their heads, but mostly everyone sat with blank expressions and stole glances at one another.

"Okay," she said, clasping her hands together. "Let's get on with it! Good luck to each of our contestants."

Everyone clapped, and Ian took center stage as Donna made her way to a seat off to the side. Ian gave brief introductions just as he had during the first round.

The second round of the contest required each chef to make a noodle soup of their choosing. Peter was known for his beef noodle soup and I was confident he'd win this round with no problems.

I sat directly behind him with Megan and Kimmy on either side of me. My parents, sister, and grandmother sat behind us. Though I'd hoped that Adam would be able to join us for the second round, he was off somewhere handling detective duties.

The judges circled the stations as the cooks busied themselves with preparing the soup bases. Peter, who liked to cook listening to heavy metal, had one earbud in and his head moved in rhythm to the beat.

My attention drifted over to Penny who was standing solo at her workstation. Looked like her cook hadn't even shown up yet. With a scowl on her face, she added seasonings and stirred the liquid in her pot.

Stella circled Penny's station and mumbled something close to her ear. Penny froze and I saw her whole body visibly tense from where I sat. The ladle stopped in the pot and she closed her eyes, taking a deep breath, at which point Stella walked away and continued on to the next workstation.

After that, I noticed that Penny seemed even more agitated than she had been earlier in the day. The connections between Joel, Penny, and Stella still stumped me, and I wondered if I would ever get any answers.

Half an hour later, the cooks had completed their assignments and the judges were each served a tiny bowl of soup. While they deliberated, the cooks tidied up their stations.

Stella, who had taken over as head judge, was tasked with announcing the winner. To get the attention of the crowd, she clanked her chopsticks against her soup bowl. The motion rather than the sound caught the attention of everyone, and the noise in the room dropped so Stella could be heard.

"After careful assessment of all the fine soups presented to us, we have come to a unanimous vote. This round goes to Peter Huang and the Ho-Lee Noodle House! Congratulations!"

The crowd erupted in applause, and my dad threw in some sharp whistles for good measure. Peter turned around and beamed at us with pride.

We took turns congratulating him before others started coming over to shake his hand and offer their praise.

Stella motioned for the crowd to quiet down. "Now that we've shared the good news with you . . . we have to share the bad news too."

The room was immediately silent, and we all waited for Stella to announce the restaurant that would be eliminated.

She held the note card in her hand and, keeping her eyes focused on it, said, "The contestant that will not be going to the next round is Penny Cho from the Bamboo Lounge."

A few people in the audience booed in response.

I caught my mother sighing with relief.

Stella nodded solemnly. "While we're sad to see her go, we thank her for participating in the contest, and look forward to seeing her try again in next year's competition!" She slid a quick glance at Penny before encouraging the crowd to applaud.

Stella dismissed the crowd after the applause died down and people began to shuffle out of the bleachers and head into the plaza. A few stragglers stopped by to extend congratulations on Peter's win.

A man I recognized as a reviewer from *Scene* magazine made his way through the circle of people and patted

Peter on the back. "I think you're going to take this contest all the way. I'm only sorry I wasn't able to get a taste of what you made today."

"Thanks, man. Feel free to stop by the noodle house any time, and I'll be sure to make anything you want . . . even if it's not on the menu."

While they talked about the different dishes that Peter could potentially make him, my attention drifted over to Penny who was in the middle of an argument with Stella. Penny jabbed her finger at the workstation while Stella remained calm, her arms crossed over her chest.

". . . sounds good to me." The reviewer produced a business card and shook his hand before saying good-bye.

"Did you hear that?" Peter asked, nudging my arm.

"Huh?"

"That reviewer guy told me he wants to do a story on me after the contest is over. He's going to do a whole spread on our menu." He held up the reviewer's business card.

"That's great news," I told him, sliding my eyes back over to where Penny and Stella were, only Stella was gone, and Penny was standing alone throwing her things haphazardly into a cardboard box.

"Dude . . . what's your deal?" Peter asked, following my line of sight. He watched her movements and chuckled to himself. "Is Penny being a sore loser or something?"

"I'm not sure . . . something is definitely going on with her. She's been acting so strange lately."

"Maybe she's having guy problems or something like that."

"I should probably check on her later."

After we packed up and cleaned the work area, Megan and I headed over to the Bamboo Lounge. The lights were off and Penny sat on the customer side of the bar with a highball and a bottle of whiskey.

"Hey . . . I just thought I'd stop by and see if you were okay."

She looked up, her eyes drifting past me to Megan.

Megan waved. "Hey, Penny . . . long time . . ."

"Hey, girls, if you don't mind, I'd like to be alone."

"What happened to your cook?" I asked, ignoring her request.

She sighed. "He bailed on me. After you stopped by earlier, he called again and told me to find another chef. He's worried that the lounge is going under and he took another job. He didn't even have the courtesy to give me any notice."

"I'm so sorry," I said, inching closer to her.

She looked down at the bottle of Yamazaki whiskey in front of her and unscrewed the cap, pouring a considerable amount into the glass. "Really, I'd like to be alone. Could we talk another time?"

I gave Megan a pointed look, and because we knew each other so well, no words needed to be exchanged. She only nodded in return and exited the restaurant.

Once she was gone, I sat down next to Penny at the bar. "I could use one of those . . ." I nodded toward the whiskey bottle.

She got up and moved behind the counter, grabbed a glass, and slid it harshly across the bar.

I caught it before it went off the side.

"No offense, but I don't see what you would need this for . . . from where I'm standing you seem to have everything going for you." She came back around and took her seat next to me, passing the bottle of whiskey. "Have what you like . . . it's on the house."

I took the bottle and poured a tiny amount into the glass she'd given me. I wasn't much of a whiskey drinker and I knew this would go straight to my head. "I'd be a whole lot better if this Norman Pan thing hadn't happened."

"It's looking that way for all of us."

"Do you think it was one of the other judges?" I asked.

"Huh? One of the other judges?"

"Yeah, you know . . . like Stella . . . maybe she did it?" I sipped the whiskey and it warmed my body as it slid down my throat.

She sneered. "At this point . . . anything is possible. That woman is horrid. Just horrid."

"What is going on with you two?"

"It's nothing . . ." Penny turned her head away from me. "She's always ruining my life, is all. I'll never be rid of her."

"What do you mean? Do you guys know each other personally?"

Penny laughed to herself. "It's a long story . . . from a very long time ago."

"Is she bullying you? Maybe we should take it to Ian and he—"

"No!" she yelled, whipping back around to face me. "We tell Ian nothing. He doesn't need to get involved. I can take care of Stella myself."

"But if you lost the contest unfairly . . ."

"I don't care. I'm out of the contest and that's that. It's done. I have to worry about finding a new head chef . . .

and repairing my business. The last thing I want is to be involved in this stupid contest. It's ruined everything."

"I'm—"

"You better go . . ." She got up from the stool, grabbing her glass and the whiskey bottle. "I've got things I should be doing right now."

"Okay, well, if you need anything, let me know. Don't forget you have friends here."

"Yeah . . . friends . . . thanks," she said bitterly. "I'll see you later." She disappeared into the back room, and I sat awkwardly staring at my whiskey glass. I downed the rest of it, which gave me a shiver, and left the empty glass on the bar.

When I went back into the plaza, Megan was waiting for me on a nearby bench. "Everything okay?" she asked.

"I don't think so . . ."

"Well, what happened in there? Did she tell you anything useful?"

"Maybe? Let's get out of here and I'll tell you in the car."

On the way home, I filled Megan in on what Penny and I talked about after she left the restaurant. When we arrived at the apartment, we decided to both take Kikko for a walk so I could think and talk it out. I always did my best thinking in one of two forms: walking or showering.

Our complex had a two-lane road that wound through the property and looped back around. We followed the loop around the maze of apartments while we discussed the situation.

"The thing that gets me is why no one will say how they know each other," Megan said. "What's the big deal?"

"The only thing that comes to mind is that they didn't want anyone to know that they knew a judge on the panel."

"But everyone knows who they are."

"Yeah, but not on a personal level," I reminded her. "Personal relationships could cause a conflict of interest . . . like they did with Norman and Walter. It's possible they didn't want to deal with the outcome of that."

"Okay, true." Megan sidestepped a fallen branch. "So what do you think it is?"

We stopped so Kikko could sniff a tree trunk.

I shrugged. "From what I've seen so far, it seems like Penny is being bullied or she's trying to protect someone and getting fed up with it. She was already upset about the contest when she arrived this morning. Then Stella talked to her while she was cooking and Penny flew off the handle."

"But what would that have to do with Joel?"

"Okay, let's say that Joel is the killer. Penny is either protecting him or he's making her stay quiet against her will. Either way Penny is hiding something from us."

"Like what?" Megan asked.

"Like what I was saying the other day . . . video of him being where he wasn't supposed to be."

"Okay, let's go with that theory. He goes to see her, and then what? Tells her to cover for him?"

"Maybe. Or she really doesn't have the tape . . . which should let her off the hook . . . but . . ." I paused.

"But?"

"But I just thought of something . . . Stella suspects something and said she overheard things she shouldn't have. So what if that something she wasn't supposed to hear was between Joel and Penny? Then she confronts Penny only to be told there isn't actually a tape, but she doesn't believe it and is trying to bully her into coming clean."

"Again . . . it's a stretch." Megan said, her voice laced with doubt.

"Well, it's all speculation. For all we know, we have it all wrong and Walter Shen and Ray worked together to get rid of Norman Pan for some reason still unknown to us."

Megan grabbed my arm, her eyes widening. "Do you think that's an actual possibility? That almost makes more sense than the other scenario."

Kikko, content with her sniffing of the tree trunk, tugged us farther down the walk. Her next target was a flowering bush that was starting to bud.

"Anything is possible. And I don't think that Opal's suspicion is totally unfounded. There's something funny about the way Walter was acting the other day for sure. And it is possible that he wanted to teach Norman a lesson."

"So what do we do now?"

"Tomorrow is the last day of the contest and Stella will be heading back to Chicago on Sunday if all goes well. I only have a few more chances left to talk with her. I know she's staying at the Ramada. Maybe I'll try and see her before the contest."

"Do you know if she ever talked with Trudeau about the fortune cookie?"

"I'm not sure. Adam hasn't mentioned anything to me. Not that he would . . . but . . . I'm hoping she did. When I go and talk with her I'll encourage her to talk to him if she hasn't already."

"Good. Because if she really does know who the killer is . . . she's walking around with a target on her back."

CHAPTER 17

The third round of the contest wasn't scheduled to start until noon, but I got up extra early so I would have time to head over to the Ramada and talk with Stella. I figured it would be easier to talk with her alone if I went to see her at the hotel. My only hope was that she wouldn't mind me stopping by unannounced. I thought about calling the hotel to make sure she was there, but I didn't want to give her the opportunity to avoid me. Especially if she had changed her mind about talking to Adam . . . then she might not want to speak to me.

When I arrived, there were a few cop cars and an ambulance outside the entrance. A few stragglers hung out in the parking lot, smoking cigars and pointing toward the commotion.

I parked the car and headed over to the group of smokers. "Excuse me, do you know what's going on here?"

A tall man with a shaved head and reddish-brown beard turned to face me. "Some chick bit it or something.

We were standing out here smoking when the cops showed up so we don't know much. No one has come out yet."

"Are they letting people into the hotel?" I asked.

He adjusted his glasses. "As far as I know . . . doesn't hurt to try."

I thanked him and made my way up the walkway to the entrance. Before I could enter, Adam barreled out of the doors.

"Out of the way!" Adam barked. "Police business." He did a double take when he realized it was me.

"Do you talk that rudely to everyone?" I asked him, a little put off.

"Lana . . . what are you doing here?"

"I came to talk with Stella before the contest," I told him. "What are *you* doing here?"

He inhaled deeply, and scooped an arm around my shoulders, directing me down the path away from the entrance. The smokers looked on as Adam veered me away.

"Adam . . ."

"There isn't going to be a contest today, Lana."

"What? Why not?"

He gave my shoulder a gentle squeeze and sighed. "There's no easy way to tell you this, but Stella was found murdered in her hotel room this morning."

As he said it, I heard the rumbling of wheels on cement. When I peeked around him to see what was making the noise, I found it to be a gurney. Strapped to it was a body bag, and inside that body bag was Stella Chung.

"This can't be happening!" Ian yelled, slamming his fists on his desk.

After I'd left the hotel, I called Megan to let her know what happened and that she didn't need to come to the plaza. She agreed to wait for me at home and I rushed to Asia Village to fill Ian in on the news. The contest was set to start in two hours and setup had already begun on the stage.

"That's what you're upset about? May I remind you that I was actually at the hotel and saw the body bag being brought out to the ambulance? Another person is dead, Ian. Be a little more sensitive!"

He took a deep breath. "You're right, I'm sorry. Please . . . sit." He gestured to the couch, and I plopped down, my head in my hands. "What do we know at this point? It was absolutely murder?"

I nodded. "Adam said there were definite signs of a struggle. She was strangled . . . just like Norman Pan. There was a broken lamp with traces of blood on the cord . . . he thinks may be that was the murder weapon because it would match the bruises on her neck."

"Oh my—" He covered his mouth.

"This can't be a coincidence, Ian . . ."

"Let's not discuss that right now. Would you like some tea?" His voice was gentle and came out as a whisper.

"More like a shot of whiskey," I said.

"I can have that arranged. Penny is just next door."

Oh my God, Penny! I thought. My brain filled with a whirlwind of thoughts. "We have to cancel the contest . . . we can worry about me later."

"Yes, of course, I'll see to it that the other judges know. Would you mind letting the contestants and stage workers know?"

I complied and stopped by the stage arena to talk with

the workers. I relayed the message as swiftly as possible so I could get back to the restaurant. I wanted to let Peter know first and then I would make calls to both Walter Shen and Stanley Gao. The toughest part of all that would be telling Peter. I knew that part of him would be disappointed. He had been so excited when we'd left the contest the day before and he was confident that he would win again today.

When I arrived, Nancy was at the podium, and Vanessa was wiping down tables. I gave a quick smile to Nancy before heading straight back into the kitchen. I wanted to tell Peter before anyone else. Then I would make an announcement to the rest of the employees.

Oh, no . . . my parents. I would have to tell my parents. The idea of it created a rock in the pit of my stomach.

I pushed that thought to the back of my mind as I entered the kitchen and saw Peter and Lou packing up boxes for Peter to take with him to the workstation in the plaza.

"Peter . . ." I said. Ugh, even my voice gave away my emotions.

Lou turned around first, his smile bright as a fluorescent bulb. "Hey there, boss!" Within a few seconds of observing me, his smile evaporated. "Boss? Is everything okay?"

Peter turned around. "Hey, dude . . . what's with the long face?"

"We need to talk . . . alone." I gestured toward the back room.

"Sure," he replied. He sounded cautious and kept an eye on me as we left the kitchen.

"Right, I'll hold down the fort here," Lou said with a

salute. "I'll have these boxes packed up for you by the time you get back."

"That's okay, Lou," I said to him. "There's no need."

Peter's eyes widened. He opened his mouth to say something, but changed his mind. Instead, he hung his head and sulked to the back office.

I broke the news to Peter as gently as possible and provided as many details as I could, which weren't very many. He nodded at the appropriate intervals and didn't say much in response. We sat in silence for a few moments before he returned to the kitchen. I knew that he was conflicted . . . I could see it on his face. He wanted to be upset because he was really hyped up about winning the contest today, but at the same time, someone had just died.

With a heavy sigh, I picked up the phone and called the others to let them know what happened. Everyone seemed extremely shocked and caught off guard by the news, but then again, it was easier to play that card without having to look anyone in the eye. As I talked to Walter and then Stanley, I wondered if I was talking to the killer. I hadn't given Stanley any consideration, but now that two judges were dead, I thought it was safe to say that it had something to do with the contest.

After I finished up with my calls, I decided to head over and let Penny in on the news. Even though she wasn't part of the contest anymore, I felt like she should know. I also wanted to see her reaction.

I couldn't lie to myself, in the back of my mind, the conversation we'd had the day before played in my head, and I thought about how Penny said she would take care of Stella herself. And now, as much as it bothered me to think it, I wondered if she had.

On the way over, I tried to come up with exactly what I was going to say. I still had trouble putting up a good front with people, and I didn't want to come across as accusatory.

The lounge didn't open until noon, so I had a little time before customers would wander in. I found her behind the bar taking inventory and rearranging liquor bottles.

"Hey." I eased my way into the bar area and gave a delicate smile. "Mind if I sit?"

She looked up from her clipboard. "Sure . . . have a seat." She stuck the pencil she was holding behind her ear. "Want anything?"

"No, thanks, I can't stay. I thought I would come by personally and—"

"Ask for an apology?" she finished. "Because you deserve one, big-time, Lana. I'm so sorry for the way I acted yesterday . . . for the way I've been acting . . . it's this stupid contest, and everything else going on. And now this thing with Stella . . ."

"Stella is actually why I came by."

Penny put her hands on her hips. "Did she send you here?"

"No . . ."

"Good . . . because anything she has to say doesn't matter to me anyhow. That woman is rotten to the core. I tried to put it all behind me, but she can't seem to stop running her mouth and bringing up things—"

"Penny . . ."

"What?" she snapped.

"Stella was found dead this morning."

She dropped her clipboard. "What do you mean dead? How can she be dead? I just saw her yesterday."

"A maid at the hotel found Stella strangled in her room this morning. I went there to talk to her about the contest . . . about . . ." I looked away. It wasn't my original intention to tell Penny why I'd gone to see Stella and I didn't know if I should tell her now. "Well . . . when I got there, the police were there with an ambulance to take the body away."

Penny covered her mouth with a shaky hand.

I had to admit, she did appear jarred by the news. Then again, how well did I know Penny . . . and how good of an actress was she? "I don't know any details, so I can't tell you much else."

She dropped her hand and placed both of them on the bar, gripping the edge. "I see."

"So . . . if anything was going on . . . now would be the time to say something."

Her eyes darted up at me. "What exactly do you mean by that?"

"You two were having problems . . . was she bullying you?"

"You think I did this?" Her expression changed to outrage. "You think I would be capable of something like this?"

I shook my head. "No, no, nothing like that. But . . . do you know who could have?"

Her eyes shifted away and she bit her bottom lip. "I can't say that I do."

"But you two knew each other. You must have known something."

"That has nothing to do with anything. She and I

knowing each other has nothing to do with whatever is happening now."

"What about Joel?"

She snorted. "What about him?"

"Why did he come to see you that day? After Norman Pan was killed he stopped by and I ran into him by the pond."

"Oh, that? It was nothing important . . ."

"Did he happen to ask you what you knew about the murder?" I asked. "Did he say anything out of the ordinary?"

"Wait a minute." She closed her eyes and held up a hand. "Are you trying to insinuate that *he* had something to do with this?"

"I'm just trying to figure this out in general. I'm not blaming anyone specifically. But this has got to have something to do with the contest."

"You have a lot of nerve, you know that?" Her eyes narrowed and she studied my face. "You come in here with all of these wild accusations, like you're the police or something."

"I'm only trying to help. This affects all of us."

"It would serve you well to keep out of it. And stop accusing people you don't know of things you know nothing about. Now, if you would please leave." She thrust her arm out, pointing at the door.

"Penny . . ."

"No . . . please go. I don't want you here." She sneered as she folded her arms over her chest. "And to think, I almost gave you an apology."

I felt partially like sulking out of the restaurant. But

the other part of me felt indignant at her behavior and I wanted to storm out declaring that justice would be served.

I chose to take the high road and leave quietly. I had to pick my battles, especially if she happened to be guilty. After all, if she was, it wasn't in my best interest to rile her.

When I got back to the restaurant, Esther, my parents, grandmother, and sister were there, congregating at a booth with Nancy. Nancy stood at the head of their table, holding an empty tray. By the looks of it, she'd just dropped off tea for the table.

Vanessa, who was on hostess duty for the day, hopped off her stool and greeted me with an exaggerated bow. Her normally out-of-control hair was pulled back in a tight ponytail at the nape of her neck. "Hey there, boss lady!"

I'll be the first to admit that I'm not good with teenagers. My mother was constantly reminding me that I needed to be patient with Vanessa. She was the daughter of a family friend and her parents were trying to teach her how to be responsible by earning her own money. I commended her for working during her free hours after school and on the weekends, but it was her mouth that usually got the best of me.

"Hi, Vanessa, how's everything going today?"

"Slow. We thought with the contest being canceled that people would stay and eat, but this place has been a ghost town today."

The restaurant was indeed lacking in customers and I worried that the disruption of the contest would bring bad press to the plaza.

My sister saw me standing at the hostess stand, and waved me over. This was going to be fun. "I'll talk to you later, Vanessa."

"Good luck with your family—your mom is super-crabby today."

"Great," I mumbled.

"Thanks for telling us about what happened," my sister spat at me as I walked over. "You could have given us a heads-up."

I slunk to the table. "Sorry, I promised Ian I would let the contestants know first."

My mother turned around, clucking her tongue at me. "Ai-ya, we are a contestant!"

"Peter and the other chefs needed to know first, Mother. I was going to call you as soon as I was done talking with everyone else . . . you just beat me to it."

She gave me a sideways glance and then shifted back around in her seat. "Well, now we know."

My dad, who was seated next to her in the booth, smiled up at me. "Don't mind your mother, Goober. She is just a little upset about everything going on around here."

"Yes! I am upset," my mother shouted. "This is too much. Too many bad things are happening. We cannot have this when your auntie comes to visit."

My sister and I shared a glance.

"It's going to be fine. If you think about it, this doesn't really have anything to do with us," I said, hoping to placate my mother.

Esther nodded in agreement. She spoke in Mandarin so I didn't understand much of what she was saying, but it sounded by her tone as if she was trying to reason with her. My grandmother nodded along with Nancy.

After that my mother sat staring into her teacup. "Your auntie always has something to say about everything. We must show her that we are doing very good. I will not be embarrassed."

I gave her a pat on the shoulder. "Don't worry, Mom. We all have sisters that are a pain."

Anna May groaned.

"Well, I just wanted to stop by and do a quick check-in before leaving for the day. I guess I'll see you guys tomorrow for dim sum?"

Everyone nodded.

I stuck my head in the kitchen and said good-bye before heading out. Megan and I had a lot to discuss.

CHAPTER 18

Because we had yet to eat that morning, Megan and I ventured to Effie's Diner for brunch. We sat in a booth facing the street, talking about the latest events and our current theories over bacon and eggs.

"My money's on Penny. It has to be her," Megan said to me after I finished telling her the entire story from that morning.

I sipped my coffee and weighed the likelihood. "Maybe."

"What do you mean, maybe?" She gawked at me, incredulous. "She's been acting strange this entire time. And the weird stuff with her and Stella? And *then,* Stella ends up dead after Penny tells you she's going to take care of it herself. Take care of what exactly?"

"Agreed. Penny is definitely at the top of my list now, but we haven't eliminated anyone else yet. Plus I don't think she killed Norman Pan."

Megan jabbed the egg yolk of her sunny-side up. "Do

we really need to look at anyone else? This whole thing seems kind of obvious to me."

"But we also both agreed we thought Joel was guilty."

"They were working together then. Maybe we had the original connection wrong. Instead of Stella and Joel working together to bully Penny, maybe Penny and Joel were working together, and Stella started snooping around. She found out too much and went to Penny not realizing that she was a killer. You did say that Stella thought she knew something she shouldn't."

"Yeah, but pretend your theory is correct. Why would Penny agree to help kill Norman? Especially in her own restaurant. It's ruining her business."

"Could have been a tit-for-tat situation. Penny helps Joel cover up the murder with Norman, and then Penny goes after Stella. And there's the whole camera thing. It's a little too convenient, wouldn't you say?"

"If what you're saying is true, Stella wasn't part of the original plan, so why would Penny agree to cover anything up for Joel?"

She sagged in the booth. "Well, that's the unknown factor, isn't it? There's that weird connection between the three of them that we don't know yet. So, if we figured that out, maybe the rest of this will make some type of sense."

"I think we need to learn more about Stella . . . where she came from . . . a time line of her principal life events. If Penny isn't going to tell us anything, and Joel is definitely not saying a word, we have to go around them."

"Sounds like a plan to me."

"But what about Ray . . . and Walter . . . ?"

"What about them?" Megan asked, polishing off a

piece of toast. "I think the three musketeers are the answer to this whole thing."

"We have to at least consider the possibility that they're involved before we completely eliminate them."

"Okay, how about *you* consider them, and I'll start digging around into Stella's past. I'm sure that now she's been murdered, there will be a ton of articles on her. Shouldn't be too hard to find out something."

I frowned. "Don't say it like that."

"But it's the truth."

"I know, that's why it bothers me."

When we got home from brunch, I went straight for my notebook, which I dutifully filled with everything new that had taken place. I made notes to talk with Adam about the fortunes Norman and Stella had received. If he didn't know about it, he needed to. It was the one thing that would definitely connect the two murders.

I wanted to tell him about Penny, but I had to be a hundred percent sure I knew what I was talking about before I said anything. After all, she was a friend of sorts, and I didn't want to throw her under the bus unnecessarily. Besides, if there was anything overtly incriminating against her, Adam would come by it with no problems.

I decided he would be my next step. I gave him a quick call and, not too surprisingly, he didn't answer. My voice mail message told him that I wanted to have dinner that night and to call me if he was free. I attempted to sound as innocent as possible.

The rest of the afternoon passed slowly. Since Megan was working that evening, we decided to give our sleuthing a break until the following day. It had begun to rain, so we opted to stay in and watch a movie until it was time for her to leave.

Probably from waking up so early and everything that happened that morning, it shouldn't have been a surprise that I fell asleep mid-movie. When I awoke, the TV was off, Kikko was lying in the crook of my knee and there was a Post-it note stuck to my pop can letting me know that Megan had left for work.

I checked the time on my cell phone and saw there was a missed call from Adam.

"Hey doll, got your message. Sorry, but it's another long night of work for me. Maybe we can catch up for dinner on Monday? Let me know what you think . . ."

I leaned back on the couch with a sigh. It was rough dating a cop. That was for sure.

Trying not to let it bother me, I typed a quick message letting him know that Monday night for dinner would be fine.

Since it was Saturday night, I wanted to make good use of the weekend night. The rain had stopped while I'd been sleeping and I now felt restless. I sent out a few text messages to see who was available. Rina responded almost instantly.

Quickly she relayed to me that there was a cover band playing at Wok and Roll and no one would go with her. She asked if I would be willing to come.

I couldn't remember the last time I'd ventured out for an evening in the Flats, so I said yes. We agreed to meet at her place and go from there.

By the time we arrived downtown, the band had already started playing. The bar and grill was packed with people, and with all the metal surrounding us, I felt like I was in a sardine can. After getting some drinks, we squeezed our way through the crowd, trying to find a suitable place to stand near the makeshift stage.

The cover band—four guys in T-shirts and jeans—mostly played songs from the eighties, but they did sprinkle in a few modern ones too. Rina bopped her head along to the music and I people-watched—one of my favorite pastimes—while I sipped my drink.

Off to the side, I watched a guy approach a displeased-looking young girl who promptly turned him down. The guy walked away sulking. It took me a minute to realize that the guy was Joel Liu . . . and the girl was Jackie Shen. What the heck were they doing here?

Then I realized the absurdity of my thought. It was a free country after all. Just because I thought Joel was a potential murderer didn't mean he couldn't go anywhere he liked. And just because I loathed Jackie—with every fiber of my being—didn't mean she couldn't do the same.

"Whatcha lookin' at?" Rina shouted in my ear.

I pointed in the direction of Joel and Jackie. "Surprised to see them here."

"Joel seems to be popping up a lot lately. I saw him leaving the plaza with Penny last night. Are they a thing now or something? He's always hanging out at the plaza. He better not get caught talking to Jackie if he's got something going on with Penny. You know that will fly all over Asia Village in no time."

I whipped around to face her. "What do you mean? You saw him at the Bamboo Lounge last night?"

She looked taken aback at my intensity. "Yeah . . .

Penny was closing up and he was there with her. They walked out together."

"They walked out together? Where did they go?"

She paused. "Out to the parking lot . . . I don't know."

I scanned the bar to see where Joel had gone, but I couldn't spot him anywhere.

Rina tugged on my arm. "Lana . . . what is this about? You're not . . . you know . . . looking into things again, are you?"

"What?" I rolled my eyes. "Don't be ridiculous."

"Lana . . . I haven't known you long, but I know *that* face."

"Something is going on with them, and I just wanted to know what it is."

"May I remind you that you almost got yourself killed last time? I'm sure that the cops can handle it . . . and if it's Joel, they'll get him eventually."

Ignoring her concern, I surveyed the crowd again, hoping that Joel would pop up somewhere, but to my disappointment he was nowhere to be seen. "I'll be right back," I told Rina.

I made my way over to where Jackie was standing, dreading every step. This was going to go one of two ways, and neither way was going to be pleasant. I could be sure of that.

"Hey, I need to ask you something," I yelled, trying to be heard over the speaker that was only inches away.

She acknowledged me without speaking.

"What did Joel want from you?"

"What business is it of yours?" She pushed off from her position against the wall. "Are things not going well with that cop boyfriend of yours? I told him he could come find me any time." Her smile was laced with challenge.

In my head, while I scrutinized the nasty sneer on her face, I counted to three. At times like these I always tried to remind myself that prison orange didn't flatter my complexion. "I wanted to let you know . . . even though you don't deserve it, that Joel is already seeing someone else. Penny to be exact," I told her. "You might want to try finding a guy that isn't already taken."

"Ha!" She slapped my shoulder. "First of all, Lee, he came up to me. And, second of all, I would never go out with the biggest loser in the Cleveland restaurant industry. I come from a family of prestige, don't forget. I wouldn't embarrass myself that way."

"Well, you did say he came up to you."

"So, the faith in Joel not cheating on that Penny woman isn't very strong, is it?"

"I didn't say that—"

"Let me ease your worried mind, Twinkie." She leaned in, her face dripping with satisfaction. "He came to ask me why my father won't return his calls."

I took a step back and assessed her face to see if she was telling the truth. "Why *isn't* your father returning his calls?"

"Do I look like my father to you?" she asked.

"What kind of business do they have together?"

"Again . . . do I look like the right party for these questions?" she asked, placing a hand on her hip. The other hand held a drink that she shook in front of my face. "I'm here trying to have a good time. You're ruining that."

We stared at each other for a few minutes until I realized I wouldn't get anything else out of her. If she did know anything more, she wasn't going to tell me. "Thanks anyway," I mumbled before walking off.

When I returned to Rina, she was talking to a tall man with jet-black hair and a decent build. She peeked around him when she noticed me coming and waved energetically. "Look who I ran into."

Freddie Yuan turned around, a crooked smile playing on his lips. "Lana . . . nice bumping into you here."

A little butterfly fluttered in my stomach. *No, Lana, no butterflies. You are with Adam whom you are crazy about. And he's crazy about you . . . right?*

I excused myself from the two, and spent some time hiding at the bar pretending to get a drink. Twenty or so minutes later, Rina popped up behind me. "Hey, what are you doing over here? Freddie was keeping me company while you've been gone, but he had to take off."

"Oh, sorry, I've been trying to get someone's attention for a drink. It's so packed . . ."

"Right . . . get me something too, will you." She rattled her empty glass at me. "I'm out."

I turned back toward the bar to get the bartender's attention . . . for real this time.

"You know," Rina said into my ear. "Freddie is a pretty interesting guy . . . and gorgeous. You have to wonder why he's single."

"He's okay," I said, shrugging off the statement.

"The funny thing is . . . he seems interested in you even though I keep trying to flirt with him."

"Me?" I glanced at her from the corner of my eye. "That's ridiculous."

"You have to have noticed by now."

"Nope . . . I haven't noticed anything."

"I'm guessing you're also going to tell me that you have no interest in him," Rina teased.

"Nope . . . no interest. I forgot he even existed."

She smirked. "Like I said before, Lana . . . I haven't known you long . . ."

On the way home, I thought about what Rina had told me. Not about Freddie—whom I refused to think about. But what she'd said about Penny and Joel. She had either just given the two a solid alibi, or further incriminated them. And, how did Walter Shen fit in . . . if he did at all?

CHAPTER 19

Sunday morning, while I was out to dim sum with my family, the text notification chime on my phone went off repeatedly. I'd forgotten to turn off the sound. My mother imposed a strict rule about no phones at the dinner table, especially on Sundays during our quality family time.

She glared at me from the other side of the table. "Lana . . . turn off your phone."

"Okay, geez, sorry," I said, reaching under the table for my purse. It was a miracle we'd been able to hear it over the noise in the restaurant.

When I gave the screen a quick glance, I noticed that it was Ian. There were three missed calls that we hadn't heard and five text messages. Something must be going on.

"What is so important today?"

I glanced up. My mother, looking impatient, waited for an explanation.

"I'm not sure. It's Ian . . ."

My mother brightened.

Though she had stopped harassing me—for the time being—about my involvement with Ian, she held out hope. It wasn't that she didn't like Adam, she actually liked him quite a bit. But, as far as marriage quality went, she thought Ian was the better pick. I tried telling her several times that it would never happen, but she wasn't giving up any time soon.

"He must need you," my mother said. "What is it about?"

I opened up the messages and read what I had missed. "I guess he wants everyone to meet about the contest today. He said he has an important announcement to make."

My sister snorted. "That man thinks that everything he has to say is important."

My grandmother asked what was going on, and my mother quickly relayed it to her.

"What time do you need to meet with Ian?" my father asked, chewing on a pea pod.

"I guess in a half hour. We're meeting at the Bamboo Lounge." I groaned. I hadn't anticipated going back there so soon.

If I left now, I would be able to make it just in time. I glanced down at my plate. It was still half full. My stomach rumbled.

"You better go," my mother said, shooing me with her chopsticks. "It is for business, so it's okay."

I pointed at my plate. "What about my food?"

"Mommy will eat it for you." She extended her hand for the plate. "You go . . . Lou can make you something to eat after the meeting."

Before I handed her my plate, I grabbed my spring roll. "Fine, but this is coming with me."

Twenty-five minutes later, I arrived at the plaza, hungry and slightly crabby. As I passed Shanghai Donuts, I inhaled the sweet smell of dough baking. I made a mental note to stop by soon and get a few pastries to cheer myself up.

I took a peek through the doors of Ho-Lee Noodle House and noticed that Nancy and Vanessa were busy serving tables. Because I was short on time, I decided not to stop by until after the meeting ended.

A little bit of apprehension filled me as I grabbed the bamboo handle to enter the lounge. The last thing that Penny said to me was she wanted me out of her sight. I was keeping my fingers crossed she would at least be able to keep up appearances if she hadn't decided to forgive me yet.

It was a little worrisome how defensive she'd become when she thought I was insinuating that she or Joel had something to do with Stella Chung's death. But then again, wasn't that exactly what I was doing? If it were me in her shoes, I probably would have reacted the same way.

I was the last to arrive. The restaurant itself was empty, and Penny stood behind the bar, wiping down the counter. She eyed me when I walked in. "The police released the party room this morning, everyone's in there."

"Thanks," I said, inching up toward the bar. "Penny . . . about yesterday . . ."

She held up her hand that was clutching the dish towel. "Please, I can't talk about this with you right now, okay? Can we just drop it?"

"Sure, okay."

I headed into the party room, and stopped at the threshold. As I took in the room for the first time since the day of the party, you'd have thought I expected the room to announce that someone had been murdered in there. Before stepping in, I surveyed the room, checking for noticeable changes, but I saw nothing.

The night of the party flashed into my mind, and I remembered where I had last seen Norman seated. He'd been so smug that night, telling me how I should do things . . . how my hair should be . . .

Who would have guessed that he'd die that night?

When I snapped out of it, I noticed that everyone was staring at me. Peter was the first to speak. "Boss, you okay over there?"

"Yeah, I'm fine," I lied.

He'd saved me a seat, and gestured to the empty chair.

I mumbled a quick "hello" to the room and sat down, hanging my purse on the back of my chair. The heat rose in my cheeks. I really hated it when everyone was staring at me.

As I settled into my seat, Ian stood up. He clasped his hands together. "Now that we're all here, I wanted to say thank you for everything you've put up with so far. I know that getting through this contest has been a piece of work. And I can assure you that it will be worth it in the end. We just have to get past these last few hurdles."

"Last few hurdles?" Ray asked. "I think we have to call this contest quits, Ian."

"Call it quits?" Ian's voice rose an octave. "Call it quits? Oh no, sir, we most certainly will not."

"Are you kidding me?" Ray asked, leaning forward in

his seat. "The judges are clearly being targeted. We have to cancel this contest immediately. I won't be next."

Freddie, who was seated next to Ray, turned to face him. "Do you really think the judges are being targeted?"

"Nonsense!" Ian interjected before Ray could answer.

Ray glared at him. "Easy for you to say. You're not one of the judges."

The door opened and Penny stuck her head in. "Ian, is it okay if I bring the tea in now?"

Ian waved her in. "Of course." He then turned his attention back to Ray. "Don't put ideas into other people's heads. You have no proof that anyone is specifically after the judges."

While the two men went back and forth, Penny made her way around the table silently. She filled the teacups for each person, and placed a kettle at either end of the long banquet table. When she was finished, she went to the door, but before she could close the door behind her, Ray stopped her.

"Hey, sweetheart," he yelled from his chair. "Bring me a Yamazaki, will you? This meeting calls for some whiskey."

She stiffened—I imagine from him calling her sweetheart—but she said nothing, only nodding and shutting the door a little too loudly.

Ray turned back around. "You're being pigheaded about this, Ian. Anyone can see that this contest has become a danger. The whole thing should be called off."

Walter Shen, who was seated on the other side of Peter, spoke up. "I agree with Ray . . . I think this contest has reached its limits. Do not carry on for the sheer sake of saving face. We know that the plaza is in trouble and you are trying to fix it."

"The plaza is not in trouble," Ian said sharply. "And you'll do well to remember that."

Walter bristled. "Young man, I have known your father for a long time and I know he is a hard man. But you do not have to do this to prove anything to him. There are other ways to fix your business."

Ian took a deep breath. "This has nothing to do with my father."

Penny returned with a highball half filled with whiskey. Ray winked at her as she set it down on the table.

"The food will be out shortly," she said, directing her statement to Ian.

Ian nodded and Penny left.

There was going to be food? Things were starting to look up.

"I think it's time to let the others speak," Ian said, holding his head. "What do the rest of you think?"

Everyone turned to look at each other, but no one said anything.

Stanley Gao swirled the tea in his cup, avoiding eye contact with anyone. Freddie traced an imaginary pattern on his cloth napkin and appeared to be somewhere else. Peter tapped his foot anxiously.

I hated to do it, but if no one was going to speak up, then I would. I cleared my throat and held up a hand.

Ian perked up. "Yes, Lana . . . what do you think about all this?"

"Why don't we postpone it for the time being?" I suggested. "None of us are going anywhere anyway. We can wait until the police have figured out what happened. Then once they catch whoever it is that did this, we can resume the contest."

"That's assuming the police will ever figure it out," Ray said, tipping his whiskey glass at me. "And if you ask me, they don't have much of a shot. They haven't even cracked into what happened with Norman yet."

"But they will," I said, giving him an icy stare. "Especially with Adam heading the case. He always figures it out."

"Not always, sweetheart," Ray retorted.

"What is that supposed to mean?" I asked, leaning over the table. I was sick of Ray Jin and his smug attitude.

"If you don't know, honey, you better ask him. Looks like he doesn't tell you everything."

Freddie perked up, now paying attention to the conversation again. He pointed a finger at me. "Wait, are you and Detective—"

Ian clapped his hands once. "Okay, that's enough. We're getting a little off topic here. Let's not worry about what Adam Trudeau has or hasn't told Lana. What they discuss is none of our . . . business." He slid a look at me before addressing the rest of the table. "Now, I think that Lana has come up with the perfect idea. We postpone the contest until the police have sorted out this whole mess. In the meantime, I can find another judge. Two if I have to," he said, directing the last bit at Ray.

Penny returned with a cart filled with appetizers. Ian adjourned the meeting while Penny filled the lazy Susan with food. I decided to slip away to the ladies' room.

When I caught a glimpse of myself in the mirror, I did

a double take. My face was bright red. I patted my cheeks. I must have been more worked up about what Ray said than I realized.

I wet a paper towel and applied it to the sides of my neck, fanning my face with my free hand. Poker face . . . still a work in progress.

After cooling myself down and once my complexion began to resemble that of a normal person, I headed back to the table. People were already filling their plates and my stomach rumbled again as my eyes skimmed over the appetizers.

I scooped a little mapo tofu onto my plate along with a teriyaki stick and a scallion pancake.

While we ate, everyone participated in idle chatter, talking about anything but the contest. Walter and Ray talked about different recipes they had come across while Freddie and Ian talked about memories from their Chicago days. Peter and I sat in silence. I was too concerned with my food. And, even though I was grateful there was something to eat, it wasn't enough to satisfy my hunger. I wondered what my chances were of having Peter follow me to the restaurant and cooking up some noodles for me before he went home. Of course, Lou was working and I'm sure he'd be happy to whip up something for me, but it just wouldn't be the same.

Once everyone was finished eating and the appetizer plates were empty, Penny returned with the cart and cleared off the table.

Ian stood, looking self-satisfied. "So it's settled, we will resume the contest once the murderer has been found. Until that time, Freddie and I will scout for a suitable judge."

Ray drained the remaining whiskey from his glass. "If I were you, Freddie, I'd stay out of the way. Helping Ian is just putting another person's life in danger."

Ian blanched. "Ray! That is enough."

"What?" Ray laughed. "The man should know what kind of responsibility rests in his hands. If you want to be reckless, that's one thing, but don't put that on someone else's shoulders."

"Once the murderer is caught, the whole thing will be behind us. There will be no one to come after the judges as you're insinuating."

"Yeah, but in the meantime, do you really want to stick your neck out?" He slammed his glass on the table. "Whoever it is, they're coming for us." His eyes moved slowly around the table. "One by one . . . we're all going to get picked off. Do you really want to be next?"

CHAPTER 20

I was flustered from the meeting and the things that Ray had said before we left. I was huddled in a back booth of Ho-Lee Noodle House with Peter sitting across from me. I didn't even have to try convincing him to make me noodles, he suggested it on his own and made food for both of us. As hungry as I felt, I was finding it difficult to eat.

"Hey, man," Peter said, looking up from his bowl. "Don't let that guy get to you. He's just a jerk."

I twirled my noodles around the plate with my chopsticks. "Do you think he's right though? Someone is going after the judges just because they're the judges?"

He tilted his head. "Maybe . . . I don't know. Norman Pan had a lot of enemies for sure. But, this Stella chick . . . what's her story? She doesn't even live here anymore. How many enemies can she really have?"

First checking to make sure no one was around, I leaned across the table and whispered, "I think there's something weird going on with Stella, Joel, and Penny . . ."

Peter sighed. "Dude . . . tell me you are not messing around with this stuff. My nerves can't take it. I am already way stressed about the contest."

I looked away. "I mean, not really. There have just been a couple of things I've noticed in passing."

"Yeah, right, you're totally playing detective, aren't you?" His voice rose in agitation.

"Keep your voice down," I hissed, taking another glance around the restaurant. "It's not that big of a deal."

He shook his head. "No way, it's absolutely a big deal. Both of them were mysteriously strangled and the last thing I need in my life is for you to end up the same way, man. Just let your boyfriend take care of it. He carries a gun and whatever."

"Why does everyone keep saying that? You know I can't. Not if it has anything to do with the plaza. And with Penny . . ."

"There's no way she's a killer. That chick seems pretty solid to me."

"Yeah, well, people can surprise you. If anyone should know that, you should."

We debated the topic while Peter finished his lunch. I decided to take mine home with me. Maybe I'd be hungry later after I'd calmed down from the rantings of Ray Jin.

We walked to the parking lot together and Peter attempted to give me a comforting speech before taking off. I told him that it helped, but I was lying.

I dug around in my purse for my car keys, and my hand brushed against something that crinkled. *What the heck?* When I pulled it out, I froze. In the palm of my hand was a fortune cookie.

It couldn't be. It just couldn't.

I held on to the wrapped cookie, and continued digging for my car keys, which I finally found. Letting myself into the car, I placed the cookie on the dashboard and stared at it like it was going to do something. Best-case scenario, it would disappear into thin air.

No such luck.

I didn't like fortune cookies to begin with. For a few reasons . . . one, I thought they tasted weird . . . and two . . . there was never an actual fortune inside. It was more often than not some philosophical nonsense. If I was going to get a fortune cookie, I didn't want it to tell me how the eyes are the window to the soul. No, I wanted it to tell me that I was going to win a million dollars.

Stalling, I started the car and stared out the window, searching the parking lot for any potential suspicious characters. Was anybody following me, waiting for me to open the cookie? I checked the rearview mirror. No one behind me.

Okay . . . I'm just going to open the cookie. It's only a cookie. It's probably nothing. Maybe it fell into my purse when I was at the Bamboo Lounge and I hadn't noticed. Although I didn't remember seeing any fortune cookies there.

I grabbed the cookie off the dashboard and ripped it open. A sliver of white paper stuck out on one side and I pulled on it slowly.

Printed on the paper was the following: *The whole secret lies in confusing the enemy, so that he cannot fathom our real intent.*

I shoved everything back into my purse, put the car in reverse, and hightailed it home.

* * *

Megan was sitting at the kitchen table on her laptop when I walked in. I shut the door behind me, locked it, and peered out the peephole. No one had followed me as far as I could tell.

I turned back around and leaned against the door taking deep breaths.

Megan scrunched her eyebrows. "Okay, what are you doing?"

"You're never going to believe what happened." I rushed to the table, set my purse down, and dug out the fortune I had received. "Look at this."

She took the tiny paper from my hand and read it. Looking up at me, she said, "I don't get it . . ."

I reached back into my purse, felt around for my cell phone and pulled it out. It didn't seem necessary to search for the quote online, but if I was going to freak myself out over this, I at least wanted to be sure. "When I was leaving the plaza, I found this fortune in my purse . . . you know . . . just like the ones that Norman and Stella got . . ." I explained to her as I typed in the quote.

"Oh . . ." Her eyes widened. "Ohhh!"

"Yeah." I slumped into the chair across from her and showed her my search results. It was absolutely a Sun Tzu quote. There was no getting around it. "I'm going to die. I'm next!"

She set the paper down on the table. "You're not going to die."

"Norman got one, and he died . . . Stella got one and she died . . . so what makes me any different?" I took the paper and carefully tucked it away in the side pocket of my purse. I didn't want to lose it . . . if anything, it was evidence.

"The difference is you have me. And the two of us together are way smarter than the two of them. That Norman guy was arrogant and he didn't think he had anything to worry about. And Stella, well, she was just plain careless. Clearly she knew something and talked to the wrong person. She should have done something about it. She probably never told Trudeau about it."

"Maybe she did." I gasped. "Ohmigod! That means I've talked to the wrong person too. At some point, I said the wrong thing to the wrong person."

"Wait . . . when did you get this?"

"I didn't notice it until I was leaving the plaza," I said.

"Okay, so most likely it happened when you were at that meeting? Unless you went somewhere else? Did you make any other stops?"

"I went to the noodle house after with Peter, but he sure as hell didn't put it in my purse. And prior to the meeting I was at dim sum with my family. It definitely wasn't there when I left for the meeting. I would have noticed it when I was digging for my keys."

"So . . . who did you sit next to?"

"Peter was on one side of me, and Freddie was on the other side."

"And we're not even considering him in this whole thing, are we?"

I shook my head. "I don't think so. He's new in town and wasn't even around the night that Norman died. And I don't think he has any associations with Stella whatsoever."

"Okay then, so what opportunities were there to slip something into your purse without you noticing?"

"I don't know, I was sitting there the whole time." I stopped. "Hold on . . . no, I wasn't. I got up and went to the bathroom while Penny was putting food out on the table. I left my purse hanging on my chair. I didn't think anything of it because Peter was sitting right there."

"So Penny came into the room, and was moving all around the table and then a fortune cookie mysteriously pops up in your purse? That can't be a coincidence, Lana. Especially after the way she acted toward you yesterday."

I shut my eyes. I didn't want it to be true. It couldn't be Penny. It just couldn't be. She had been in the plaza with us for the past year . . . I had drinks with her and hung out at the Bamboo Lounge at least once a week. "There has to be another explanation. Both Walter and Ray were there too . . . it could have easily been one of them."

"True . . ." She tapped her fingernails on the tabletop. "Well, that definitely eliminates Joel, wouldn't you say?"

"I guess so." I paused. "Unless he and Penny really are partners . . ."

She threw her hands up. "How are we ever going to eliminate anybody?"

"We have to find that connection between the three of them and see if it would have any relevance to what's happening."

Megan pointed to her computer. "I'm reading up on Stella right now. She's had an interesting life, to say the least."

"Okay, you keep digging online. In the meantime, I'm going to try and get some info out of Adam. We have a date tomorrow night, so I'll try to casually bring up the case and see what I come up with."

"Shouldn't you tell him about this fortune showing up in your purse?"

I shook my head. "Not yet. If I show him this right away, he's definitely not going to tell me anything. He'll be too worried about me being in danger."

"Do you really think he's going to tell you anything anyway? He's not exactly open about things to begin with."

"I have to at least give it a shot . . ."

She focused back on the computer screen. "Lana." Her voice was firm as she said my name. "I think what you have to do is accept the fact that all roads lead back to Penny Cho."

CHAPTER 21

Monday morning came and went and I hardly noticed. This is an unusual occurrence for me since Mondays always seem to last forty-eight hours. But I was too preoccupied with everything roaming around in my brain that I had gone through the entire morning on autopilot.

When Nancy came in, I retreated to the office and shut the door. I told everyone that I was going through receipts and managing the books, but what I was really doing was thinking. Thinking about what Megan said to me the afternoon before. *All roads lead back to Penny Cho.*

If I really sat back and thought about it, I didn't know much about Penny besides the fact that she had moved up North from Florida where she'd owned a small restaurant that hadn't done all too well. After a major hurricane devastated her home, she wasn't able to keep up with the restaurant or the repairs needed on her house. So, with what little she had left, she decided to move to Ohio and start from scratch.

It always seemed like a legit story, and I'd never questioned it. There wasn't any reason to. But now I began to wonder if there was another reason for her move.

Most of our conversations centered around business at the plaza, or she would ask me questions about myself . . . like how things were going with Adam, or what was new with Megan. But never really anything about herself. I didn't know if she lived alone, had a roommate, what her hobbies were, and up until the recent rumors about her and Joel, I didn't know if she was even dating anybody. She always managed to steer our chats back around to me without offering up too much about herself.

A little while after lunch, I decided to stop by for a visit with Rina, and see if she knew anything about Penny. I wondered what type of conversations they'd had, if any.

On my way over to the Ivory Doll, Freddie Yuan waved to me from the community center and came toward the doors to greet me. I wasn't ready for another encounter with him and I thought he might want to rehash things that were said at the last meeting, so I gave him a quick wave and rushed over to meet my friend before he could stop me.

Rina was watching me from the entrance of her store. She welcomed me with a big hug and giggled in my ear. "What was that all about? I think I actually saw you jog a little bit."

"Nothing . . ." I pulled away. "Just excited to see you is all."

She grinned. "Uh-huh . . ."

A few women lingered around the store, comparing face powders and reading ingredient labels.

"Do you have a minute?" I asked, nodding toward her customers.

"Sure." She led me off to the side farthest away from the other women. "What's up?"

"What do you know about Penny Cho? Personally, I mean."

Her eyebrows scrunched. "Penny? Lana, what's this about? Tell me you're not still snooping into this case."

I didn't want to tell her about the fortune cookie. I knew that it would only make her worry. "I was thinking about it earlier this morning and I realized I don't know that much about her outside of the plaza. Do you?"

Rina took a minute to think. "No, not really. Usually she turns the conversation toward me. And I don't like to pry with people, so I never push. If anyone knows that people like to keep things private, it's me."

"See, that's the thing . . . she does the same with me when we talk. Other than knowing she moved up here from Florida, I don't know anything else about her."

"Florida, yes." Rina nodded. "She likes to talk about Florida. Hurricanes and all that."

"You wouldn't want to do some digging for me, would you?" I hated to ask, especially since there was no telling if Penny was someone safe to be around. But I figured Rina talking to Penny at the lounge would be harmless.

"Oh no, absolutely not," Rina said, taking a step back. "I am not going to encourage this."

My shoulders slumped. "I understand."

"I don't think you do, Lana . . ." Rina shook her head at me. "Because I know you're going to keep investigating anyway."

"Well, I can't just leave it," I told her. "Two people are dead and the killer could be right under our roof."

My voice must have risen because the two women who were on the other side of the store turned around and gawked at us.

Rina smiled awkwardly at them, and ushered me closer to the entrance. "Hey, remember that restaurant you have to manage?"

I pursed my lips at her.

"Why don't you go back there and take care of that instead of worrying about this nonsense. Adam and his guys will get it figured out. Don't you worry." She shooed me out of the store with a wave of her hands.

"Fine . . ."

"Oh, and don't forget about our coffee date tomorrow. We can go to Shanghai Donuts instead of Starbucks so you can satisfy that sweet tooth of yours." She gave me a wink and turned around to tend to her customers.

I sulked all the way back to the restaurant.

After work, I rushed home to shower and get ready for my date. Adam told me that we were going to Michael Symon's restaurant, Lola. Having never been there, I was excited to sample the menu because of all the great things I'd heard about the place.

I prepped and primped for about an hour until the doorbell finally rang. Kikko went into a frenzy of yips and growls as she pawed at the front door.

"Calm yourself, woman," I lectured her as I opened the door.

Adam stepped in, embraced me in a giant hug, and

lifted me off the ground. I buried my head in the crook of his neck and inhaled his signature cologne. He smelled of cinnamon and sandalwood.

"I feel like I haven't seen you in forever." He set me down and gave me a gentle kiss.

"I just saw you on Saturday."

"Yeah, but I didn't really get to *see* you." A devilish grin spread on his lips and he squeezed my sides.

A giggle escaped against my will, and I chastised myself for it.

"Are you ready to go? I'm starved."

On the way downtown, we played a mini-version of catch-up that was mostly me telling him about things going on at the restaurant. As usual, he barely said anything about his own work."

Twenty minutes later we were walking down Euclid Avenue, making our way over to East Fourth Street. The early evening air was crisp and smelled like spring. It was one of my favorite smells, and I wished the walk to Lola was a little bit longer.

The restaurant was decently packed for a Monday, but not overly crowded. We were seated at a table off to the side of the entrance.

After we had reviewed the menu, ordered our drinks and food, I decided to begin my covert snooping.

"You know, something has been bugging me about Stella Chung," I said, attempting to use my most sincere and innocent voice.

His eyes narrowed. "Is that so?"

"Yeah, she came to me a few days before she was . . . murdered, and asked about talking to you."

He perked up in his seat. "She did?"

"You mean she never did come talk to you after all?" I was a little shocked, but after her telling me she didn't really trust the police, I had my suspicions that she might try and keep the fortune-cookie episode to herself for as long as possible.

"No, she never did." He took a healthy swallow from his glass. "What did she say?"

I fiddled with my napkin. "She showed me a message that she'd gotten . . ."

"On her phone?"

"No . . ."

"Lana, don't make me drag it out of you."

Sighing, I said, "It was a fortune . . . but it wasn't a regular fortune-cookie fortune. It was a threat."

"I found that in her things," he admitted. "I wasn't sure if it meant something. It didn't seem like a typical fortune."

"I told her that she should talk to you right away. Especially since Mr. Pan received one before the contest."

"He did?" His voice rose in surprise. "Why didn't I know about this?"

I shrank in my seat. "I don't know. Maybe Ian forgot about it? Norman gave it to him after the first round. I don't think either one of us thought much of it at the time."

Adam scowled at the mention of Ian's name. "Do you think that he would have held on to it? It's a fortune-cookie paper; that type of thing could get lost easily."

I could feel my face getting hot like I was in trouble. It had never occurred to me that Ian wouldn't have the slip of paper that was given to him by Norman. What if he'd thrown it away thinking it wasn't anything of significance?

"Lana, I need you to call Ian and ask him about it right now. I need to know if he still has it."

"Now? While we're at dinner?"

"Yes, right now," he said more firmly.

"Okay, okay." I pulled out my phone and dialed Ian's number. After three rings, he answered. Quickly, I relayed the situation to him and asked if he had the fortune-cookie paper that Norman had given him.

"Well," Adam mouthed to me.

I nodded a yes.

"Tell him that I will pick it up tonight. Where can I meet him?" Adam whispered.

I relayed the message to Ian who said he would be working late at the plaza. He assured me he would wait for Adam to arrive.

I thanked him and we hung up.

Adam sat back in his seat. "I don't want to jinx it and say this is a lucky break . . . but this feels damn lucky."

"See, aren't you glad I brought it up?" I beamed.

"Actually, I am. This confirms we are dealing with the same person for both murders. And we can assume that the killer knew both parties on a personal level, so there must be some type of connection between them." His gaze drifted off and I could tell he was morphing into 'all-business Adam.'

"Why do you say the killer knew them on a personal level?"

"Because Stella had drinks with this person. We found two glasses and a bottle of whiskey in her hotel room. One glass must have been broken in the struggle, and I'm guessing it was the killer's because we found her prints on the other glass. Aside from that, we have nothing. The broken glass was so destroyed we're probably not going to get anything off it. The whiskey bottle, all the surfaces and the door handles were wiped clean. There was a partial print on the lamp cord, but it's probably worthless."

"A bottle of whiskey, you said?"

"Yeah, a half-empty bottle of Yama—" He stopped, slapping himself in the face. "Why am I telling you this?"

"Casual conversation?" I shrugged.

He groaned. "Let's talk about something else."

"But maybe if we talk it out, you'll come up with more ideas," I suggested.

The server came with our food and set the plates down in front of us.

Adam reached for the salt shaker, giving me a quick glance. "Nice try, Lana."

The rest of dinner was pleasant. He managed to successfully get my mind off recent happenings, talking about ideas he had for summer plans. If he could manage the time away, he wanted to have a weekend getaway with me. We spent the rest of our meal talking about various locations that we'd both like to visit if we got the chance.

We stayed for one drink after dinner, and then he said we needed to leave so he could meet up with Ian.

I stopped in the ladies' room knowing that crossing my legs the whole way home was not going to cut it. The bathroom was immaculate and might have been nicer than my apartment. At times, I wished there was such a job as restroom connoisseur. I would have a blast rating all the bathrooms in the city . . . and there were quite a few that would make it on the . . . well, you know what list I'm talking about.

When I returned to the table, my purse that I had left

on my seat was now on the table, and Adam was livid. I know because when he gets mad, his lips disappear into his mouth, and his eyebrows hang really low over his eyes. In a way, he kind of looks like Burt from *Sesame Street*.

"What did I do now?" I asked, trying to make a joke.

It didn't work.

"Lana, what is the meaning of this?" He held up the fortune-cookie paper.

No! I had forgotten to take the slip of paper out of my purse! "You went through my things?"

"I was looking for gum . . . now answer the question."

I sulked. How could I be so careless? "It's nothing . . . it—"

"When did you get this?"

"Yesterday," I mumbled. "I was going to tell you, I swear."

"Funny that it didn't come up during this entire dinner . . . or say . . . yesterday!"

The couple sitting down next to us turned our way.

I put my head down. "Can we not do this here?"

"Fine, we need to go anyway." He got up from the table and slipped the fortune-cookie paper into a tiny, plastic resealable bag he pulled from his pants pocket.

"Do you keep baggies in your pocket all the time?" I asked as we left the restaurant.

"You never know when you're going to need one." He took long strides the entire way to the car and my short legs had a hard time keeping up. "Come on, we have to get to the plaza."

"We?"

"Yeah . . . as of now, I'm not letting you out of my sight."

CHAPTER 22

By the time we made it to Asia Village, the shops were closed and the parking lot was empty and darkened except for a few security lights. Adam parked right outside of the main doors and ushered me inside.

We found Ian in his office jotting down notes in a ledger. “Lana, what is so urgent about this fortune?” He looked up, his eyes automatically locking on Adam. “Detective Trudeau . . . nice to see you again.”

“Likewise,” Adam replied. There was little feeling behind the word.

Ian pulled open a desk drawer and took out the slip of paper. “After everything that happened with Norman, I completely forgot about it. It’s been sitting in my desk this entire time.”

Adam took the paper from him. “Did you discuss this with anyone?”

“No, like I said, it’s been in my desk drawer this whole time,” Ian said. He nodded toward me. “Lana was with me when Norman brought it over. It was just a handful of us standing there. I meant to talk with the waitstaff about it, but I never got the chance."

"Good. The fewer people know about this the better." He took another plastic baggie out of his pocket and slid the paper in, securing the zip seal. "Now, if we can just figure out what all of these secret messages mean."

"They're Sun Tzu quotes," I told him.

His eyes narrowed. "Sun Tzu quotes . . . ?"

"Yeah, you know . . . *The Art of War.*"

"Huh, well, that's a first for me. Does that have any significance to either one of you?"

I sighed. "Well, clearly the one I got means that I'm next on the chopping block. But no . . . I don't know what using Sun Tzu quotes means. If it meant anything to Norman, he didn't say so. Stella had no idea what it was about. She didn't even recognize the quote."

"Wait, you got one too?" Ian asked, stepping in front of Adam. He grabbed my shoulders and lightly shook me. "Lana, what have you gotten yourself into?"

"Why don't you let me worry about that?" Adam removed Ian's hand from my left shoulder. "I'm not going to let anything happen to her."

"I should certainly hope not." Ian removed his other hand and turned to face Adam head-on. "You'll have hell to pay."

"Is that so?" Adam straightened his back and lifted his chin. "And what exactly are you going to do about it, Sung?"

Ian snickered. "Oh, I don't mean me, Detective. I'm talking about Mrs. Lee."

* * *

We'd barely spoken on the way back to my apartment. Adam was deep in thought and not willing to share. In the passing streetlights I would catch a glimpse of his expression. His face was hardened, his jaw clenched.

Megan was still at work, so it was only Kikko that met us at the door. Adam gave her a pat on the head before he slumped onto the couch. He leaned his head back and scrubbed his face with both hands. Since the beginning of the evening a five o'clock shadow had appeared and there were dark circles under his eyes.

"Do you want some coffee? I could make some," I offered.

"No, I should try and get to sleep. Tomorrow is going to be another long day."

"Oh, okay. Well, I can walk you out, I'll bring the dog."

He snickered. "First of all, that little wrinkle of a pooch isn't going to protect you from a rabid squirrel. And second of all, I'm spending the night. There's no way I'm letting you out of my sight. I'll try and get some police detail on you tomorrow, but for tonight, I'll be your guard."

My eyes widened. He was staying the night? He hadn't stayed the night since . . . well, since the last time I got myself into trouble.

With the way our schedules kept conflicting with one another, there hadn't been any time for cozy sleepovers or long evenings that carried into early morning. We'd only been on a handful of dates in the time that we'd been seeing each other.

"That's okay with you, right?" he asked when I didn't say anything.

"Yeah, I just . . . have to walk the dog." I grabbed for Kikko's leash and fastened it onto her collar. "Come on, Kikko." I rushed out the door before he could offer to come along. I needed a moment to myself.

Outside I took a deep breath while Kikko sniffed around a fire hydrant. Adam was going to spend the night. He'd never offered to spend the night, or asked, or suggested that I spend the night at his place. I'd never even been to his place. Everything so far had been very much innocent. And since I was shaky about getting involved with someone too fast, it had been fine by me.

My mind was racing. Did I have acceptable pajamas to wear that didn't involve a T-shirt with a stupid saying on it? Had I remembered to shave my legs? Would I snore and keep him awake? Would *he* snore and keep *me* awake? It had been a long while since I'd shared a bed with anyone other than Kikko, and I was starting to feel like I was out of practice at being in an adult relationship. Were we even in a relationship? What *was* this?

Breathe, Lana. It's going to be okay.

When I got back inside, I found Adam sprawled on the couch. His demeanor had changed from the car ride and he appeared to have relaxed a little bit. Lying on his back, he'd kicked his shoes off and had his head propped up with his arms. He watched me while I removed the dog's leash and hung my keys on the brass hooks hanging by the door.

It suddenly occurred to me that he might intend on sleeping on the couch like the last time he stayed. I started to feel silly for even considering that we would both sleep in my bed.

"I hope you're not a blanket hog," he said with a wry grin. "My feet turn into icicles while I sleep."

My stomach leaped into my throat. "No, I don't think I do—"

He seemed to sense my anxiety. "I can sleep out here if that would make you more comfortable."

"No!" I said a little too eagerly. I tucked my chin in. "I mean . . . of course not. Don't be silly."

He laughed. "You seem a little jittery there. You okay? I know this whole thing with the fortune cookie can't be easy."

"Yeah, I'm just going to straighten up my room a little bit, and then we can go to . . . bed."

In one swift motion, he was up from the couch and at my side. His arm looped around my waist and he pulled me down on the couch, nestling me into his side. The heat from his body seeped through my shirt. "Sit with me a minute, okay?"

"Okay." I could hear the nerves shaking my vocal chords. *Why are you such a spaz when it comes to him, Lana?*

"This is kind of important, and I've been waiting for the right time to tell you this . . . but I don't think the right time is ever going to present itself."

My stomach dropped. He really wasn't helping me relax. One of the worst feelings in the world is when someone tells you they have to tell you something . . . at least for me. My natural instinct is to think of the worst-case scenario. And, in this case, it was that he didn't want to be involved with me anymore.

"If you don't want to see me anymore . . ." My bottom lip quivered with the words. Secretly, I'd been thinking it for weeks. And now with this whole thing going on, and me getting myself into trouble yet again, I could see him being completely fed up with me and my shenanigans.

"How can you say that, Lana? I wouldn't be here right now if I didn't want to be." He squeezed my shoulder.

"You're just doing your job," I suggested. "You're here to make sure nothing happens to me."

"Sweetheart, I hate to break it to you; this is a little above and beyond the call of duty. So no, it's not that I don't want to see you anymore."

I took a deep breath trying to calm my nerves.

"But there is something you need to know about me . . ."

My stomach sank yet again. My mind went down the list to the next possible worst-case scenario. "Oh my God, you're married, aren't you?" I shifted away from him and stuck my hands between my knees. Things started to make sense . . . the distant behavior and lack of communication, it all started to come together. "I should have known. A handsome guy like you wouldn't be single. And that explains why I've never been to your place . . . oh my God, it explains so much." I looked at his hands. "Why don't you wear a ring? And—"

"Lana!" Adam put his hands on my shoulders and turned me to face him again. "I'm not married."

"Oh . . ." My face reddened.

"The reason why we haven't spent much time together . . ." His hands dropped from my shoulders. He rested his elbows on his knees and steepled his fingers in front of his face. "The reason that we haven't . . ."

My heart was beating and I could feel the pulse thick in my throat. Whatever he needed to say was clearly difficult for him. I'd never seen him act this way before. I inched myself closer to him and rested a comforting hand on his thigh. "You can tell me anything," I assured him. "I'm not going to judge you."

He closed his eyes and let out a deep breath through his nose. "When I was little . . . I was eight . . . I lost my dad. He was . . . murdered . . ."

An involuntary gasp escaped my throat. "What?"

His eyes opened, and when he turned to me, I noticed they were bloodshot. "He was killed during a robbery at a gas station."

I didn't know what to say. The words *I'm sorry* felt like they wouldn't do the subject matter justice. I gave his thigh a gentle squeeze and decided to stay silent, letting him finish what he wanted to say.

"At the time, there had been a string of gas station robberies happening in the area. They would take everything in the cash register, kill the owner, and shoot out the cameras."

"Oh my . . . that's terrible . . ."

"We were on our way out of town. My parents and I were headed to Marblehead for the weekend, and we stopped to get gas. My father went inside to pay and get snacks while we waited in the car."

I covered my mouth, stifling another gasp. How horrible! Adam had been there when his father was killed. I couldn't imagine what that would do to a person, especially someone so young.

"When I heard the gunshots, my mother told me to get down and hide on the floor in the backseat. The next thing I remembered was people yelling and tires peeling out as they took off. Sirens were going off in the distance . . ."

He stared at the door of the apartment, his eyes glazed over. I knew that he was imagining it all over again in his head. I knew that he was there.

My heart sank, and I could feel tears welling up in my eyes. "You don't have to—"

He held up a hand. "No, just let me get this out. I need to do this.

"I stayed there like that until the cops came . . . I remember my mother trying to get me out of the car. But I couldn't move. One of the first responders was finally able to convince me to get off the floor of the backseat. My father never came back out to the car . . . I already knew he was dead without my mother having to explain anything to me.

"When they finally got me out of the car, they took us to the police station and tried to question us, but we hadn't seen anything that could help them. I didn't even notice any of the other cars in the parking spots or at the pumps and neither did she. They never did catch the guys who did it.

"After that, my mother and I went to live with my grandparents and they helped raise me. Things were rough on my mother for a long while, but our family helped keep us together. I don't know what we would have done without them.

"That's why I became a cop. I might not have been able to get justice for myself or my family. But I wanted to get justice for others . . ." He glanced up at me. "And that's also why I've been avoiding your question for so long. Not many people know about what happened. The guys at the station know, and I suppose anyone who dug into my past would know, but I don't make it a point to tell people."

"Adam . . . I'm so sorry . . ." I said the words even though they made me cringe. I needed words with more power, more feeling.

"If we're going to go any further with this, it's important that you know this about me. I come with baggage, Lana. I come with a lot of mental baggage. It destroyed my last relationship. She couldn't deal with how protective I could become. One night . . . she didn't come home and I had cops searching for her everywhere. I was losing my mind trying to find her."

"Where was she?"

He smirked. "Turns out she was cheating on me. She was at the *other* guy's place that night. Said she needed a man who treated her like a grown woman. Apparently, all my worrying made her feel like a child."

"Ugh . . . that . . ." Again, I found myself at a loss for words.

"I know you know that feeling. We talked about it when we first met."

"I remember." He was referring to the story I'd told him about my previous relationship and the unshakeable feeling that stays with you after someone you trust cheats on you.

"So . . . yeah . . ." He laced his fingers together. "You're always worrying about me not wanting to be with you . . . you don't say so, but I know it. I can see it on your face. The look of insecurity you'll get . . . or the tone in your voice when I tell you I can't make a date because of a case. It's not a line, Lana . . . it's the truth."

"I know." It came out as a whisper.

"And, I really do worry about you."

"I know," I said again. "I also know now why it affects you so much."

"Loss scars you . . . deeply," he said, looking into my eyes, no doubt trying to read my mind. "I don't want any more loss . . . I know that's not reasonable . . ."

"There's nothing wrong with having hope."

"In my head, you're my girl. I think from the minute I saw you come out of those double doors, I knew . . . you're my girl. I've tried to hold on to that moment . . . I've tried to keep you at a safe distance so I wouldn't lose you. But I realize we can't stay in that space forever. It's not realistic."

My insides were screaming. This was a completely different side of Adam, one that I'd never seen. For all the times we'd spent together, I knew that more was going on in his head, but I never knew that it could be all this. From the moment we'd met, I had never been sure how he'd felt about me and now I'd learned what was holding him back.

"So . . . the real question is . . . do you still want to be with me?" As he asked the question, he transformed from a grown man full of confidence and assurance to a little boy with his heart on his sleeve. His eyes were filled with doubt and apprehension as he waited for me to answer.

I propped myself up on my knees and wiggled myself close to him, wrapping my arms around his shoulders. He leaned into me, his head resting on my shoulder. I kissed the top of his head. "Of course I do. You're my guy, Adam. Baggage and all."

CHAPTER 23

When I awoke, Adam was sitting on the edge of the bed staring out the window through the half-opened blinds with Kikko by his side. She stared at him waiting for action.

"Whatcha doin?" I shifted under the blanket, propping myself up with my elbow.

"I hope I didn't wake you," he said over his shoulder. "I didn't sleep that great."

"Because of our conversation from last night?" Even though I'd been exhausted from the emotional evening we'd shared, it was hard to fall asleep. I'd spent at least thirty minutes reciting the alphabet over and over in my head.

"No, this fortune-cookie thing has me stumped. I don't like that feeling."

I hoisted myself up and leaned against the wall. "Probably you're thinking about it too hard. Try focusing on something else and maybe the fortune-cookie angle will come to you."

He stood up and paced the length of the room. "But why Sun Tzu . . . why the *Art of War*? If it didn't mean anything to Stella, then what was the purpose? Had it meant something to Norman Pan? Why did he take the fortune to Ian of all people?"

Kikko followed him with her eyes.

"Well, whoever it is, obviously they're declaring some type of war."

"War on what? The contest? And why go to all this trouble?"

"It has to mean something to them and they just don't realize it," I suggested. "Or maybe the guy is just a fan of Sun Tzu."

"Or woman," Adam shot back.

"True . . ." My thoughts swirled back to Penny Cho. "Whoever it was must have wanted the victims to know who they were in advance."

He turned to me. "Yeah, but then how does that relate to you? Does anything strike you as odd about this Sun Tzu angle at all?"

I shook my head. "It doesn't ring any bells with me."

"Then there's a different message here . . . some type of connection to the other fortunes that were given out."

Throwing the blanket off me, I swung my legs over the edge of the bed and stuffed my feet into the fuzzy slippers Megan gave me last Christmas. "If we're going to talk motives, I need coffee."

"I should head into the station. I need to check in with the chief and talk this out with him. And I need to enter this stuff into evidence. I could get into some serious trouble for not bringing this in right away."

"Just tell them you didn't get any of it until this morning."

Adam wrapped an arm around my waist as I stood. "Miss Lee, are you trying to make a liar out of me?"

"No, but I don't want you to lose your job either."

"The sentiment is much appreciated." He gave me a kiss on the forehead. "Listen, there's something I want to talk about with you before I leave."

"Okay . . ."

He pulled me over to the bed, and we sat on the edge, facing each other. "I've been thinking about our conversation from last night."

I couldn't say that I was surprised, my own mind was replaying the whole evening from top to bottom. Part of me was still processing everything.

He scrubbed his chin with the back of his hand. "I don't want to make the same mistakes I've made in the past and end up pushing you away. I know I have to let you make your own decisions."

I wrapped my hand around his bicep and gave him a reassuring squeeze. "I know you know that. I don't look at your protection and concern as a burden. But I do need you to trust that I'm capable too."

He nodded. "Can you promise me one thing?"

"Anything."

"We always make it a point to communicate. If you're getting into something, I want you to tell me. It's better that I know about it than you going behind my back."

"But aren't you just going to tell me to stay out of it?" I asked.

Adam smiled. "Yeah, but when have you ever listened to me?"

After he left, I tiptoed around getting ready for work so I wouldn't disturb Megan. I hadn't heard her come in and that meant it must have been pretty late.

Before Adam left, he'd called the station and asked one of his buddies to come keep an eye on me until I made it safely to the plaza. When I was letting out Kikko for her morning tinkle, I saw an unmarked car parked at the end of the lot. A middle-aged man with aviator glasses watched me as I circled the grassy area with Kikko. It was Officer Wilkins, the same guy who'd questioned me the night of Norman's murder. From what I could see, he was dressed in plainclothes and there was nothing to give away the fact he was a cop. His sandy-blond hair was tousled and the beard that was beginning to form made it seem like he'd just gotten out of bed. I waved at him, but he pretended not to see me, turning his head in the other direction.

Wilkins followed behind me all the way to the plaza, and I curbed the urge to wave at him again as I entered Asia Village. It probably wasn't the best idea for me to give away the fact that someone was keeping an eye on me. Kinda defeated the whole purpose.

On my way to the restaurant, Mr. Zhang came waddling up to me as I passed Wild Sage. His demeanor was always affable and slightly on the curious side. He peered at me through his bifocals, assessing my appearance. "Young Miss Lee, how are you this morning?"

"I'm doing well, Mr. Zhang, how are you today?"

He nodded. "I am also well. Do you know if your grandmother will be stopping by today?"

"I'm not sure, any particular reason you're asking?" I tried not to smile.

He chuckled. "She is a very beautiful and wise woman. I would very much like to know her."

"I could talk to her for you . . ."

Mr. Zhang blushed. "Oh no, please do not mention it, Lana. I will find my own way."

"Well, if you ever change your mind . . ." I started to walk away, but realized who I was talking to. Speaking of wise, Mr. Zhang was pretty adept in that department. I realized he would be able to give me some insight into the whole Sun Tzu thing. He might suggest a possibility that hadn't been considered yet. "May I ask you a question?" I turned back around to face him.

"Of course, anything. Mr. Zhang is always here to help."

"Do you think it would be odd for someone to quote Sun Tzu in this day and age? People who would do that probably are into history or something, right?" After my earlier conversation with Adam, I began to wonder about the specific connection myself. I had decided on the way to work that we could narrow down our possibilities to people who would be interested in Asian history. Although around here that could still be quite a few people.

He shook his head. "Sun Tzu is very popular in the business world. Many people seek his teachings to run their companies. Cindy Kwan could tell you the same. I imagine she sells a lot of books in this style."

Great. So in light of that information, none of the possible suspects could be eliminated. Everybody involved so far was a business owner, and any of them could have read the book for their own purposes.

I thanked Mr. Zhang and went on my way to Ho-Lee Noodle House. I needed to start narrowing things down if I was going to get anywhere with this case.

The morning proceeded with nothing of importance occurring. The Mahjong Matrons came in as usual, and gossiped over their pickled cucumbers and rice porridge. I refilled their teakettle at least twice before they decided to head out for the day.

On my lunch break, I stopped by the Modern Scroll and talked with Cindy Kwan about *The Art of War* and she confirmed what Mr. Zhang had told me earlier that morning. It was a very popular book in the business world, and she sold plenty of copies.

Of course, my questioning her about the book led her to ask me whether I was still investigating the recent murders.

"So, clearly the murderer wasn't Stella like I originally thought," Cindy said, leaning over the counter. "My money's on that Joel guy. For sure. Hands down." She slapped the counter for emphasis. "Especially with him lurking around the plaza lately. I think he's been here every day since this mess started. Tell me, Lana, when's the last time you saw Joel here before that?"

"Rina mentioned that too," I told her. "But don't you think it would be stupid of him to bring more attention to himself? He's already under suspicion because of the way he acted during round one."

"Maybe," she said, tilting her head in consideration.

"However, at the same time, he could be trying to keep tabs on what's happening around here so he can be one step ahead."

She did have a point, and I tossed it around in my head while I took a quick skim through the mystery section of the store. Arguing with myself about whether or not to purchase anything, I left the store empty-handed. I made myself promise that I wouldn't buy any more new books until I had this whole thing solved. That would be my reward.

I ventured over to visit with Rina and confirm the time of our coffee date, but she had her hands full with an abundance of women perusing her store. It made me smile to know that her business was doing well. After the loss of her younger sister, Isabelle, it was important for Rina to have something positive in her life. Moving to Cleveland was a big step for her, and I'd hate to see her fail and return to New York. In the short time we'd known each other, we'd gotten pretty close and losing her as part of my daily routine would be both sad and disappointing.

Continuing my loop around the pond, I caught sight of Freddie Yuan and sped up my pace, hoping that he wouldn't stop me. Now that I knew the real reason for Adam's distant behavior, I felt guilty at ever entertaining the idea of another guy.

I had almost passed the community center successfully, but before I could completely get away, I heard a "Hey, Lana!"

I cringed, but turned around. He'd said it so loudly there was no way I could deny having heard my name.

Freddie walked over to greet me. His smile was killer and I silently scolded myself for thinking so. "Hey, there!"

"Oh, hi, Freddie . . ."

"So listen . . . I was thinking . . . it was really nice seeing you away from the plaza the other night."

"Yeah . . . you too."

He rubbed the back of his neck, flexing his arm muscles in the process. "It occurred to me that we should have drinks sometime. You know, just shoot the—"

"I have a boyfriend!" I blurted, diverting my attention to the pond. Could I be any more awkward?

Freddie let out a nervous laugh. "Oh, my bad. I didn't realize. Anybody I know?"

"Maybe? I'm dating Detective Trudeau . . ."

"Oh, wow . . . a detective . . . how could I compete with that?" He scratched his chin. "Well, hey, can't blame a guy for tryin'."

"You know who you should ask out? Rina," I told him. "She mentioned she thinks you're very attractive." I pointed in the direction of her store. I knew she was going to kill me for this, but I would deal with the repercussions of that later.

His head turned in the direction that I pointed. "Oh . . . Rina. Yeah, she seems like a cool chick. Kinda straitlaced for me though . . . but I'll think about it. Anyway, no hard feelings on my end. If you change your mind though . . . or things go south with the detective, you know where to find me." He winked before jogging back to the community center.

Before I turned around to head back to the restaurant, I noticed Ian standing at the door of the property office watching the exchange. Great, just great.

* * *

After lunchtime, business slowed, so I snuck into the office and called Megan to fill her in on what just happened with Freddie Yuan and the conversation I'd had with Adam the night before. She snickered before making some inappropriate catcall comments.

"It's not funny," I scolded her.

"But it kind of is," she replied. "This is the way of life, my friend. You finally found yourself a great catch, and all of a sudden these other guys come out of the woodwork. It's classic."

"I feel awful though."

"Don't. You didn't do anything wrong. So you found another guy attractive. Big deal. Things with Adam haven't really presented themselves in the right light. This conversation you guys had last night was huge. And, it's a game changer. He's not someone to bring a woman into his life lightly. Now you guys are getting somewhere."

"True . . ."

"So, enough boy talk. I have been waiting to tell you this all day. I found out something about Stella that you're going to find superinteresting."

"What? I can't believe you didn't bring that up first. Do tell!"

"Okay, so you know how I said there would be tons of articles on her because of her death?"

"Yeah . . ."

"Last night on my break, I was scrolling through yet another article about how she came to be a hotshot chef and it mentioned again how she went to that fancy culinary school."

"Right, the Loretta Paganini School of Cooking."

"Yeah, so the person writing the article asked whoever

from the school to provide some pictures of Stella for the paper. And you'll never guess who is caught in the background in one of the photos."

"Who?" I asked, inching to the edge of my chair.

"Joel Liu."

CHAPTER 24

"You have got to be kidding me! So he and Stella go *way* back then."

"That's not all," Megan said. "After that, I started to think about our little trio of suspects, and dug around some more with the school as my connection. Sure enough, Penny Cho attended the school too."

My eyes widened. "Really? Penny went there too?"

"Yup. Pretty interesting stuff, huh?"

"I would say so." I stood up from my seat at the desk feeling anxious. With this new information, we knew for sure that they had been connected in the past. Going to school with people could be a bonding experience or it could be the perfect recipe for enemies.

"What are you thinking?" Megan asked, breaking the silence.

"Sorry, just thinking about the possibilities this opens up. This could change the dynamic of everything we thought we knew."

“I agree. I say we keep digging into these three and see what we turn up. Even though Walter Shen is a jerk, he’s probably just that . . . a jerk.”

“True, but I don’t want to eliminate Ray Jin just yet. There’s something odd about him that isn’t sitting well with me. The way he’s been acting about the contest hasn’t been consistent. I’m not sure if I’m reading something into that, so I want to check it out.”

“Well, if Joel did kill Norman Pan, then it was because he’s mad about the contest, and Ray won the contest last year . . . allegedly because of dirty dealings.” Megan let that statement hang while I made my own assumptions based on her theory.

“So if this theory checks out . . . Ray could potentially be the next target,” I said.

“Exactly. And maybe because he has a guilty conscience he suspects it and that’s why he’s been acting so erratically.”

I took a deep breath and sat back down in my chair. “Okay . . . do you think I should warn him?” Something needed to be done. Being at the restaurant doing nothing was going to make me a nervous wreck.

“I wouldn’t bring it up just yet. From what you’ve told me so far he sounds a little on the angry side, and if you approach him, he might try to retaliate. You said he was already trying to pin the murder on Joel anyway, didn’t you?”

“Yeah, he’s not being shy about his feelings on the subject.”

“How about we solidify this new theory of ours first? If we can get something concrete on these two, then you can take that to Trudeau and let him deal with the rest. It'll at least put the investigation in the right direction."

While she spoke, I came up with a plan that I could put into action immediately. Penny was too mad at me and had made it clear that she didn't want to talk about it further, so I doubted I could learn anything more from her. Megan was right about not approaching Ray too soon, so that left one weak link. Joel Liu.

"Here's the plan," I told Megan. "I'm going to confront Joel about him talking with Jackie Shen."

"What do you mean? How does anything involve that girl?"

I'd forgotten I never had the chance to tell Megan about what I'd seen when I was out with Rina at Wok and Roll over the weekend.

"Ohhh, that's a good angle," Megan said after I filled her in. "Then maybe he'll admit he has a history with Penny and you can find out what happened with the three of them."

"Yeah, if I pretend to be concerned about him trying to mess around behind Penny's back that should get him talking. The concerned-friend role usually works."

"But what if he says that he's not with Penny and leaves it at that?"

"If he says they're not romantically involved, then I'll throw Jackie under the bus and tell him she mentioned that he's been calling Walter Shen . . . and we'll see if that takes us anywhere. If he gets too defensive about it, we'll know that something's up with them and we can officially bump Walter back to the top of the list."

Megan sighed with relief. "Lana . . . we're getting close to something. I can feel it."

When we hung up, I felt a sense of satisfaction. This knowledge could take us somewhere. Hopefully that somewhere was in the right direction.

The restaurant was still pretty slow, and Nancy seemed to have everything under control. Taking the bank deposit with me on my way out, I swung by to see Rina and cancel our coffee date, promising that we'd get together another day. Right now, I needed to pay a visit to Joel's restaurant.

As I'd anticipated, business was slow for Joel as well. I thought about the last time I'd been there and the fact that Stella had met with him shortly before her death. Even with Wilkins in the parking lot as my shadow, I needed to be careful. There was no telling what type of situation I was walking into.

The same hostess was standing near the door when I walked in and I wondered if Joel had the means to hire any other staff. It was beyond me how he was able to pay anyone to begin with.

The hostess smiled cheerily at me. "Back again, I see. Would you like a table? Or will you be taking out today?"

I returned the smile as I stepped up to the hostess stand. "Actually, I only need to speak with Joel today. Is he available?"

The smile fell from her face. "Let me see if he's free."

While she went to search for Joel in the back, I glanced around the dining room, giving it a more thorough scrutiny than I had on my previous visit.

The place needed some updates. Most of the vinyl booths were beginning to tear and crack, the wallpaper was peeling at the seams, and the lighting was horribly dim. If Joel managed to keep himself in business, he would definitely need to make some improvements before things got any worse.

A few minutes passed before the hostess came back. She wasn't as chipper as she'd been when I first arrived. "Joel will see you now," she said with little inflection.

"Thanks." I gave her a polite nod and headed through the restaurant to the back where his office was located. I thought it was a little rude of him not to come out and greet me, but I wasn't going to split hairs over it. At least he wasn't avoiding me.

The kitchen was exceptionally clean and I attributed that to the lack of the business. The cook seemed bored, and I caught him scrolling through something on his phone. He hardly flinched as I walked by.

Joel was sitting at his desk, staring off into the distance, drumming his fingers on the arm of his chair. When I walked in, he shifted his eyes toward me, but made no other acknowledgment.

I sat in the chair across from his desk, saving my smile for a better use. "I won't be long; I just wanted to ask you one thing."

He sat up in his chair and folded his hands over his waist. "Is it another ridiculous accusation?"

"Are you dating Penny?"

He blurted a laugh. "You're joking, right?"

"Why is that so funny? You've been seen together a lot lately. There's a rumor floating around the Village that the two of you have been quite cozy."

"That damn plaza of yours," he said, shaking his head. "It's worse than a tabloid."

"If you would just answer the question, things would move a lot faster. If you are dating, I don't see why it would be such a big deal to tell me."

He sighed, leaning his head back. "No, we're not dating . . . we're just friends."

I took a moment to consider how I wanted to word my next question. If he wasn't dating Penny, then I would have to move onto the Walter Shen angle as I'd considered earlier. I would have preferred that Joel told me he was in fact dating Penny. Any other explanation for why he was hanging around the plaza would be better than the alternative.

"You came all this way to ask me that? You could have asked Penny that. Or is she sick of your ridiculous nonsense too?"

"No . . ." I grumbled. "There is something else I wanted to ask you about."

"Out with it then."

"Why are you so interested in getting a hold of Walter Shen?"

"Ah . . . so that's the real reason you came here. And tell me exactly, what business is it of yours?"

There truthfully was no reason for it to be. I hadn't thought through that part of it and my mind was drawing a blank. What *was* my purpose for caring?

We stared at each other, and the longer the silence lasted, the worse my brain functioned.

"How about being honest with yourself on why you're really here?" He checked his watch. "I have things to do."

I wiped my palms on my pant legs. "Okay, fine. I thought it was awfully suspicious that you were talking with Jackie the other night, so I asked her about it. At first, I thought you were hitting on her. Then she told me that you wanted to speak with her father . . . and it struck me as odd, considering you and Walter Shen have never been friends. He's disrespected you just as much as Norman has. With current circumstances, I have to wonder if—"

"You're not going to let this whole thing drop, are you?" he asked.

Mild relief washed over me. I was glad he didn't let me say the actual words. "No."

He took a deep breath and ran a hand through his hair. "If I tell you something, can you try and keep it to yourself for the time being?"

"Depends on what it is."

"Then no deal." He folded his arms across his chest. "If you can't keep your mouth shut—"

"All right, fine," I said. If he had something worth hearing, I needed to know what it was.

"I have your word?"

"Yes. I'll pinkie-swear if you want me to."

He groaned. "Not necessary. Just remember that you promised to keep this between us."

"Okay." I wanted to tell him to quit stalling, but if I rushed him, he would probably back down on me.

"The reason why I have been trying to contact Walter is because I wanted to enlist his help in getting my restaurant back in shape. He's a very experienced man, and if there's anyone that can help me put my business back together, it's him."

"Why would he help you?"

"Publicity. I pitched an idea to him about notifying the media that a long-standing local restaurant owner was helping one of the little guys. We could do a whole segment on it in local papers and it would give both of us more business."

"And he accepted the idea?"

"Originally he did, but since then I've tried calling him several times and he refuses to return any of my calls. I don't know what scared him away."

"That's the big secret you're telling me?"

"No, the big secret is that Stella Chung, Penny, and I all go way back. Farther back than anyone realizes."

Pretending that I was learning this for the first time, I widened my eyes. "How far back?"

"Back to culinary-school days."

"And you decided to keep this a secret because of the contest?"

"Not really." He sat back in his chair, focusing his eyes on the wall behind my head. He refused to make eye contact with me, and I wasn't sure if it was because it was a hard story to tell, or he was lying to me. "We had a falling-out, and haven't seen each other since school. Of course I've seen Penny around town since she moved back, but we've never confronted each other. This contest was the first time we've all been in the same place at the same time."

"You and Penny seem pretty friendly now."

His eyes flitted toward me momentarily. "Outward appearances can be deceiving."

"Okay, so what happened that split the three of you up so much you pretend not to know each other?" I thought about Megan's love-triangle theory. If she was right, I would never hear the end of it.

"The three of us, we were best friends. The best there

could be. We met on the first day of culinary school, bonded, and immediately became inseparable."

"If you were such great friends, what horrible thing could have happened to make you separable?"

"Stella." He smirked. "She was always a little bit on the outside, keeping one foot partially outside the group. Because of her family situation, I think she always thought she had something to prove, that she needed to work harder than the rest of us. And she always did. Penny and I would go out partying on the weekends, and Stella would stay behind and practice cooking techniques and recipes. While Penny and I grew closer, Stella kept us at arm's length. I still considered her one of my best friends, but there was always something she was holding back."

"So, she was a real go-getter . . . what was the problem?"

"You're not a very patient person, are you?"

"I wouldn't say it's my strong suit."

Joel laughed, and it was the first genuine expression he'd shown during my encounters with him. "A girl that's honest . . . I like it."

I gave him a small smile of appreciation. "Please . . . continue."

"Right . . . well, there was a job opportunity coming up, a cook-off of sorts was planned with a fine dining restaurant located in Chicago. They were going to give us a chance to work in their kitchen for a summer, and if we did well we could keep the job. All we had to do was create an original recipe to their specifications that really wowed them."

"How many job openings were they offering at this restaurant?"

"One."

"Tough competition."

"Exactly, and three friends all gunning for the same job? I'm sure I don't have to tell you how ugly that could get."

"I'm guessing Stella got the job, considering her last place of employment."

"You would be correct."

"But I don't understand the problem. Okay, so Stella got the job, what's the big deal? Even though you're competing against each other, as friends you should be happy for her, right?"

"It's not the fact that Stella got the job . . . it's *how* she got the job . . ."

CHAPTER 25

I was on the edge of my seat—both literally and figuratively. "How did she get the job?" Right away my mind went to sleeping with a teacher or bribing one of the chefs . . . or maybe even sleeping with the restaurant owner that was offering the position. I had been watching too many movies and reading too many books.

"Stella is a great chef, don't get me wrong, but there was one thing she lacked . . . and that was creativity. She could never come up with a solid recipe of her own. They were good, but they weren't great.

"And she wasn't one to lose a competition. So, her solution became stealing someone else's recipe . . ."

He let that hang there for a minute, and my mind continued to dance in circles, coming up with possible scenarios of the different ways this story could go. But, since Penny seemed to hate Stella so much, I knew there was only one logical explanation. "She stole Penny's recipe."

The confidence in my voice surprised me but the minute I said it, I knew I was right.

"And that, as they say, is that," Joel said. "Each of us who applied for the position took turns having our recipes sampled by the restaurant owner and a few teachers. Stella was scheduled before Penny and me. Penny had no idea what was even happening until the chef and the teachers accused her of stealing her recipe from Stella."

"Why didn't they believe that the recipe was hers and not Stella's?"

"I guess when Stella presented her recipe she told the restaurant owners that it was a re-creation of a long-standing recipe in her family. Stella had always been a good storyteller, so I'm sure the performance she gave them was quite impressive.

"Penny, on the other hand, was missing proof that the recipe belonged to her. She wasn't the most careful person and was a bit on the old-fashioned side when it came to certain things. She preferred to handwrite all of her recipes on index cards, and keep them on her desk. Anyone could have access to them. She never thought once to hide anything or back up her recipes on a computer. At least if she had done that, there could have been a way to claim ownership of the recipe. But she trusted Stella wholeheartedly and so did I.

"By this stage of our friendship, we were all sharing a tiny apartment. One night while Penny and I were out having dinner, Stella went to her room, and stole the recipe card from her box. She rewrote it in her own handwriting, and there was nothing to prove that Penny came up with it on her own."

"Wow." I sat back in my seat, shaking my head. "Talk about shady. How could you do that to your own friend?"

"After that, things weren't the same and got ugly really fast. We moved out of the apartment a week later and went our separate ways."

"How did this affect you?" I asked. "I feel like you got caught in the middle of this."

"I did. Both of them were mad at me for not hating the other more. Stella didn't want to admit what she did and tried to convince me that I should be mad at Penny. She kept up the whole story about how that recipe really came from her family. But I knew Penny, and I knew Penny would never steal anything from anybody. She was too honest.

"Meanwhile, Penny wanted me to completely cut off Stella. I knew that I probably should have, but truth be told, I felt sorry for her. She was a very lost young girl and didn't have many friends to begin with. Of course, it doesn't excuse what she did, but nevertheless, I felt bad for her. If she ended up with no one as a friend, I didn't know what direction in life she would end up taking. Years later, I see there was nothing to worry about. She did just fine on her own in Chicago. I don't know what types of personal relationships she was involved in while living there, but it was clearly her career that mattered most."

Now that Joel had come clean about the situation, I was wondering how much of this story was true and how much more I could press him for. He didn't seem to have a loyalty to anybody in particular. "Do you think that Penny . . . ?" I couldn't make myself finish the sentence.

He sighed. "I know what you're going to say because

I've considered that too. I don't know what to think anymore, to tell you the truth. After everything that happened with Norman, I was so sure that Ray was somehow involved in this whole thing. Stella even thought so."

"She told you that?"

"Yes, that's why she was here the other night. We both thought Ray was up to something. Stella said she had some kind of proof, but she wouldn't tell me what it was. She thought maybe Penny knew more than she was letting on and tried to convince her to give up any info she might have. If something was caught on her tapes in the lounge, Stella wanted to use that as evidence."

"Penny told me that the cameras aren't actually functioning. They're only for show."

He nodded. "Yeah, that's what she told us too, and I believed her at first . . ."

"At first? What made you change your mind?"

"Stella being murdered."

"You think she's hiding something and Stella found out what it was?"

"Maybe. Either way, Penny got awful weird when Stella and I started asking her questions. I decided to let it go, but Stella couldn't drop it."

"And now . . . what's going on now? Like I said earlier, the whole plaza is talking about how they see you guys together a lot."

"She needs a friend, and I'm trying to win her trust back. And, to be truthful with you, I'm trying to figure her out. If she comes clean with me then maybe I can convince her to turn herself in. What happened between her and Stella has been weighing on her since school. She tried running away from it and starting a new life in Florida, but obviously that didn't work. Then she comes back here, and she has to see Stella all over again when things seem to be going so well for her. I'd hate to think of what she'd be capable of if she thought Stella was trying to compromise that."

I thought Joel trying to get Penny to admit to any wrongdoing was a pretty risky idea, especially if he believed there was a chance she might have done it. But I decided to keep that to myself since that would be the pot calling the kettle black. "I should go," I said, checking the time on my phone. "I appreciate you telling me all of this. It really explains a lot of what's been going on. If anything else develops, would you mind letting me know?"

He stood up at the same time I did. "Sure. If you think it will help Penny in some way. I don't know if she actually needs the help or I'm looking at this the wrong way. Regardless, I want to be there for her until this whole thing is resolved. I'll sleep a lot better knowing that she's innocent."

"You and me both." I turned back around as I opened the door. A cool breeze came through, and I realized how warm I'd become sitting in his office. I took a deep breath. "If you happen to get any weird fortune cookies, make sure to contact Detective Trudeau right away."

"Weird fortune cookies? What does that mean?"

"It means your number is almost up."

I drove back to Asia Village in a daze, Wilkins a few cars behind me. Either he thought there was something strange about me going to Joel's restaurant, or he figured it was just a normal part of my day. Whatever he thought, I hoped he didn't mention it to Adam.

After our discussion, I knew that Adam wanted me to relay these things to him, but the angle that I was digging into didn't feel solid enough for me to report just yet. Once I put together a few more pieces, I would let him in on what I was up to. Besides, there was no reason to worry him unnecessarily.

The conversation I'd had with Joel was not something that I'd expected and I didn't know what to do with myself. I also wasn't sure if I could entirely trust his story. He could be trying to set me up so I wouldn't look into him anymore. But with all the details he'd given, I figured parts of it had to be true, at least.

True or not, everything with Penny did seem to line up. I also found it suspicious that she had conveniently left out all the details of her life before moving to Florida. She had never come right out and said that she'd lived in Florida her whole life, but by the way she talked about it, you kind of got that impression. There was definitely no mention of her ever having lived in any part of Ohio.

When I got back to the restaurant, business was still slow, and I hid out in my office trying to get some work done. But it felt impossible considering all I could really focus on was what I should do with the information I'd obtained.

There were still too many loose ends to tie up, and I needed to be sure that Penny was who Adam should be looking at. Even though Joel's story confirmed a solid reason why Penny would want to go after Stella, it still didn't explain the Norman Pan angle.

This led me back through the list of potential suspects and the only person I hadn't really given much thought to. Walter Shen. Over the past handful of days as I'd pondered the possible motives and suspects, I hadn't felt too strongly about him being the killer. I didn't see him taking the time to plant menacing fortune-cookie messages on the people he intended to kill. But I had to be one hundred percent positive that I could cross him off my suspect list.

I didn't want to go back to his restaurant alone. He gave me the creeps because, guilty or not, he reminded me too much of Mr. An. And I had a feeling that the direct approach wasn't going to work on him like it had with Joel.

Sending Megan a quick text, I asked if she was free for dinner later that night. When she responded that she was, I told her that we had a mission to carry out . . . dinner at the House of Shen.

CHAPTER 26

We pulled up in front of the House of Shen a little after seven thirty P.M. The dinner rush was wrapping up, and we were able to find parking without a problem. I took a couple of deep breaths before opening the car door.

Megan observed me from the passenger's seat. "Are you going to hyperventilate or what?"

"I hate coming here. I hate Walter Shen . . . I hate his daughter . . . I hate their stupid restaurant."

"Are you sure you want to do this? I can always come back with Nikki or something?"

"No, it's okay. We're already here and I just have to suck it up."

"That's my girl," Megan said with a wink. "Now let's eat, I'm starving."

The restaurant was what I like to deem "comfortably busy." There were just enough people there to assure you that it was a good restaurant, but it wasn't packed.

When Jackie realized that it was us, the ready-made smile on her face dropped. "*Now* what do you want?"

"We want to eat dinner. Is that okay with you?" I glanced around the dining area. "You are still open, aren't you?"

Jackie huffed. "I suppose. You probably need to eat some decent food anyway." She pulled out two menus from beneath the counter and turned to lead us into the dining area.

The booth she took us to was right outside of the restrooms. "Your server will be right over," she said with a smirk.

I gave her a good nostril flare before sliding into the booth. "Of course . . ."

Megan plopped down across from me. "Ignore it. Besides, we're closer to the back . . . maybe we'll catch something in action."

"Like what?" I grumbled, picking up my menu. The menus they had were nicer than what we had at our restaurant. The covers were black with the name of the restaurant engraved in red. The pages inside were made of a thin rice paper, with ornate writing both in English and Chinese characters. "We need menus like these. I hate to admit it, but these are way classier than what we have."

Megan picked up her menu and inspected the design. "It does give it a sort of fine-dining feel. Maybe now that you're running things, your mom will let you pick new menus."

"Doubtful. I can't imagine how much it would cost to have something like this printed." I scanned the soups, feeling myself get agitated over nothing in particular.

"So what's the plan exactly?" Megan looked over her shoulder at the kitchen doors.

"I'm not really sure. We have to eliminate him somehow. I can't even think of a legitimate reason to talk with him. I have no business here."

"It's too bad you don't have some official contest news to discuss with him. That would at least be a way to get him talking."

"We could make up a story of some kind . . . say it's for the contest. It's not like he'd know the difference. He doesn't seem to be a huge fan of Ian, so I don't see him going out of his way to discuss it with him."

We sat for a few minutes, reviewing the menu, and plotting what kind of excuse we could drum up to get Walter talking to us. I was really kicking myself for not thinking this through before we got to the restaurant. I hated to waste a trip.

But, the truth was, I was getting impatient with this whole thing and I was grasping at straws. My investigation was going in circles, and I didn't feel closer to figuring anything out than I had before.

One thing I did know was that most likely Penny was guilty of something. I just didn't want to believe it. I thought about all the times that I had sat across from her at the bar in the Bamboo Lounge and it made me cringe. Had I been hanging out with a killer this entire time?

The server came and took our drink order and asked if we wanted appetizers. Both Megan and I ordered tea and hot and sour soup.

"You know what I've been wondering," Megan said after our tea arrived. "Would all of this still have happened if the contest didn't exist? We still don't know if this is contest related or not. If someone was after both Stella and Norman, they got pretty lucky, wouldn't you say? I mean, she doesn't even live here. So, would that person have gone to Chicago and killed her there at some point? Do killers do that sort of thing?"

"I don't know. This could have just been a good opportunity that presented itself. Stella has ties to this community, maybe the killer was just biding their time until she came back?"

The server returned and we placed the rest of our order. Megan ordered kung pao chicken, and I ordered my usual Mongolian beef dish with white rice.

When the soup came, I did my usual critique. The brown base was a nice, thick texture, and there was a decent ratio of tofu to bamboo to mushrooms. All in all, it was a decent soup. Was it better than Peter's? Never.

Megan slurped her soup. "Have you come up with any ideas on what we're going to say to Walter yet?"

"No . . . I just keep thinking about how this is a waste of time, and whether I like it or not, Penny is probably the guilty one."

"I'm on board with that, but can you really believe this Joel guy though? I mean, seems pretty convenient that he's telling you all of this now. He could be the one pulling the strings and trying to pin it on her because he knows that she has a motive the police would find very interesting."

"But why wouldn't he have taken that information to the police already? He could have easily thrown the spotlight on her. Besides, I kinda believe him."

"Why though?"

"Because when I told him about the fortune-cookie thing, he appeared genuinely surprised. He was totally clueless as to what I was talking about."

"Maybe he's a good actor. He could have been faking it. You fake being surprised all the time."

"I was looking him right in the eye though. He didn't flinch or pause or anything." I sighed. "I don't know. Either way, she's at the top of the list."

"Where is Trudeau with the whole thing? Has he said anything useful to you about it?"

"Not really. The original murder weapon used on Norman hasn't turned up, there were no prints found in Stella's room, and he can't seem to find any actual concrete evidence. The only thing he has going for him are those stupid fortunes."

"Did he find any fingerprints on the wrapper or the cookie paper?" Megan asked.

"So far, nothing. This person was meticulous about covering their tracks, which makes me think they've had a long time to think about this."

The server returned with our food. As she was bringing the food out, Walter Shen came out of the kitchen carrying an oversized tray above his head. He took careful steps as he made his way into the dining area.

"Dad!" Jackie yelled from across the restaurant. "Don't do that!" She ran over to meet her father, and took the tray from his hands. "What did I tell you about lifting this stuff? It's too heavy and you're going to hurt yourself."

"Bagh!" Walter swatted at her arm. "You worry too much."

Jackie scoffed and strutted away with the tray.

Megan turned to me. "What the heck was that all about?"

As the server set our food on the table, she said, "Mr. Shen has a shoulder injury and he's not supposed to be lifting anything heavy."

"How long has he had problems with it?" I asked.

"Maybe ten or so years. But you know how some men can be . . ." She gave us a wink. "Stubborn as all get out."

We thanked her for the food, and stared at each other after she left.

"Well," Megan said, waving her chopsticks at me. "That solves that. If he can barely lift a tray on his own, there's no way he'd have the strength to strangle anyone, especially someone the size of Norman Pan. At least we eliminated one person."

The part of me that wanted to narrow things down was relieved. But the part of me that wanted to stay in denial about Penny was not.

When we got home that night, I sat down with my notebook and logged in everything that I had learned throughout the day. I drew a line through Walter's name and added a note about his shoulder injury.

Ray and Penny sat at the top of my suspect list. The two of them had something in common: both of them only benefited from one of the parties being dead. If Joel's accusations from the previous year were true, Ray would benefit from not having Norman Pan around anymore. With him gone, no one would ever be able to prove that Ray fixed the contest by bribing one of the judges. But there was nothing for him to gain by having Stella out of the picture. They had no associations, and Stella did mention to me that she'd never met him in person prior to the contest. Unless there was a missing piece we weren't aware of and Stella or Ray had been lying.

The same scenario went for Penny. Norman wasn't anyone for Penny to be concerned about, but if she was the murderer, she did have a good reason to get rid of Stella . . . revenge.

I wanted to cross Joel's name out indefinitely. But I was still holding on to what Megan suggested about Joel potentially being involved. He did have information about Penny that he could use to his benefit. It didn't completely track since he could go to the cops with it, but with him being an unreliable source in the eyes of the police department because of his own feelings toward Norman, he might not want to seem like he was trying to take the attention off himself. Usually people who blamed others tended to look more on the guilty side.

Another big question lay with the act of murder itself. Did Penny have what it took to go through with it? Not just mentally, but physically. Overpowering Stella would have been no problem, as she was a petite woman and Penny could most likely take her out. But a man of Norman's size would be a little more difficult.

However, both parties were drinking prior to their deaths and Norman had had a considerable amount. I pondered that thought and wondered if there was any significance to it. Just in case, I wrote that down too.

With Walter Shen technically eliminated, I thought I would feel better, but I didn't. There were parts of me that worried he could have orchestrated the whole thing and convinced someone else like Joel to carry out the task.

Maybe the goal was for me to suspect Penny so that I would turn the focus on her and not on them. Everyone involved knew I was dating Adam. What if they wanted him to be persuaded to investigate a certain angle? They might think that could be accomplished through his nosy girlfriend.

Joke was on them though. If they knew anything about him at all, they would know he never listened to my theories anyhow. He was the professional, and I was just a gal with an overactive imagination and a ratty notebook.

CHAPTER 27

Sleep did not come easily. I tossed and turned thinking about the various possibilities concerning the murders. Kikko was not happy with me and she left to go sleep in her doggy bed during the middle of the night. I fell asleep just as it was turning light out, and the alarm went off all too soon.

Stumbling around, I prepped my coffee and got ready for work, not feeling too much like being social. I thought about calling in sick, but my mother would throw a fit and probably come check on me only to find out that I was perfectly fine.

After giving myself a pep talk with little result, I decided I would go in to work for the shortest time possible. Once Nancy arrived at eleven, I could bail and attempt to do something useful on the case. I kept my fingers crossed that business would be slow.

On my way into work, Adam called my cell phone.

"Seems your theory about Ray Jin fell through," he said when I answered.

"What do you mean?" I stopped at a light and watched intersecting traffic pass by.

"Ray called the station last night and said he also received a fortune cookie. He's flipping out saying that someone is coming after him."

"What did the fortune say?" I asked.

"I can't remember word for word, but it had something to do with the enemy hiding in plain sight."

A tingle ran down my spine. "Where is he now?"

"He just left the station. He came in this morning to make an official statement. We had cruisers driving by his place last night, but there was no activity. Have you seen anything unusual?"

"No." The light turned green and I proceeded down Lorain paying more attention to the road than to the call, which was hard considering Adam was now telling me that Ray had also received a fortune cookie. There were two of us with targets on our backs. "Everything has been normal. No weird cars . . . except your guy, of course."

"Wilkins is a good guy," Adam said. "He's a good friend of mine who owed me a favor. And don't wave at him anymore. The whole point is not to let anyone know that you're being followed."

"I know . . . I thought about that after the fact." I sighed. "So, what now?"

"Nothing, you let me deal with that. The fact that there are two fortunes out there means that the killer is getting anxious. They're going to slip up, and when they do, I'm going to be waiting."

"You sound like a movie script," I said playfully.

"Lana . . . this isn't funny. I need you to take this seriously. I don't know who this person is and they can sneak up on us at any time."

"I *am* taking this seriously. I'm the one who's in danger, remember? Just trying to add some levity to the situation."

"Add levity to the situation all you want, but I want you to stay away from anyone involved with the contest until I get this squared away."

"I promise I won't do anything stupid," I told him. "Don't forget about me being capable."

He grumbled, warning me to be careful, and told me he needed to get back to work.

I must have been extremely distracted the rest of the way to work because without realizing it, I'd arrived at the Village parking lot. I sat in my car staring at the entrance. If I had a fortune cookie, and Ray had a fortune cookie . . . then that meant Penny was the last woman standing.

"It just doesn't feel right," I said to Megan. I was hiding out in my office and decided to give her a call once I'd prepped the dining area. I only had about fifteen minutes before I needed to open the doors. I could hear Peter banging around in the kitchen through the wall and it was grating on my already tense nerves. "It can't be Penny. It has to be a mistake. How could she do all of this?"

Megan, who was groggy and had been disturbed from sleep by yours truly, mumbled into the phone. "I know you don't want to believe it, but we're running out of other people to blame. Her name keeps coming up, and she has a pretty good motive for wanting to kill Stella."

"But now me and Ray too? It doesn't make any sense. I'm going to see Ray later this afternoon. I have to talk to him about that fortune."

"Do you want me to come with you? I could call in sick."

"No, you better go to work today. You've been taking a lot of nights off and switching shifts for me lately. Plus, he might be more willing to talk if it's just me and him."

"Okay, well, call me when you're finished there. Or better yet, stop by the Zodiac for a drink. I'm sure you can use one after all this chaos."

"Well, if I do stop by, I won't be alone. Officer Wilkins will be there too . . . in the parking lot, of course."

"Oh, right . . . that guy is still following you around, huh?"

"Yup, Adam said he'll be around for as long as he needs to be."

"Well, maybe he can have a drink with us. He's gotta be tired of sitting in that car."

My time was up and I said good-bye, promising her that I would check in later. I opened the doors and the Mahjong Matrons hustled inside, peppy and ready to start their day. I was hopeful their cheery dispositions would rub off on me, but that ache in my gut would not go away.

Normally when I'm anxious to get things under way, time seems to drag, and I spend more time checking the clock than actually being productive. However, that was not the case on that particular morning.

The restaurant was busier than normal, and I sped around the dining room trying to keep up with orders and cashing people out. Food and supply deliveries came in succession and on other days they went pretty smoothly. But the vegetable guy lost control of his stack of boxes and red peppers, shitake mushrooms, and heads of cabbage went all over the kitchen and that in turn slowed Peter down, causing him to burn a few orders that needed to be remade.

I was ready to rip my hair out by the time Nancy arrived. And with lunchtime right around the corner, business did not let up. Nancy and I buzzed our way around the dining area trying to keep the flow of people in check.

Finally when the lunch rush died down, I slipped into the office and hurriedly prepped a bank deposit. I swung by Nancy's table to let her know I was on my way out. She was in the middle of taking an order for a young couple who'd just been seated.

Out of the corner of my eye, I noticed someone standing at the front. I decided to seat them before I left, so they didn't have to wait. When I got closer to the front, I realized that it was Penny standing at the hostess station.

I stopped mid-stride. What was she doing here? I thought about my call with Adam that morning. He'd said he thought the guilty party was starting to get anxious. Was Penny coming to get me?

"Lana," Penny said, when she noticed I was staring at her.

"Hi . . ."

She took a step closer to the podium. "Would you mind if we talked?"

"Right now?" My hand clenched the deposit bag.

She nodded. "It won't take long . . . what I have to say . . ."

"Uh, sure. Did you want to talk in the back room?"

"Actually, I was thinking we'd talk at the lounge. Maybe have a drink?"

My hand was shaking and the zipper on the deposit bag rattled.

Penny looked down at my hand. "You okay? Too much coffee this morning?"

A nervous laugh escaped. "Yeah . . . you know me and my coffee."

We stared at each other.

If I didn't go with her, she would know that I knew. Did it really matter at this point? Then again, what if she wasn't guilty and she was going to tell me something that would break the case? She hadn't exactly been forthcoming in recent weeks, so the chances of that happening were slim.

How badly did I want to know what she needed to say? Adam's warning about staying away from everyone involved with the contest ran through my head. I knew he was right, but I also knew that whatever Penny planned on telling me wasn't going to be something she told the police.

In the end, my curiosity won. "Nancy," I yelled. "I have to run over to the lounge with Penny. If you need me, that's where I'll be . . . just come get me." I gave Nancy a pointed look, but of course, she had no idea why.

Sitting inside the empty establishment felt completely different now that I viewed Penny in a negative light. I realized how there was no direct line of sight to the entrance and the feeling of isolation was unbearable.

Penny shuffled around behind the bar, grabbing pieces of strawberry, raspberry, and blueberry from a plastic container. She dumped them into a blender on the counter and added some ice. "I found a new cook," she said as she opened a cooler and pulled out a carton of orange juice. "He's going to start next week."

"Well, hey, things are looking up!" I said this with a little too much enthusiasm and it clearly sounded fake.

She stopped what she was doing and turned to face me. "Are you feeling okay? You really drank that much coffee?"

I chuckled. "It's been a long morning."

She gave a dismissive shrug and continued with her drink concoction. She turned on the blender and the crunching sound of ice filled the bar. When she was done, she poured the mixture into two tall glasses. "Try this . . . I just found the recipe online." She dropped a maraschino cherry on top and slid the glass across the counter.

I took a sniff and smelled the sweetness of the fruit mixed with vodka. "What is this?"

"A Blushing Dragon. I think I'm going to add it to the menu after I tinker with it for a bit."

It felt obvious that I was waiting for her to take a sip first. Did I really think she was going to poison me? Possibly. It wouldn't be the first time that someone tried.

She sipped her drink and I let go of a breath I didn't realize I was holding. "So," she said, leaning against the bar. "I don't want to keep you long; I know you have things to do. But I didn't want to wait to talk to you anymore. Our argument has been eating away at me."

Instead of responding, I tasted my drink. Not bad.

"I want to apologize for my behavior. I know that I've been acting strange lately, and I need to explain."

"Okay . . ." I twirled my straw in the glass, my heartbeat quickening.

"Stella and I . . . we have a long history together . . ." she started, choosing her words carefully. "We used to be best friends even."

I wanted to stop her there because I already knew this story. Of course she didn't know that, and I needed to see if she would tell me the same story that Joel told me. If their stories matched up, maybe I could trust her. Maybe.

She went through the same details that Joel had, almost a little too closely. And, as she talked about their time in school and the contest, I started to wonder if it sounded a bit rehearsed. But then she added something I wasn't expecting.

"After Norman died, she came to me and told me she thought she knew who did it, but was afraid to say anything until she was one hundred percent sure. She kept asking me for video footage of the night of the party because she wanted to double-check something. But when I told her that the cameras don't actually work, she flipped out on me. She kept hounding me and told me she was running out of time."

"She actually said those words?" I asked.

"Yes. She told me that she needed solid proof to take to Detective Trudeau. Apparently she was worried that what she had on her own wasn't enough to convince anyone of anything. She said she needed to be careful and needed something that would prove the person was guilty without a shadow of a doubt."

"Did she tell you what she knew?"

Penny took another sip of her drink. "Not in detail. She mentioned something about an argument she overheard. But she didn't tell me anything more than that. She was afraid of someone, that much I know."

"Did she happen to tell Joel any of this?"

"Joel? Why would you bring him up?"

"Because . . ."

"Have you talked to him?"

My cheeks flushed. "Maybe just a little."

She huffed. "I suppose you didn't have a choice. I know how you are . . . always trying to solve things happening around here. I just wish you wouldn't have."

"Why not?"

"Because that's the main reason why I asked you here. I think it's Joel . . . I think he's been playing me this entire time. I think he could be the killer."

CHAPTER 28

The expression on Penny's face contorted after she'd said the words out loud. I could tell that it pained her to think that a friend could be capable of something so horrid. Even if that friendship had been lost over the years, it was still someone she'd spent significant time with and thought she knew.

While she attempted to collect herself, I considered the possibilities of what she was telling me. Focusing on the bottles of alcohol that were on the shelves behind her, I tried to let thoughts come as naturally as possible. The bottles were lined up neatly in three rows and a neon light from underneath the glass bottom illuminated the bottles in bright blue. Vodkas were grouped together, then rums, then whiskeys. Whiskey . . .

Penny broke my concentration. "I would never hurt anyone, Lana . . . no matter what they did to me. If anything, I wanted my success to shine through. That was my way to get back at Stella . . . to become better than her.

In the meantime, I've been trying to keep an eye on Joel since Stella was killed, just to see if I could catch him in a slip-up, but so far nothing. I'm concerned about his behavior."

"I think you're just as crazy as I am," I said. "Spending time with people you think could be guilty of murder."

Her eyes narrowed. "What do you mean by that?"

"Oh! No." I waved my hands at her. "Not you. I wasn't talking about you. I meant when I was digging into what happened with the others."

"Ah," she said with an understanding nod. "Well, you know what they say about keeping enemies close and all." She paused. "You know, so far no one has bothered to ask me, including your boyfriend, but I do have an alibi for that night."

"You do?"

"I didn't want to say anything because it's still a little early, but I've been seeing someone. We were on a date that night, and I'm sure he'd have no problem verifying that."

I was surprised to hear it, and under normal circumstances, I would have questioned her more on this potential beau. However, I needed to stay focused on the task at hand. "I have to ask . . . did Stella say anything to you about a fortune?"

"A fortune?" Penny asked. "What kind of fortune?"

I noted the genuine confusion on her face and sighed with relief. Alibis were great and all, but they weren't too helpful until they could be verified. "A fortune-cookie fortune."

"No, she never mentioned anything like that."

"And you've never gotten one yourself, have you?"

She shook her head. "No . . . what is this about? What does any of this have to do with fortune cookies?"

I explained the fortune-cookie situation to her and said that both Norman and Stella received a cookie before their murders. I left out the part where I had gotten one too.

"Something about that rings a bell, but I can't think of why."

"I asked Mr. Zhang about it, and he said Sun Tzu's *The Art of War* is referenced a lot in the business world. You've probably heard it in passing."

"Ooh, no." She snapped her fingers. "I know! Norman used a lot of Sun Tzu quotes when he was writing articles for some culinary magazine."

"He did?"

"Yeah, other people in the food industry have told me he went through this whole phase of quoting Sun Tzu in almost all of his articles and he would sometimes use them in his reviews. I guess he stopped doing it a few years ago, but I'm sure you could still get your hands on some. I bet they're online."

I took a sip of my Blushing Dragon and considered what this could mean to the case. Clearly, someone had been trying to pass along a message to Norman before they killed him. But what was the purpose of giving me, Stella, and Ray a fortune as well? There was no apparent significance for us.

After I finished my drink, Penny and I spent a few minutes catching up before I had to get going. I left the Bamboo Lounge feeling a weight lift off my shoulders. It seemed safe to assume that Penny Cho was off my list.

* * *

I drove to the bank and noticed Officer Wilkins cruising a few car lengths behind me. He followed me to the bank, waiting in the parking lot, and continued on with me when I returned to the plaza.

If I went to see Ray, I wondered if he would think it was something unusual. When I'd gone to see Joel Liu, he thankfully hadn't seemed suspicious about it. But I was almost certain Adam would have told him about Ray Jin and his fortune cookie of doom by now.

Back in the restaurant, I hibernated in my office, searching the Internet for proof of the Sun Tzu quotes that Penny mentioned during our conversation. Norman had written so many articles and reviews that it felt nearly impossible to find anything that would relate. I wished Megan was here to do the search instead; she was so much better at digging up dirt on the Internet than I was.

Perhaps if I typed in the actual quote that Norman received along with his name, I could find it that way. When the results came up, I blinked a couple of times to make sure I was seeing it right.

I was.

The quote had been used in one of Norman's articles about running a restaurant and the difficulties in owning your own business in the current cultural climate when everyone wanted to be their own boss. He used examples of local entrepreneurs and among the names mentioned were Joel Liu and Ray Jin.

That quote and their names, and the fact that Norman received that specific fortune, could not be a coincidence.

And if Ray also received a fortune, then that left one guilty party. Joel.

I could smack myself for even believing his story. But he'd been so convincing. And he'd kept to the truth, piggybacking off Penny's story the entire time. He was probably using her to see how close she was to figuring things out. When I'd spoken with him, he was very gently trying to steer me in the direction of blaming her.

"Ugh!" I slammed the cover of the laptop down and started to pace the small area behind my desk. Now what?

I decided to do the responsible thing and call Adam right away. With this new evidence, there was no reason not to fill him in as soon as possible.

Adam picked up on the second ring. "Everything all right, babe?"

"Yeah, it's better than all right. Wait . . . why did you ask me that?"

"You hardly ever call me during the day; I assumed something was wrong."

"Oh." I shook my head as if he could see me. "Anyway, I know who the killer is."

There was silence on the other end.

"Did you hear me?" I asked.

"Yes, Lana, I heard you." He sighed. "I thought we both agreed you would stay out of it and let me handle this."

"Well, yeah, but—"

"No, Lana . . . no buts."

"Oh, come on, don't you wanna at least hear who I think it is?"

He groaned into the phone. "Okay, tell me, who do you think it is?"

"It's Joel Liu. I have proof. There's an article with the same quote that was in the fortune that—"

"Let me stop you there. Joel Liu has an alibi for the night of Stella Chung's murder."

"He does?"

"Yeah, he was at the movie theater in Valley View. He has the ticket stub, and we have him on camera."

"But he could have left the movie theater."

"We thought about that, but we see him on the tape again leaving shortly after the movie is over."

"But he could have left and come back. How long was the movie?"

"Lana, it's not possible. The time to get to where he needed to be and back would not have worked out. Look, I'm sorry your theory didn't pan out, but I really have to go. We can talk more later tonight if you want, okay?"

"Okay," I said, pouting.

After I hung up with Adam, I continued to pace. It had to be Joel. It just had to be. I needed to get home, and check my notebook. I was close to something, I could feel it. If scouring over everything again, piece by piece, was what I needed to do than that's what I would do.

On the way home, I called Megan to tell her about the recent developments.

"I still think he was working with someone. We should revisit there being two murderers and them killing one person each," Megan said.

"Who would Joel work with though?" I asked as I pulled into the parking lot of our building.

"Penny."

"No, she's not involved. After talking with her today, I am almost one hundred percent certain she has no part in this whatsoever. Plus she said she was on a date."

"Almost is not good enough, Lana. And besides, she could have lied about the date. Don't believe her wholeheartedly just because you don't want it to be her. We have to stay objective, remember?"

I huffed. "You're right. I'm home. I'll call you back later."

"Just come see me at work. Are you going to sit there all night staring at that notebook? We can go over stuff together later. Two heads are better than one."

"I don't know, I'll think about it."

We said our good-byes, and I rushed inside to let the dog out. When we were back from our short walk, we both sat on the edge of my bed, and I started from the first page of my notes and worked my way through.

There were a couple different angles I could entertain. One was the bribery angle. Stella had mentioned hearing something going on between two people. Was Joel bribing someone? Could it be Ray?

I thought about the rumors that had circulated after last year's contest. All of a sudden, after insisting on his claims of contest tampering, Joel had dropped the whole thing and disappeared into the proverbial shadows. And even with all of his shortcomings regarding the restaurant business, he'd managed to stay afloat. Of course, the rumors continued to exist on their own, but they began to die down as time passed, nothing new came of it, and people got bored.

Maybe Joel was bribing Ray about knowing last year's contest *was* rigged, and Norman found out about it; that would explain Stella overhearing things and getting involved. Being a previous friend of Joel's, she might have tried to convince him not to participate in illegal activities and maybe she thought enlisting another old friend—Penny—would help convince him to do the right thing. But little did she know that Penny was on the wrong side of it. If Penny was working with Joel, that would give Joel an alibi. Penny could have easily gone to Stella's hotel, and later claimed that she'd been on a date. Like she said, no one had even bothered to ask her anything yet . . . because all eyes were focused on Joel.

And a guy like Ray? He would never admit to being blackmailed by someone like Joel Liu. You could see it in the way he looked at him. Ray definitely thought he was superior.

This new theory led me to believe that Penny was involved somehow, after all. Maybe Megan was right. Joel took out Norman . . . and Penny . . . Penny took out Stella. She already had reason to, after everything that happened between them in the past.

I smacked the notebook shut, and the sound scared Kikko who flounced off the bed. I knew what needed to be done. I had to talk to Ray and get him to admit that he was being blackmailed by Joel. My only hope was that Joel was working alone and I was wrong about Penny.

CHAPTER 29

It was close to nine P.M., and Ray would be closing his restaurant soon. I got ready as quickly as possible, throwing on a T-shirt and jeans. Anything that I hadn't worn to work would do. Wilkins was out in the parking lot, and I wanted to give him some type of story about why I was going to Ray's restaurant, but I wasn't supposed to approach his car. There was no real way to communicate with him, and I would just have to wing it. Hopefully he wouldn't choose to follow me into the restaurant this time.

While I drove, I kept an eye on the rearview mirror, and sure enough, he followed behind at least two car lengths away. When I turned into Ray's restaurant parking lot, he did not turn in with me. Instead, he opted for the next parking lot over and it happened to be a bar. Good thinking on his part.

As I got out of the car, I slid an eye in his direction, and he stared back at me without making any type of acknowledgment.

The restaurant was nearly empty and a woman about my age was busy wiping down tables when I walked in.

She turned in my direction when she heard the bells above the door chime. A soft smile spread over her lips, and she sauntered up front, abandoning her cleaning supplies at the table. "Good evening, just one tonight?"

I smiled in return. "Actually, I was hoping to speak with Ray. Does he happen to be here still?"

"Of course, he's always here." She chuckled. "There aren't any problems with a takeout order, are there?"

"No, no, nothing like that. I just really need to talk with him if he's free."

"Sure, I'll go get him."

Next to a booth for waiting customers, there was a fish tank with a couple of exotic fish and I watched them swim around, rehearsing the story I had planned in my head. First, I would tell Ray about the fortune cookie and how I had gotten one too. Then depending on what he said, I would either get straight to the point or I would take the scenic route, and explain all the strange behavior going on with Joel. They weren't friends anyway, so I wouldn't have to worry about Ray being offended or sticking up for him.

A few minutes went by before the woman returned with Ray trailing behind her. He seemed a little surprised to see me, but didn't make any mention of it.

"Miss Lee," he said, giving me a slight nod. "What brings you by?"

I glanced at the woman, who'd returned to her cleaning duties. "Would you mind if we talked in your office?"

His brows crinkled low over his eyes. "What's this about?"

"I think it would be best discussed in private."

He stared at me for a minute, not sure what to make of my request. With resolve, he shrugged and extended a hand toward the door leading to the back room. "After you."

His office was a mess. Stacks of papers, books, and folders were lying on his desk, on top of his filing cabinets, and on the two guest chairs he had on the opposite side of his desk. On top of one of the filing cabinets that was stacked with folders and books sat a half-wilted plant in desperate need of water. The other filing cabinet was topped with various half-empty bottles of liquor.

"Sorry about the mess," he said, shutting the door behind him. "I don't usually have anyone back here besides staff."

I felt sorry for the staff. "No problem."

He shuffled around in the cramped space, and removed a stack of magazines off one of the guest chairs. The top magazine was the latest copy of *Cleveland*. "What's all this about? You seem pretty . . . concerned."

Immediately, I noticed that he wasn't. I would think after getting a menacing fortune cookie like the one I had received, he would at least be a little unnerved. "I wanted to talk to you about the fortune you got the other day."

He raised an eyebrow. "The fortune I got? How do you know about that?"

"Ad— Detective Trudeau told me about it."

"He did, did he?" He smirked. "The perks of dating a cop, I suppose."

"That's not why he told me." I sat down in the seat he'd cleared while he took the stack of magazines over to the other side of the desk, turning his back to me. "I received one as well."

He slowly rose from his bent position, but didn't say anything. "You did . . ."

"Yeah . . . so I wanted to talk to you about it. I think I might have some ideas on what's going on."

Ray's shoulders visibly tensed, and he turned, his eyes meeting mine. "And what exactly do you think is happening?"

My stomach dropped. What if I was wrong about the bribery angle? I would sound completely stupid if Joel wasn't actually bribing Ray. "Well . . . Joel, he's been acting pretty strange, don't you think? He clearly had a problem with Norman Pan. And Stella, she must have seen or heard something that made Joel nervous . . ." Even though she was dead, I felt weird outing her secrets to Ray.

"Interesting theory. I can see how you would come to that conclusion." He moved around the desk, leaning against the edge of it right in front of me. "Have you told your boyfriend this theory of yours yet?"

"Sorta. We don't talk much about his work or any of the cases that are still active. He doesn't like for me to get involved."

"I don't blame him." He folded his arms across his chest. "A young girl like yourself . . . you shouldn't meddle in such horrible things."

"I can handle myself." My chin rose a little. I hated when people told me what I shouldn't do. I tried to ignore it. "He did say that Joel has an alibi for the night that Stella was murdered, but I think he could have easily faked it."

He was staring at me so intently that I had to look away.

My eyes roamed around the office and I noted the decent collection of liquor bottles that he had lined up. Guess someone really liked to let loose during work hours on the regular. I paused, one of the bottles caught my attention. A whiskey bottle to be exact. It was the same brand of whiskey that Adam had been reluctant to tell me was found in Stella's room. And, it was the exact brand that Ray asked for during the meeting at the Bamboo Lounge. Yamazaki was pretty distinct.

He twisted around to follow my line of sight. "See anything up there you like? I could get some glasses if you feel like having a drink."

"No, that's okay," I mumbled. "I drove here, and I should be going soon anyway. I only wanted to stop by and uh, you know, talk about Joel."

"What is it that you need from *me* exactly? Sounds like you have this pretty much under control."

"I, um . . . well," *Think, Lana, think!* "Maybe he threatened you? That whole rumor thing he started last year . . . maybe he's coming after you because he thinks you cheated in the contest."

Ray blinked. "The rumor . . . ah, the rumor . . . yeah, Joel. That guy. He's a piece of work. I think you have every right to assume he's the one behind all of this. I should have thought of it myself."

The expression on his face was so intense, my eyes kept drifting away. I attempted to read some of the book titles off the spines that were showing, but I was having a hard time focusing my vision. The office felt stuffy and the clutter he had lying around was beginning to make me feel claustrophobic.

"Maybe you could get me a glass of water?"

"Sure." He stood up from the edge of the desk, and opened the door letting in a cool breeze. "I'll be right back."

"Ice too," I said.

He smiled. "No problem."

Ray shut the door behind him, and I took a deep breath and slouched in the chair. This was a mistake. He was creeping me out and I had no idea what I was talking about. In my head, I imagined that we would talk about the fortune cookie and then he would add some dialogue. Maybe he would tell me about how it made him so nervous that he was looking over his shoulder ever since he received it, or that he was checking around corners, and hearing things that weren't there. But nothing. He said nothing of the sort. This wasn't going how I planned at all.

I checked my cell phone. I'd only been at the restaurant for about twenty minutes, but it felt like two hours.

My attention shifted back to the stack of magazines and books that were on top of the filing cabinet. I wondered if he'd kept the issue with Norman Pan's Sun Tzu-themed review. I didn't hear anything going on in the kitchen, so I decided to take a quick peek at what magazines were in the pile before he came back.

As fast as possible, I rifled through the magazines, checking the issue dates on each one as I flipped through the pile. The ones I held in my hand were more current issues, none of them appeared to be from the right year.

I started to put the magazines back on the shelf when I noticed one of the books that had been hiding under them. It was a thick hardcover in black with red foil lettering. And the lettering read: *The Art of War.*

My breath caught in my throat. Setting the magazines

down on his desk, I reached for the book, running a hand over the cover feeling the impression of the foiled script.

I always flip the pages of a book, I can't help myself, and that's exactly what I did at that moment. When I fanned the pages, I noticed there were highlighted passages marked in yellow. I stopped on one of the pages and read the highlighted quote.

It read: *If your enemy is superior, evade him.*

With a gasp, I dropped the book, and cringed at the sound it made. It was the same quote that Stella had received in her fortune cookie. Quickly, I picked the book up from the floor and held it to my chest, my eyes sliding to the door. What do I do now? This was evidence. I had actual evidence in my hands.

I heard some rustling around in the kitchen and knew I had to make my move quickly. I set the book down on the desk, picked up the magazines and placed them on top of the filing cabinet where they were. I grabbed the book and tried shoving it into my purse, but the book was too big; I had a small cross-body bag with me instead of the jumbo-sized handbag I carried on a normal day.

Crap.

In a panic, I searched around the office. If I could stash it somewhere and then tell Adam where it was hiding, then maybe he could come back and get it.

But it was too late. The doorknob turned and Ray stepped inside, catching me red-handed with his dirty little secret.

He pursed his lips and shut the door behind him, never taking his eyes off me. "Now what the hell are you doing with *that*?"

CHAPTER 30

If the room wasn't hot before, it was definitely hot now. My shirt was clinging to my body, and my hands felt clammy against the book cover. I shifted my weight from one foot to the other.

Ray held the glass of water, his hand shaking ever so slightly, causing the water to splash over the sides. "I asked you a question, Lana."

I held up the book, trying to keep my own hands steady. "I was thinking maybe I could borrow this? I've been so fascinated with this type of stuff lately. You wouldn't mind, would you?"

"Oh, I would mind. That's my favorite book." He sneered. "So . . . I leave you alone for a few minutes and you go through my things? Is that any way for a guest to act?"

A nervous laugh escaped from my throat.

He was inching closer to me, and I slid my feet

backward, shimmying myself around the corner of his desk. I kept moving until the desk stood between us.

I was shaking. In the past there'd always been someone to save me, there had always been someone there. They might not have arrived until the last minute, but what mattered was that they were there. This time was different. The only person who knew where I was sat in a bar parking lot next door, and by the time he realized something was wrong, it would be too late.

"You really shouldn't have done that, Lana," Ray said in a calm voice. "Now, I can't let you leave here . . ."

"I won't tell anyone," I promised him. "You can have your book back, and I'll just be on my way. Like it never happened."

He laughed. "Oh, Lana . . . I know you. I know your track record. I've read the stories in the *Plain Dealer*. This is your thing, isn't it? You're like one of the Scooby gang . . . only . . ." He paused, looking around the room. "Doesn't seem to me like you have much of a gang."

"I'll scream," I told him. "Your employee will hear me and come to see what's going on." At least that's what I hoped. The walls in Ho-Lee Noodle House weren't all that thick, and I was praying they weren't here either.

"What employee?" Ray set the water glass down on his desk. "I sent her home about five minutes ago."

My eyes darted toward the door. There was no way to get to it with him standing where he was, and now that I knew we were alone in the restaurant, I kind of wished that Wilkins would have followed me in.

"The genius of this whole thing is that no one is ever going to guess it's me." Ray puffed up his chest. "Norman and I were friends . . . and I have no connection to

Stella . . . and you . . . ha, I'll be gone before anyone realizes what happened to you. How far do you think I can make it by nine A.M. tomorrow morning? I should at the very least be able to make it through three states. I've been told I have a lead foot."

"Why then?" I asked, trying to stall. "Why kill your friend? Why kill Stella? Why do any of this?"

"Norman . . . ah, good ole Norman. We weren't always friends, you see." He sat down in the seat he'd originally cleared for me and seemed to relax as he leaned back in the chair. He didn't have a concern in the world. "Norman's friendship came after the money started flowing . . ."

"You *were* bribing him then!"

"I had to. His articles on my restaurant were hurting business. It was common knowledge that he was crooked . . . so I took advantage of that fact and proposed a deal. It was an excellent partnership."

"Well, if it was going so great, then why kill him? Your business turned around, and winning the contest last year helped your image. You had it made."

Ray leaned forward. "Because he got greedy. He wanted too much money . . . an unthinkable amount. He told me that if I didn't pay him, he would out my attempts to pay him off. You call being indebted to someone like that 'having it made'?"

"Wasn't he worried about the backlash?" I asked. "I mean, if he was accepting the bribes, it would come back on him and his credibility. His entire career would be destroyed. Every review he'd ever written would then come into question."

"I can tell you with certainty that Norman wasn't

worried about it. He's paid off a few people himself. As they say, it helps to have friends in high places. On top of that, he was very careful. He only accepted cash payments and covered his tracks very well. He planned to retire on that money . . . *my* money."

I clutched the book tighter to my chest. "But then why kill Stella, what did she have to do with this whole thing? Were you bribing her too?"

"I did try . . . I will tell you that." He laughed. "She wouldn't take my money though. And it's a shame. All I wanted her to do was forget the conversation she overheard. One small task." He shook his head. "And she couldn't even do that."

"So you killed her for overhearing about blackmail?" This tracked with what she had told me, and what others had witnessed without realizing what they were seeing. Stella really had been on to something.

"Not about the blackmail. Unfortunately, she heard me threaten Norman's life. I warned him. I tried to save him . . . but that stubborn old man would not back down.

"Then he winds up dead . . . and she's got her eye on me. I couldn't have that."

"So the fortune-cookie thing . . . I don't get it. Why go to all that trouble?"

"I wanted Norman to know that I was coming for him. That the things he'd written about me were not forgotten. I wasn't planning to continue with it, but I needed to connect the murders so no one would suspect me. Like I said, there is nothing to associate me with Stella other than us being judges on the same contest panel.

"I thought that would be obvious, Lana. Killing Stella was a two-for-one deal. It would take the suspicion off me, and it would connect the murders. I had no reason to kill her . . . at least not one that anyone knew about . . . except Norman, of course. But with him out of the way, there was nothing standing between me and getting the hell outta dodge.

"However, you've put a kink in my plans. I thought giving you that fortune would shut you up. I saw the way you were looking at everyone . . . trying to figure out who was responsible for ruining your precious little contest.

"Then, I decided to play the victim card myself. After I gave my fake fortune to your boyfriend, I planned to leave town on the premise of fear. People dropping like flies . . ." He rubbed his chin. "Although, I suppose you could add to that story . . . sweeten the pot.

"I can see it now," he said, stretching out his arm and imitating a headline banner. "Local detective's girlfriend brutally murdered in the back of a Chinese restaurant."

"In the back of *your* restaurant," I reminded him. "They'll know it's you."

"No . . . because you see, 'I saw the killer, Officer, and Lana stepped in and risked her life to save my own. It was that woman and her boyfriend . . . the Bamboo Lounge owner and the crazy man from the noodle contest.'" He smirked. "It's going to be a great story. And, hey, on the plus side, you'll go down as a hero. It's the least I could do for you."

I shivered. He was insane. The way he talked, this was all a big game to him. I had to get out of here. Maybe if I could reach one of the bottles on top of the filing cabinet, I could bash him over the head with it.

He watched me weigh my options, and he smiled to

himself. “Not so fast, Lana.” In one swift motion, he rose from the chair, and leaped toward me.

I shrieked as his hands wrapped around me and he squeezed me until my bones hurt. I stepped on his foot, and his hold weakened enough for me to shove him with my shoulder. He stumbled backward, a look of annoyance on his face.

As he rushed me again, I took the book I’d been holding on to for dear life, and swung my arms back as far as I could.

He groaned as he lunged at me, and with all my strength, I swung the hardcover book, hitting him in the side of the head.

The force of the hit caused him to fall and smack his rib cage on the desk. He fell to the ground, hitting his head in the process. With one hand holding the side of his head, he tried to stabilize himself.

In the meantime, I stepped over him as fast as I could and whipped open the door. I flew through the restaurant, and as I made it out of the kitchen, I heard him stampeding behind me.

“Get back here, you little b—”

Before he could get the rest of his sentence out, I ran out the front door. I was waving my hands over my head as I headed in the direction of Wilkins’s car, praying that he for once in his life would acknowledge me.

He did.

He got out of the unmarked car, and for the first time since he’d been following me, he spoke. “What the hell is going on?”

Ray exited the restaurant, consumed with rage and trying to capture his escapee.

Wilkins, without hesitation, pulled out his gun, and aimed with the precision that comes from being a professional. "Hands in the air! I. Will. Shoot."

Ray halted and raised his hands in the air.

"Get in the cruiser, Lana," Wilkins barked without removing his eyes from Ray.

I did as I was told, and watched as he inched his way closer to Ray who was slowly starting to kneel to the ground.

Wilkins checked him for weapons, and then pulled out a pair of handcuffs from somewhere in his sports coat. I saw his lips moving and I imagined he was reading Ray his rights. Afterward, he pulled out his cell phone and made a call, which I guessed was for backup.

I took deep breaths, still clutching the book to my chest. I didn't want to let it go. It was the only thing I had at the moment that felt tangible.

Minutes passed before two cruisers showed up. When they had situated Ray in the back of one of the cars, Officer Wilkins came back to the car. He sat down in the driver's seat, and stared out the window. Without looking at me, he said, "Man, Trudeau is going to be so pissed at you."

We'd left my car at Ray's restaurant because I was too shaken to drive. Megan told me she would get it later so I didn't have to go back there. In the meantime, Wilkins took me to the police station so I could make an official statement and they submitted *The Art of War* into evidence.

Megan met me at the station to take me home. Adam

had things he needed to wrap up so he let me know that he would meet us there when he was finished.

I didn't talk on the way home and Megan didn't pry. She knew that I would tell her what happened when I was ready.

While I sat wrapped in a blanket on the couch with Kikko dutifully by my side, Megan ordered an extra-large pizza and a giant bucket of wings. It had become our post-capture tradition.

The pizza guy came and went, and I hadn't moved from my position on the couch since I'd gotten home. Megan had set out plates, shots of whiskey, and napkins. When she was done, she sat on the couch next time in silence. And the three of us stayed like that until there was a knock at the door thirty minutes later.

Megan got the door, and Adam stepped inside appearing larger than life. He stared at me from the threshold, and I stared back, not knowing what to say.

He turned to Megan. "Can you give us a minute?"

"Sure, I'll call Nikki and see if she can take me to Lana's car," she said before disappearing into her room.

After I heard the door to Megan's room shut, I held up a hand to Adam. "I already know what you're going to say. I said I wasn't going to do anything stupid, and I ended up sticking my nose into something I shouldn't have. I didn't realize how close I was . . ." I paused. "I'm sorry."

He walked over to the couch, and sat on the edge, his knees brushing against my leg. "Actually, I'm proud of you."

I straightened. "You are?"

"Yes, you defended yourself. You were in a tough situation, Lana, and you defended yourself. I'm not happy about how you got to that point, but I'm proud to know I have a girlfriend who doesn't give up."

For the first time that night, a tiny smile appeared on my face. "You said the g-word."

He wrapped an arm around my shoulders and pulled me toward him. "Maybe I did."

The tension from my body released, and I let myself relax against his strong frame. I was safe now. The whole thing was behind me, and I could move on. Life could go back to normal.

Adam kissed my forehead. "And, besides, it was kinda cool when the guys at the station were giving me high fives because my girl's got a mean right swing."

EPILOGUE

The following week after things settled down at the Village, Ian got his wish and the noodle contest continued. With Ray out of the picture, Ian needed to request yet another judge, and this time, it was a member of the OCA. They weren't messing around anymore.

We were now back in the bleacher seats, and the contest arena was packed with people awaiting the final results of who would take home the grand prize. As I surveyed the crowd, anxious for the judges to finish their deliberations, my mind wandered over the various things that had taken place since Ray's arrest.

News of the horrible ordeal and its outcome made national news, and Ray was quickly coined the "Fortune Cookie Killer." Details about his life and dirty dealings were in every major newspaper the day after his arrest. The police hadn't found the original murder weapon used on Norman before detaining Ray, but it turned out to be a cell phone charging cord. On the night of the murder, Ray had conveniently dumped it in the toilet tank at the Bamboo Lounge where he was confident no one would look. Adam found it exactly where Ray said it would be, wrapped around the chain that connected to the handle.

Since I'd survived Ray's wrath unscathed, three local papers asked for my personal account. With reluctance and the advisement of my sister, I gave them the full story so there would be no chance of speculation about what really happened. I've never enjoyed being the center of attention, so when the interest started to wane in the public eye because *another* ridiculous thing had happened in the political world, I was more than relieved.

Penny and I were slowly returning to normal, and she and Joel rekindled their lost friendship. He stopped by the plaza every day to visit, and was becoming quite the regular face among the Asia Village family.

Penny's new cook was a natural, even adding a few interesting new appetizer dishes to her menu. To her extreme delight, business was status quo at the Bamboo Lounge once again.

Adam and I were doing better than good, and things finally felt like they were moving in the right direction. Call me an optimist, but I think he was getting used to the idea of me and my Nancy Drew habit. My only wish was that those days of sleuthing were now behind me for good. Being a restaurant manager was plenty to have on my plate. After everything we had been through so far, I imagined that we could withstand more than an ordinary couple.

Speaking of couples, somewhere during the chaos that had been going on around us, Mr. Zhang mustered up the courage to ask out my grandmother. And, when I say "ask out," I mean hang out at the plaza together. It was a small step, but I found them spending a lot of time together at Wild Sage or down at the community center watching the Mahjong Matrons win game after game. They were a cute pair, and I think it somewhat relieved my mother that my grandmother was occupied for a few hours each day.

With my mother's newfound free time, I thought she might try and reclaim her responsibilities at the restaurant. Turned out she was taking this retirement thing seriously, and the restaurant was mine to run indefinitely with no interference from her. I knew she must have pulled a mom trick or two without my realizing that she intended for me to take over the restaurant all along.

Kimmy grabbed my shoulder and gave me a hearty shake. "Hey, pay attention, Lee, I think they're about to announce the winner."

Megan leaned over Adam who was sitting on the opposite side of me, "Yeah, where are you anyway? Back in la-la land?"

I laughed. "Just thinking about how crazy it's been lately. Hard to believe it's all behind us now."

"Yeah, shhhh," Kimmy hissed in my ear. "Donna's walking up to the microphone. This is it!"

Adam pinched my arm and we both laughed.

Donna, in her elegant manner, approached the microphone and flashed a ruby-painted smile at the crowd. "Ladies and gentlemen, it is with great pleasure that I announce the winner of this year's contest . . . finally."

A few people in the crowd chuckled and our little group of Ho-Lee Noodle House staff shared a glance. I turned my attention to Peter who was standing in front of me. He was tapping his foot impatiently, and I could imagine the anticipation was getting the best of him.

For the last entry in the contest, each chef was tasked with making what they considered to be their signature dish, and Peter's was an egg-noodle recipe covered with Taiwanese meat sauce that consisted of ground pork simmered to perfection in seasoned stock. I didn't know anyone who made a better version of it.

Donna slid a finger through the sealed envelope in her hand and pulled out a piece of paper. When she read it, a small smile spread over her lips and she looked up at the crowd with satisfaction. "It gives me great pleasure to announce this year's winner as Peter Huang from Ho-Lee Noodle House! Congratulations to them and his winning dish!"

The crowd erupted in applause. Kimmy jumped up from her seat and attacked Peter in a massive hug. His mother, Nancy, was next to join in the hug, and I think I saw her shed a tear, her face the true vision of pride. We all surrounded Peter, congratulating him on his success as Donna came over with the trophy. It was a golden noodle bowl with a pair of chopsticks resting on the brim. Peter held the bowl in his shaky hands and beamed. Success was his and I couldn't be happier.

Out of the corner of my eye, I noticed that Jackie was approaching our huddled celebration. Her mouth was set in a frown and the flat stare she gave me as we made eye contact spoke of pure dissatisfaction.

Before she could approach Peter, I stepped in front of her, blocking any chance she had of talking to him. I didn't imagine she had anything nice to say and I didn't want his moment ruined.

She folded her arms across her chest, glaring at me. "I came over to say that you got lucky this year. That's it. We'll take that trophy back from you next year. You can mark my words, Lee."

I'd like to say that I was a bigger person, but there was a part of me that reveled in the fact that she was clearly bothered. I remembered a few things she'd said to me in recent weeks and decided to give her a taste of her own medicine. With a large smile, I said, "Well, if you want someone to show you how to make *real* noodles so you stand a chance of winning next year, you know where to find us." I patted her on the shoulder and gave her my best customer-service smile.

I turned my back to her as her jaw dropped.

Kimmy overheard the conversation and promptly gave me a high five. Thankfully, she'd been the only one to notice the exchange, and I returned to our happy little group as if nothing had happened.

After the crowd dispersed, everyone went back to Ho-Lee Noodle House to celebrate our victory and I decided to take a break from the chaos and walk around the Village before rejoining the party.

I took an extra minute to stand in front of the bookstore. I'd barely had any time to make my usual weekly trip and I reviewed the books Cindy placed so lovingly in the window displays.

There in the center of the right window stood a black hardcover book with red foil lettering. *The Art of War* was the spotlighted feature and copies of the book were selling faster than Cindy could shelve them.

It has always fascinated me how books of all styles and genres can have such an impact on a person. A book can shape someone; change their life, inspire or re-create them, entertain them, or influence them.

In Ray's instance, one book completely devastated his life and led him through pain, success, and ultimately his downfall. But it's not just the power of words at work; it's what you as a person choose to do with them. Ray, who'd been so filled with hate and revenge, let everything be consumed by it.

I slipped into the store, and went over to the display, picking up Sun Tzu's classic. As I fanned through the pages, my eyes skimmed over the words that had been created so long ago. I imagine if Sun Tzu were alive today, he never could have imagined his words would be used in such an odd way.

As I stood there staring at the book, I thought about how much change had occurred in a matter of months and how I'd gotten to this point.

Without intending to, I'd become the manager at our family business, started a new relationship, and could finally see brighter days ahead. And though most of what happened wasn't part of my grand scheme, somehow it had all become okay with me. Life is never as you expect it, and things come your way that you hadn't planned. That's just the way it goes and I was no exception to the rule.

I set the book down and grinned. No matter what, in some way, shape, or form, books have always saved my life. And that was okay with me too.

Turn the page
for a look ahead to

Wonton Terror

---

the next Number One Noodle Shop Mystery,
coming soon from Vivien Chien
and St. Martin's Paperbacks!

CHAPTER 1

"The Poconos or Put-In-Bay?" I waved two travel brochures in front of my good friend and restaurant chef, Peter Huang. My boyfriend, Adam, was planning a weekend getaway for my upcoming birthday and he'd left me in charge of location selection. The only problem was that I couldn't make up my mind.

Peter and I, along with many others from the surrounding community, were standing in a parking lot on a blocked off Rockwell Avenue in preparation for the first Asian Night Market of the summer. Rockwell, located in between the two intersecting streets of E. 21st and E. 24th, was barricaded from traffic to host the weekly outdoor event. Every Friday during the summer months, local businesses—some Asian and some not—set up a booth to display their merchandise or food. The event always started at sunset and went until eleven p.m.

And as restaurant manager of the Ho-Lee Noodle House, I, Lana Lee, was tasked with the duty—by my mother—to accompany Peter, to at least seventy-five percent of the events.

Not that I minded in the least. Would I take hanging around outside on beautiful summer nights over being cooped up in our family's restaurant? That would be a yes.

The evening was just beginning and the market wasn't yet opened to the public. Peter was busy prepping our rented grill and workstation. My job was to handle the cash flow and take the orders. He had given me specific instructions not to touch his grill, and without a fight, I complied. Instead, I busied myself with the travel brochures that Adam had passed on to me the other day. When it came to stuff like this, I was never good at making a decision.

"I don't know, man, I've never been to either one before." He leaned over the grill and the black baseball hat that he wore sat low, covering his eyes. "Flip a coin or something. That's what I always do when I can't decide."

I grumbled at the color pamphlets in my hand. "I don't know why he can't pick where we're going. It was his idea to begin with."

Peter chuckled. "If you pick something lame, maybe he'll pick something else."

"Hmmm . . . not a bad idea . . ." I stuffed the brochures back in my purse underneath our workstation counter. As I stood up, a food truck pulled into the parking lot and maneuvered itself carefully near the fence adjacent to our location, next to two other trucks that had arrived earlier.

The truck nearest the stage sold bubble tea in every flavor known to man, and was sure to bring long lines, especially in this heat. The truck now located in the middle spot sold barbecued meat on sticks. Since what they sold was easy to carry while walking around the night market, they could also be counted on to pull in a lot of business.

The vehicle currently parking, Wonton on Wheels, was owned by Sandra and Ronnie Chow—friends of my parents since I could remember. Sandra and Ronnie were always getting into one business venture or another, but they were new to the food service industry.

A little over a year ago, they jumped on the food truck bandwagon and so far it seemed to be going pretty well for them. Even though the married couple had been friends with my parents since I was little, they'd grown apart over the years and we hardly saw them anymore. My mother used to drag me to their house to play with their son, Calvin, who was only a few years older than me. I remembered him being something of a bully. My dad would try to convince me that Calvin teased me because he liked me, but at that age I couldn't have cared less. After all, boys were "yucky."

Sandra, a rail-thin woman with sunken cheek bones and a sharp nose, hopped out of the passenger's seat and inspected her husband's parking job. After she made a loop around the vehicle, she stood near the driver's side window and gave him a thumbs up.

"Good thing we didn't bother bringing any wontons with us," Peter said, watching as the couple worked to set up their truck. "They're totally going to steal the show."

As far as Asian food trucks go, Wonton on Wheels was a genius idea if I ever saw one. They prepared wontons in a variety of ways: on skewers, as salad cups, fried, steamed, and of course, as soup. I had sampled a couple varieties myself . . . you know, for research, and found that I was a fan of their steamed wontons in chili sauce.

Thinking about them made my mouth water. I decided to focus on our station instead. Maybe at some point, I'd get the chance to slip away and grab myself a couple of wontons.

After the register portion of the booth was set up just the way I wanted it, I checked the time and noted there were about ten minutes left before the general public would be allowed through the barricades.

Sandra had wandered off from the food truck and was now standing at a booth diagonal to both of our spots. She was chatting up a woman who appeared to be peddling handmade jewelry. The woman locked eyes on me and waved me over. Sandra turned around to see who the woman was waving at and smiled when she realized it was me.

I smiled in return and waved, letting Peter know that I would be right back.

When I approached the jewelry stand, the woman came around to the front of her table and grabbed both of my hands. She was a petite woman with chubby cheeks that reminded me of my mother. "Waaaa . . . Lana Lee!" She leaned back and gave me a once over, nodding in approval. "You are so grown up now!"

I kept the smile on my face, unsure of what to say. I didn't recognize this woman at all.

"You do not remember me, but I was good friends with your mother when you were a little girl. My name is Ruby."

"I'm sorry, I don't remember. But it's nice to meet you . . . again."

"That's okay." Her eyes darted back to the Ho-Lee Noodle House booth. "Is Anna May here too? I bet she is a beautiful woman now."

"No, she's working at the restaurant tonight."

Anna May is my older sister and she's okay looking as far as I'm concerned.

Ruby pinched my cheek. "Your mother must be so proud of you."

"I hope so . . ."

She stepped aside so Sandra and I could say hello.

"It is so nice to see you, Lana," Sandra extended her hand. "It has been a very long time."

Most of the older generation Asians are opposed to hugging, but I can't help it, I'm a hugger. I blame my dad for that one. So forgetting my manners, I wrapped my arms around Sandra. "Nice to see you, too."

Sandra winced.

I jumped back. "Oh, I'm sorry!"

"It's okay," she replied apologetically. "I hurt my back this week. It is nothing serious."

Ruby tsked. "You hurt your back . . . again?"

The two women exchanged a look that was lost on me.

"So . . ." I said, feeling slightly out of place. "Is this your first time at the night market?"

Both women nodded.

I inspected the table of jewelry Ruby had displayed. "These are gorgeous."

Organized in velvet trays were cloisonné earrings, jade bracelets, rings and necklaces made with opals, mother of pearl, and turquoise. She even had a selection of Chinese hairpins and hair combs.

"Thank you," Ruby admired her table of accessories. "I make everything by hand."

"You should talk to Esther Chin about carrying some

of these in her shop. I bet these would sell like crazy at the Village."

"Perhaps I will talk with her," Ruby replied.

"Speaking of crazy, be prepared for tonight," I warned them. "It gets so jammed with people, they can barely get through. Last year we ran out of food within—"

"Sandy!" A gravelly voice shouted from behind us.

The three of us turned in the direction the voice was coming from and saw Ronnie Chow standing near the back of the food truck. He was short, chubby and sweating like he'd just run a marathon. He waved his arms frantically at his wife. "Get over here now!" Ronnie yelled. "Stop messing around and gossiping. We have work to do!"

"Okay, I'll be right there," Sandra said in a sheepish tone. When she turned to face us, I noticed that her cheeks were pink with embarrassment. "I will talk with you later."

The two women exchanged another look before Sandra walked off.

When she was out of earshot, I turned to Ruby. "Is everything okay?"

Ruby shook her head, disappointment etched in the soft lines of her face. Her eyes stayed on Sandra as she approached her husband. "This is how Ronnie behaves. I don't know how Sandra can handle him." With a heavy sigh, she turned away from the couple and walked back around her table.

I continued to watch the couple while Ruby busied herself making the final preparations to her jewelry stand. I gathered that Sandra and Ronnie were speaking harshly to one another by their jerky body language and strained expressions. Ronnie pointed at their food truck and then pointed at the food truck next to them. I saw her look around him, fold her arms across her chest and turn on her heel to head back in their truck. When she turned away from him, she mumbled something to herself before disappearing onto the other side of the vehicle.

I said my goodbye to Ruby and wished her luck with her first evening at the night market before making my way back to Peter.

"What the heck was all that about?" Peter asked.

"Oh, I guess that lady at the jewelry stand was a friend of my mother's when I was a kid."

"No, I didn't mean that . . . I meant them." He tilted his head toward Wonton on Wheels.

"I have no idea, but I was wondering that myself."

CHAPTER 2

To be clear, the path that I ended up on isn't exactly how I saw my late twenties going. Less than a year ago, I was determined to turn myself into some kind of corporate hotshot who wore stiletto heels and fancy suits. Never mind that I have yet to find a pair of stilettos I can wear longer than fifteen minutes without staggering in pain.

But an unforeseen turn of events that began with an ugly breakup and continued to spiral led me down a road I couldn't have anticipated. That's life, right?

Before I knew what happened, I was working at my parents' Chinese restaurant, Ho-Lee Noodle House, as their day shift server, sporadically dyeing my hair unnatural colors—I'm currently purple, by the way. Now a handful of months later, I'm managing the family business while my mother enjoys an early semi-retirement, dating a detective with the Fairview Park police department, and wondering what color to dye my hair next.

Things were going good, I felt happy and my life—though on a different track than intended—was starting to feel back to normal. As the crowd began to enter the streets, I took a moment to appreciate my current plane of existence. It was good to be me.

Rockwell Avenue was soon filled with masses of people moving from one tented booth to another in search of handmade goods, local services, or menu samplings from nearby restaurants.

Asia Village, the shopping plaza that housed my family's restaurant, was well represented amongst the busy street. Aside from Peter and me, Kimmy Tran from China Cinema and Song, an Asian entertainment store, was two tables away from us selling CDs and Chinese movies. Esther Chin, who owned Chin's Gifts, was somewhere down the street peddling her porcelain knickknacks, music boxes and jade jewelry. Jasmine Ming, from Asian Accents hair salon, was showcasing a table of hair treatments, shampoos and nail care products while Mr. Zhang, from Wild Sage herbal shop, was at the opposite end of the street enlightening people on proper usage of herbal remedies and elixirs.

Even Penny Cho from the Bamboo Lounge was present, handling the onstage entertainment that was set up at the end of the parking lot. As the night continued, dance and musical acts would be performed on the main stage that sat in front of an eating area packed with picnic tables. Once that began, our little tent would have a long line of people waiting to purchase spring rolls, dumplings, and fried noodles.

The beginnings of that line formed in front of our stand, and before I had time to truly appreciate the event,

Peter and I were slammed with food orders. While he worked to keep the food pans stocked with the most popular items, I filled plates with customer requests and cashed them out as quickly as possible.

It was a humid night and the air felt stale around us. The heat coming from the grill and below the pans wasn't helping matters. I made a mental note to remember clip fans for the following week.

The performances began around seven p.m. and opened with a group of women dressed as geishas that wowed the crowd with a traditional Japanese dance. It was so beautiful that most of the crowd in the surrounding area paused to watch, and Peter and I got a break from serving customers. When the act was finished, applause erupted all around us and within seconds the momentum of the hungry visitors continued.

Peter inspected the inventory below the counter, opening lids and counting what we had left. He shook his head. "Dude, we're almost out of dumplings already. I thought the spring rolls would be first to go."

We were only halfway through the night. I pulled out the small notebook I kept in my purse and made notes on what items we would need to adjust for next week's market. "I wonder if anyone else is running out of food yet."

My eyes traveled over to Wonton on Wheels which had a line that was at least ten deep. Sandra was manning the window by herself, and when I glanced over to the front of the truck, I noticed that their son, Calvin, had arrived and was having what seemed to be a very heated discussion with his father.

Despite the fact that I was not a fan of Calvin's, he'd

turned into a decent-looking young man. He was tall, thin with a little bit of muscle, and kept his jet-black hair short and shaved on the sides.

His full lips were turned down in a frown and his arms were crossed over his chest in defiance of his father. From small snippets I'd heard around the plaza, Calvin was constantly butting heads with his father, who was dead set on turning his son into an entrepreneur like himself. But Calvin wasn't having any of it, and had immediately enlisted into the Navy when he turned eighteen.

He didn't last long, though, and ended up getting out after a couple of years. Since then he'd been filling his time by going back to school and picking up odd jobs. Last I'd heard, he was working as a food delivery truck driver and drove routes that took him all over the Midwest.

I lost sight of the argument and quickly forgot about it when our next wave of customers came by, keeping us busy for the next hour. In that time, Peter's mom and our split shift server, Nancy Huang, showed up to lend a hand. The three of us worked in harmony with Peter cooking, Nancy filling the plates and me cashing out the customers.

I felt chipper, as we worked. It was going to be a great summer and Ho-Lee Noodle House was sure to gain tons of new business being at these weekly events. As a marketing tool, I'd ordered postcards with a picture of our restaurant on the front and our menu on the back to pass out with each order.

As the night trickled to an end and the crowd started to thin out, Peter, Nancy, and I began closing up shop.

Nancy, one of my mother's best friends, was a dainty woman with soft features. Her voice at times was barely above a whisper and the beauty of her youth had carried well into middle age.

She and Esther Chin were my honorary aunts, and I wondered how things would flow when my real aunt, Grace, came to visit this summer.

Nancy placed a gentle hand on my shoulder. "I see Sandra Chow talking with Ruby at her booth. It's been a long while since I've seen Ruby. I think I will go say hello."

"Yeah, I talked with them earlier tonight. I don't remember Ruby at all."

"When she moved to the east side she didn't come visit anymore. Everybody is always so busy."

"Were she and Mom close?" I asked.

Nancy tilted her head in consideration. "For a short time, yes."

Momentarily, I pondered if there might be any interesting back story, but if there was anything to be told, I was sure I'd hear about it through the grapevine. "Okay, well, we're almost all packed up here. I'll come and get you when we're done and ready to go."

She nodded and turned to leave.

After she'd joined the other two women, I busied myself with straightening up the cash box and the slips containing our orders. The order forms had been another one of my ideas to help keep track of what sold best and what was less popular. I gathered them with a rubber band and slipped them in the cash box before locking it.

When I looked up, I saw Calvin ambling over to our booth.

"Well, if it isn't Lana Lee . . . all grown up." He laughed as he extended a hand over the register.

"Calvin," I said, reaching for his hand. "It's been a while, how have you been?"

"Not too bad. Not too bad, at all." He glanced down at my hand. "Firm handshake you got there. You're not a delicate flower, that's for sure."

I smiled in return. "That I am not."

He nodded in approval. "Right, so you're working for your parents now or somethin'?"

"I actually manage the restaurant . . . wasn't part of my master plan, but it's paying the bills. What are you up to these days?"

He gave Peter a quick eyeball before answering my question. "I just quit my job as a trucker and started working in an auto repair shop. I got sick of being on the road all the time, ya know?"

"I can imagine that would be hard."

A scraggly man in a dingy t-shirt and torn jeans came walking up to us from the direction of the food truck area. He stood behind Calvin and peered up at the makeshift sign we had hanging from the top of our tent. "Ha . . . Ho-Lee Noodle House . . . for real? That's the real name?"

I pursed my lips. "Yes, that's the real name. And, we're closed now, sorry."

Calvin chuckled. "Easy there, Sunshine, that's my Uncle Gene."

"Oh!" I blushed. "Sorry, I didn't realize . . ."

"No sweat . . . I don't believe we've had the pleasure." Gene stepped up to the counter next to Calvin and gave me a goofy grin. "I'm Gene Tian. Nice to meet you."

As the words left his mouth, I could smell alcohol on his breath. Clearly he had taken advantage of the beer tent.

"Nice to meet you," I replied, not bothering to offer my hand.

"My apologies for interruptin' your conversation, but I need to exit stage left with my designated driver over here." He slid his eyes in Calvin's direction. "Come on little nephew, time to get out of here."

"Okay, cool, just one sec," Calvin turned his attention back to me. "So, I was thinkin' maybe—"

"Hey . . . C . . . we gotta go . . . ASAP!" Gene grabbed his nephew's arm and yanked hard. "I need to use the facilities and I ain't usin' those port-o-Johns, ya dig?"

Calvin rolled his eyes. "All right, let's go then." He waved a hand at me. "Maybe we can catch up another time, Lee. I'd sure like to hear how your mom roped you into taking over the family biz."

"Sure, stop by the restaurant some time," I offered. "I'm there all week."

He winked and ran after his uncle who had already started hightailing toward the exit.

"Interesting dudes," Peter said as he finished cleaning off the grill. "That one guy for sure had way too much to drink. Good thing his nephew is takin' him home."

"Odd that I've never met or heard of Gene before," I said as I watched them disappear down the road. "I wonder whose brother he is."

"Maybe he's visiting from out of town for the summer or something," Peter suggested.

"Speaking of," I said, turning toward Peter. "My Aunt Grace is going to be here in a few days . . . I want to prepare you for my mother's crazy behavior."

"Oh man, is she gonna be all micro-managey at the restaurant? Because we've gotten into a nice groove since

Mama Lee has been out of the picture. I mean, I love your mom and everything, but my chi is flowing so much better now."

I laughed. "You've been talking to Mr. Zhang again?"

Peter shrugged. "Guilty as charged."

I inspected our tent and was satisfied with our progress. All Peter had to do was pull up the trailer so we could haul away our grill and we'd be on our way home. I was already daydreaming about slipping into my pajamas and basking in the comforts of air conditioning.

Peter seemed to come to the same conclusion and dug in his pocket for the keys. "I'm sure there's a line out of the lot, but I'm going to make my way over there anyways. If my mom wants to leave just tell her I'll call her tomorrow."

"Okay, I'll be here." I told him.

Right as Peter turned his back to me, he paused, his body straight as a rod.

"What's wrong?" I asked.

I heard a crackling sound, and Peter's head turned in the direction of Wonton on Wheels. "OH sh—"

Before I could fully understand what was happening, Peter grabbed me and knocked me to the ground. A large boom and the sound of hail followed. From my place on the ground, I could see flames lighting up the parking lot. Wonton on Wheels was on fire. . . .